MURDER IN CHINA

An addictive crime mystery full of twists

ROY LEWIS

Arnold Landon Mysteries Book 20

Originally published as *Dragon Head*

Revised edition 2022
Joffe Books, London
www.joffebooks.com

First published by Constable & Robinson Ltd
in Great Britain in 2007 as *Dragon Head*

This paperback edition was first published
in Great Britain in 2022

ISBN: 978-1-80405-421-5

NOTE TO THE READER

Please note this book is set in the early 2000s in England, a time when social attitudes were very different.

PROLOGUE

A soft wind came sighing off the South China Sea and the moon rose high, riding pale silky clouds tinged with the pink of dawn. The night had been humid but the light breeze that ruffled the palms had brought relief to the early risers who strolled along the Rua da Praia Grande. This had once been the waterfront esplanade of Macau, and in the early evenings it was still a location for strolling tourists, heading for the cluster of restaurants in the Portuguese section. The area of the Leal Senado had been pedestrianized, and in the dawn light beggars huddled there, waiting near the cathedral for their ragged days to begin.

Against the lightening sky the residential blocks, luxury apartments lining the far shore, began to glitter into life, lights twinkling in the darkness beyond the long arch of the bridge to Taipa Island, as Ricky Chan stepped out of the brightly lit entrance to the casino, still busy with night-long gamblers surging around the tables, ten deep in places, T-shirted, wearing frayed jeans, addicted to the Chinese vice.

The dark limousine was waiting for him as he came down the steps; the uniformed driver took a finger to his peaked cap and reached for the rear passenger door but Ricky Chan raised a hand. The man froze obediently and Chan walked past him, strolling contentedly towards the water-front, a cigar in his left hand, head back, enjoying the soft breeze that came in from the sea, ruffling his dark hair.

He was fifty-three now, and a happy, satisfied man. He had achieved his dreams, and a safe, glittering future lay ahead of him. A young couple walked past him, arms around each other, and he smiled at them, bowed his head in a gentle greeting. The sight of the young lovers made him think of his own home life. He had not seen his wife for seven years. She was still in Fujian, where she had returned after their ten years together in Hong Kong, but she was comfortable, he kept her well provided for, and his three daughters were now grown women. He had maintained his honour with her, and like all Chinese wives she understood, and accepted, that a man in Ricky Chan's position would have concubines, almost as necessity, for his emotional and sexual needs as well as for his status.

He paused at the rail, looked out over the dark, ruffled sea and nodded in satisfaction. He enjoyed Macau: the old-est European settlement in China, it retained an old-world elegance and way of life. Forty-five minutes away on the high speed jet-foil, Hong Kong was a different proposition. Vibrant, crowded, busy and exciting, it formed a clear con-trast to Macau with its firmly rooted nineteenth-century appearance. The pace of life was slower here, the Portuguese influence bringing a Latinized gentility into the midst of ori-ental mystique.

He took a deep, contented breath. He recalled the days when, as a young man, he had first entered the smuggling trade. They had made big profits in those days, running Western luxury goods into China, on board the *dai fei*, speedy grey-painted, fibreglass-hulled speedboats. The *dai fei*, Big Wings . . . He remembered them with affection, the excite-ment of the chase when the British patrol boats had come out of the Fragrant Harbour in the darkness, hunting them down, the twisting and turning among the myriad islands, the gunboats firing warning shots across their bows . . . The *dai fei* still plied their trade, of course, although he himself no longer had any part in it. These days the Big Wings ran different goods into China, including top of the range cars — BMW, Mercedes-Benz, Lexus, Audi and Porsche. And new developments were in the wind. He understood the trade was expanding to run vehicles into South Africa, Zambia, Tanzania and Kenya, the Caribbean, Canada and USA.

For himself, he had other fish to fry.

He turned, leaned against the rail, chewed at his cigar thoughtfully. He continued to enjoy Macau, once each year, after the conclusion of the necessary business, maintaining underworld contacts, looking for new opportunities on his annual return to Hong Kong. It was almost like a pilgrimage for him, coming back to Macau each year to relax, recapture a little of his lost youth at the gaming tables in the casino. He could have flown in by helicopter, of course, but he still clung to the old ways, travelling on the jet-foil, gambling on board, then returning at dawn to Hong Kong to conduct a little business, seek out old business friends, before returning to the United Kingdom, to direct his new empire, and be with the Western woman who was his dearest concubine and the son who would one day succeed him.

And to enjoy his new-found status, having achieved his goal, in spite of the efforts of his rivals to dethrone him. He grunted, dropped the cigar, ground it under the heel of his expensive, highly polished shoe. He thrust thoughts of his rivals away from him, preferring to dwell on the memory of the woman. He would never marry her, of course, and his son would not have his name but that mattered little. The training, that was the important thing for the boy: training for his heritage. The world was changing; new opportunities were presenting themselves, a future Dragon Head would need to possess different skills if he was to succeed. It was like Macau itself: the two-century-old streets were still clogged by day with handcarts and rickshaws, cars and lorries and the ubiquitous motor cycles, throttles roaring, exhausts pumping out noxious fumes that caught at your throat, but Macau was in the process of inevitable change. In a few years, it was known, the territory would revert to China. New systems, new bosses, new corruptions would steal in. He himself, tomorrow, would be talking to new men in Hong Kong, men in plain, ill-cut suits who would have crossed through the China Gate hours earlier. He sighed. The old days were gone. China was reclaiming her own.

But he had achieved success in another, barbarian country. He turned around, raised his head. The limousine still waited, a gleaming symbol of his status. Slowly he made his way back towards it. The gambling had been exciting. It was time now to return to his hotel: a shower, a brief sleep and then he would take the ferry back to Hong Kong. In three days he would be back in England.

He was still thinking about England when he settled into the deep leather seats of the limousine. He experienced a grim satisfaction as he thought about his enemy. The lawsuit had been something the man had not expected: problems were traditionally settled between societies, and within societies, by internal agreements or internal warfare. Bringing in the courts, or using the police, these were unusual tactics. But there had been warnings enough, and Ricky Chan was satisfied: his following was loyal enough to support him. His enemy was finished: he would have lost face by the lawsuit. It meant he would probably steal away, back to China . . .

The limousine headed back to the hotel. Dawn was breaking and the traffic was already building up in the narrow streets. The car slowed, and Ricky Chan leaned back, half closed his eyes. He became aware of the limousine slowing further, then coming to a stop. His eyelids flickered: the red traffic light glowed at them. He closed his eyes.

As a consequence, he never saw the two Japanese-manufactured motor cycles that came weaving through the traffic: even if he had, he would have paid little attention because motor cycles were numerous in the streets of Macau.

Nor did he see how they took up station, one either side of the limousine. The chauffeur became aware of them, saw the pillion passengers draw Chinese military-issue automatic pistols from within their jackets, and he opened his mouth to scream a warning but it was already too late. There were sharp, cracking, explosive sounds as the dark-helmeted pillion passengers emptied their weapons into the limousine at point-blank range, catching both men in a deadly crossfire. The glass shattered under the hail, the limousine driver died instantly, two bullets entering his skull just below the rim of his peaked cap. He slumped forward across the wheel, the horn blaring harshly in the traffic-laden street.

In the back seat Ricky Chan felt the first bullet plucking at his throat; he heard the snapping sound of the weapons and he began to rise, images of death rushing into his mind, brief panic clutching at his chest. But there was no time, none to reflect, none to regret, none to remonstrate. The windows were shattered, fifteen seconds had elapsed, and Ricky Chan was dying, choking on his own blood, his dreams and expectations dying with him.

Men on the street were diving into doorways after their first, shocked paralysis. The lights were changing, the motor cycles roaring off, weaving through the still stationary traffic. They left behind them a slow stain of exhaust fumes, blue in the morning air. The horn of the limousine still blared; excited onlookers clustered around, a few people got out of their cars, but no one ventured to approach the vehicle, or look in at the dying man in the back seat, and the dead man at the wheel.

It took the police almost half an hour to clear a way to the limousine. Their immediate verdict was that there was little they could do: it had been a well-timed, meticulously planned hit that had been executed with precision.

A few hours later they had identified the dead men. A call was put through to Hong Kong, to private addresses in the Walled City, outside official channels. That afternoon three dark-suited men came in from Hong Kong and spent several hours at the police station, closeted in a private room with well-placed officials.

The Portuguese governor acted quickly to calm public concern. He made an announcement: there was no cause for panic, tourists should not worry, this violence was strictly a feud within the criminal underworld, and would be dealt with swiftly and efficiently by the local police. The perpetrators would be brought to justice within days. He made no reference to the criminal statistics in Macau, said nothing of the number of fatalities, the corpses found floating in the river from time to time, the robberies that continued in the narrow streets. Open security measures were stepped up, naturally, for a few days: policemen in flak jackets wandered the streets around the Lisboa, armed with sub-machine guns. Little attention was paid to them, and by the end of the week, life had returned to normal, with the underworld societies operating as before, in secrecy, dealing in power and avarice as they had done for centuries.

In England there was a brief flurry of violence, a degree of blood-letting, a settling of old scores and, eventually, the eerie calm that always descended after such a storm led to new agreements, delineation of territories, election of officials, so that men could carry on doing what they did best, under cover, in secret: the things they had done for two thousand years, since the foundations of their Chinese societies.

CHAPTER ONE

1

Arnold Landon hunched in his jacket, and turned up the collar against the east wind that was driving in off the sea. It was a sharp, clear day, blue sky, cloudless, but the wind was icy. The clarity of the air meant that he could see the distant outline of the Farne Islands but the sea was too choppy for them to wander further in that direction, even had they wanted to. Beside him, leaning against the wheelhouse of the former fishing boat and sheltering from the wind, Karen Stannard, forsaking for once her head of department desk in Morpeth, looked fairly miserable, clearly regretting her decision to accompany him. It had been bravado, of course. She was not prepared to admit that she was reluctant to undertake anything he was prepared to do. Her view was that she was as good as any man in the Department of Museums and Antiquities, and especially Arnold. He understood what drove her, and it gave him a certain grim satisfaction now to perceive her discomfort.

'From here, across towards the cove and to the right of those cliffs,' he said, pointing, 'that's where the information centre would be located. There's a tumbledown jetty there on the beach; it would need repairs and extension but the idea would be to provide school parties and summer tourist boat trips to come out here, towards the Black Needles, to show where the *Vendela* went down in 1737.'

Karen turned her head to glance in the direction of the sullen surge of white-capped water that denoted the existence of the sharp, treacherous rocks away to their left. The wind tugged at her hair, flicked it about her eyes, and she raised a hand to brush it away irritably.

'It's all a pipe dream anyway,' she said. 'I don't see that we're going to be able to afford completion of the information centre.'

Arnold glanced at her doubtfully. 'I thought the funding was already in place. The council—'

'The council is in raiding mood,' she interrupted him. 'Yes, we were promised the funding, we produced the plans, prepared the budget and instructed the architects, but my guess is that when we get back to the office we'll find that suddenly things have changed. The new government guidelines on transport, and the cutting back of grant-in-aid has caused a flurry in the political dovecotes. The Chief Executive left a message on my desk on Friday: he wants to see us on Monday morning, and I'd be more than surprised if it's something other than bad news.'

'But I thought it was all in place,' Arnold protested.

'When the financial crunch comes, where does the axe fall first?' she demanded scornfully. 'Libraries, and museums. What they see as the soft, easy options. And anything progressive, out of the ordinary, imaginative . . . You know what they're like, Arnold. You've been in the business long enough to know. I'm damned sure that when we get back to Morpeth, the news from Mr Powell Frinton, our revered Chief Executive, will be clear enough. Cut unnecessary expenditure, halt all new projects, tighten our belts, get rid of part-time staff . . . you know how it goes.'

'We've had a lot of support from the Education Department, and the Tourist Board,' Arnold demurred. 'Won't that help swing things our way?'

'It won't be enough. Those departments don't carry enough weight, when money is scarce.' She crouched closer against the wheelhouse as the boat swung, circling the Black Needles, and they began to head back towards the cliffs. She glared doubtfully at the cold surging water above the rocks, and she shivered. 'This was a bloody stupid idea, Arnold, coming out here. I could have appreciated the project sufficiently just by standing on the cliff tops. I'm frozen. Hey, get over here, stand closer to me, shield me from that wind.'

She was the head of department. Obediently, Arnold left the bulwark he had been clinging to and lurched across the deck to stand beside her. Her shoulder leaned into his. He was slightly taller than her, and he looked down at her. Her glance held his for a few moments: he had never made up his mind about the colour of her eyes. They seemed to change with her mood — sometimes green, sometimes hazel — but this morning they seemed grey, and thoughtful. For a moment, as she leaned against him, his mind drifted back to a night in a hotel, when she had been vulnerable, warm, receptive. She had cast away her antagonism that night, broken free from her struggle to demonstrate that she was better than any man she knew. But it had been a brief interval. The following day she had quickly reverted to her professional self, and since then their relationship had returned to one based on competition, distrust and wariness. Yet for a moment, as she leaned against him, seeking protection . . .

He dragged himself back to reality, too careful to fall into such a mental trap, particularly if he was setting it himself. He looked away. 'The wind would have been a lot worse that night,' he commented, 'when the *Vendela* broke up on those rocks. It's a pretty horrible scene to contemplate, men struggling in the icy water, the sea crashing over those rocks . . .'

'Life often can be pretty horrible,' she complained. 'Like now. Arnold, get this damned boat back to shore before I freeze to death.'

* * *

10

He suggested they might stop for lunch at Alnwick but she replied, curtly, that she had better ways to spend her Saturday, so they drove back to Morpeth in a silence that was hardly companionable. Arnold was used to Karen's mood swings. There were times when she could be unbearable; there were others when she used her unquestioned beauty to dominate, manipulate, obtain concessions from the toughest of her peers. She remained an enigma to him, nevertheless. He had known her in the warm darkness, and he had suffered her tongue-lashings in the office, her cool, adversarial attitude in public meetings. He knew that rumours about the nature of her sexuality were unfounded, he admired her professional competence, and he guessed he probably knew her better than anyone else of their acquaintance. Yet she still remained difficult to predict. Mentally, he shrugged the thought away: it was best simply to take Karen as she was, and not worry about what she might do next.

'Do you ever get fed up?' she asked him suddenly.

He glanced at her in surprise. 'About what?'

'Life. Your job. The bloody department,' she replied angrily.

The question brought him up short. He hesitated. 'I suppose there are times . . .' He fell silent again as he thought about the matter. It was difficult to respond to the question: naturally, there were occasions when he felt disgruntled, not least when Karen herself attacked him without good reason, but he could not really contemplate doing anything other than the work he undertook. It satisfied him, gave him freedom to wander the fells and sea coasts of Northumberland, to indulge in his personal passion, delving back into lives long since ended, societies that had risen and died, exercising his imagination and professional skills, abilities his father had nurtured in him long ago on the Yorkshire hills. It was not exactly about being happy, because he had experienced loss in his life, failures in relationships and one in particular, but, broadly speaking, he was content.

'I just feel undervalued,' she raged suddenly, glaring out of the side window. 'No, not that really, just, well, it's always a battle to get things done, complete what I want to get accomplished, do what I know to be the right thing. It's always a bloody struggle, dealing with fat, egocentric politicians with sweaty hands, worrying about budgets, having to defend policies in committees who neither understand nor care about what we're trying to do.'

'You can't be certain the *Vendela* project will get dumped,' he offered, guessing this was the immediate cause of her unhappiness.

'I'm not just talking about the *Vendela* project,' she snapped irritably. 'That's only one thing, an example of what we have to put up with. It's just that I feel constrained, tired, limited in scope. I can do better things, Arnold. I'm not stretched, I'm frustrated, dealing with little people with pea brains, pompous fools who are overblown with self-importance. I'm fed up, Arnold. I'm thinking of getting out.'

A Porsche, sleek and black, overtook them, accelerating smoothly away down the dual carriageway. Arnold watched it go. 'Have you got anything else in mind?' he asked.

She did not answer him directly. 'I've been too long in this bloody job,' she muttered.

By inference, he could have taken it as a criticism of himself. He had been at the department twice as long as Karen. He did not pursue the matter. And Karen lapsed into a sullen silence that was broken only when he dropped her at her apartment. As she got out of the car she gave him her thanks, somewhat gracelessly, and went into the lobby of the apartment block.

Arnold drove into town, left the car in the parking area outside the Black Horse and went inside to the lounge bar. It was busy: there was a noisy group of young men watching a football match on the large television set mounted on the far wall, but he managed to find a table. He ordered a drink, and a pub lunch. He felt vaguely depressed. It was partly the result of Karen's general ill humour that morning, partly the thought that perhaps Karen was right. Both she and he had been in the department too long. Maybe, like her, he should be thinking of fresh fields. But, lacking academic qualifications, and possessing professional expertise in only a limited area of activity, he did not, he concluded gloomily, have a wide range of opportunities open to him.

There was also the sudden thought, unbidden, that if Karen Stannard left the department, something would go out of his life.

He remained in a gloomy mood all weekend. He took a walk along the coast at Seahouses but a misty rain swept in and he took little pleasure in the excursion. On the Monday morning he went to his office early and dealt with various files concerning projects that were nearing completion: the Roman bridge dig at Chollerford, the Celtic grave at the foot of the Cheviots, the footings of the destroyed medieval abbey, probably Premonstratensian, in the hinterland beyond Amble. But the *Vendela* kept intruding into his thoughts. He hoped Karen was wrong; he hoped the project would not be axed. He glanced at the clock. He would soon find out: the meeting with Chief Executive Powell Frinton was scheduled for ten o'clock.

Portia Tyrrel wandered into his room shortly before the meeting was due to start.

'Nice weekend with the boss?' she asked him slyly.

She was inclined to tease him. There were times when he felt caught in a pincer movement between the head of department and her assistant. They were both beautiful women, but very different. Where Karen was tall, cool elegance, with russet-gold hair, eyes of indeterminate colour and classical features, Portia was Eurasian, wearing her dark hair short. She was perhaps five feet two in height, small-breasted, slimly built with pale-olive skin tones and dark, almond, luminous eyes. She seemed to possess a natural confidence that was displayed in most situations. She was the daughter of a Singaporean mother and a Scottish father. Raised in Southeast Asia, she had come to England to read for an Oxford degree, followed by a postgraduate course at Cambridge before joining the department at Morpeth. She worked as Karen's assistant, but there was a competitive edge to their relationship, and while there were rumours that Karen might have lesbian tendencies — probably spread by disenchanted would-be Lotharios in the department — there was no doubt where Portia's tastes lay. The general view in the department was that she was a man-eater.

'We didn't spend the weekend together,' Arnold replied, falling into her trap irritably. 'It was just a morning trip up the coast to view the site of the *Vendela* project.'

'Oh, I don't know,' she commented, giving him a sideways glance. 'You should be more careful, Arnold. Jaunts with the boss into the Northumberland hinterland, it can give rise to gossip.' She paused, reflecting. 'Besides, I thought that project was going to be put into mothballs.'

'Then you know more than I do,' Arnold replied, rising to his feet.

She stood innocently in the doorway, forcing him to brush against her as he left the room. Her almond eyes looked up to him mischievously. 'I'm just telling you what the rumours are on the next floor down. I tried to discount them, of course, suggesting that you and Karen were not just off on a social visit, but with the chat about the *Vendela* project . . .'

He heard her chuckle lightly as he marched off down the corridor towards the Chief Executive's office. When Powell Frinton's secretary ushered him into the inner sanctum he saw that Karen Stannard was already there. She wore a crisp white open-necked shirt, and a dark skirt. She sat very upright in her chair, slim, long legs crossed elegantly, her skirt just short enough to reveal them to advantage. She could never resist using her appearance to get her own way, but right now her eyes were angry as she flicked a glance in his direction.

The Chief Executive, Powell Frinton, displayed no emotion. He was a person not given to showing his feelings; a careful, precise man and a lawyer by training, he maintained a reserve in his professional dealings with his staff and with his political masters. He maintained an air of control; his features were narrow, his appearance desiccated, the eyes behind the horn-rimmed glasses unreadable. He waved Arnold to the chair beside Karen. When he spoke there was a hint of an unaccustomed weariness in his tone. 'Miss Stannard and I have had a word, while we waited for you, about the *Vendela* project.'

'The whole department is very excited about it,' Arnold said hopefully. 'And both the Tourist people and the Education Department are convinced that the centre would be a great asset for the area. The Tourist Board even suggest it could quickly raise a great deal of revenue.'

'Quite.' Powell Frinton frowned wearily. There was a puffiness about his eyes that Arnold had not noticed before. 'But I believe Miss Stannard has already intimated to you that there will be problems over the project. The reality is that the council has pared down budgets so much that it would seem there is no way forward for us in the short term.'

And Arnold knew that a project delayed would be a project lost. There would always be newer opportunities in the future that would soak up the money falling available. He glanced at Karen; her features were composed but there was an angry glint in her eyes. He was about to make some comment in protest at a decision he knew had already been made but he was forestalled.

'I have already discussed the *Vendela* project with Miss Stannard, and she has given me her views. Forcefully. But that is not the reason why I called this meeting, Mr Landon,' Powell Frinton said in his dry, slightly rasping voice. He leaned forward, resting his bony fingers on a file in front of him, and remained silent for a few seconds. Arnold eyed him curiously: he had known Powell Frinton for some years but he saw him rarely, and in the months since their last meeting the Chief Executive seemed to have aged, subtly. His lean cheeks seemed to have become more cadaverous; his skin was yellowish, his eyes more deep-set. In addition, he seemed to move more slowly. Always a man of deliberation, he now presented an air of weariness. He raised his head and looked at Arnold with pale eyes. 'You have heard of Lady Mannington?'

Arnold hesitated, glanced at Karen and became aware she also had thought the meeting was about the *Vendela*. He nodded. 'Vaguely. She was the widow of an MP, who died recently. They lived at Mannington Hall, up near Otterburn. Quite wealthy, I believe. Childless. But beyond that . . .'

Powell Frinton leaned back in his chair, and linked his bony fingers together. 'The Mannington family were Irish in origin. They came into their wealth in the seventeenth century, managing to survive the Cromwellian barbarities, and thereafter built up a considerable trade in Dublin and Waterford. About 1850 the Mannington family bought properties in Northumberland, having made investments in the coal industry, owning mines formerly operated by the Delaval family. Then, as was the way with aristocratic families in those times, they turned to politics, and Sir Wilfred Mannington took his seat in the House of Lords as a life peer in the fifties. He died about ten years ago. His widow, Lady Mannington, as you intimated, died recently.' He paused, inspected his bony fingers with little interest. 'As a result of a letter I've received, I've been in communication with the firm of solicitors who are dealing with the estate of Lady Mannington. Following on from that conversation, I've arranged a meeting with a representative of the firm, a Mr . . . ah . . . Penrose. He will be arriving any moment. I thought it appropriate, in view of the brief discussion Mr Penrose and I had on the phone, that you should be present at the meeting.' He hesitated, glanced at his watch, then lifted the phone to speak to his secretary. 'I think we could have the coffee served now . . . Ah, he is already in the building? Please direct him to my room immediately.'

Karen Stannard straightened in her chair, flashing a glance towards Arnold that told him she was as puzzled as he was. 'May I ask—' she began, but Powell Frinton held up a hand. There was a light tapping on the door, and the Chief Executive's middle-aged secretary ushered a short, balding, portly, dark-suited man into the room. 'Mr Penrose,' she explained. 'I'll bring in the coffee immediately.'

Powell Frinton rose politely, extended his hand to the solicitor and introduced Karen and Arnold, before offering Penrose a seat. When the Chief Executive returned to his own chair Arnold thought he detected a slight wince of pain as he lowered himself into his seat. 'I've already mentioned to my colleagues your situation as executors of Lady Mannington's estate,' he stated, 'but I've not given any details as to the reason for your visit.'

Penrose nodded, lifted his briefcase on to his lap and opened it. He extracted a sheaf of papers, and what seemed to be a sales catalogue. The door opened behind him, and he paused, his lawyer's instincts regarding confidentiality making him wait until the secretary had brought in the tray of coffee, placed it on the desk in front of Powell Frinton, and retreated. There was a further delay while the cups were distributed and then the solicitor coughed lightly. When he spoke, his voice was light and reedy.

'I suppose I should begin with a certain apology for the delays that have occurred in contacting you, Mr Powell Frinton. I can only plead that the difficulties of dealing with such a large estate as Lady Mannington's have made delays inevitable. The rigour of the law . . .'

'I quite understand,' Powell Frinton intervened, one lawyer to another.

'The estate is considerable, and it's taken us quite a time to prepare an appropriate inventory,' Penrose continued. 'Apart from Mannington Hall itself, there are certain other properties in Northumberland and Ireland that have to be disposed of, various bequests to a number of charities, it's all been quite complicated. And then, it's only recently, when we were dealing with the inventory, that we realized there had been a late codicil to her will which, while not having been overlooked, exactly, certainly was . . . shall we say, not quite appreciated in *impact* terms?'

There was a short silence as the solicitor looked at the faces of each of his audience in turn. Arnold managed not to smile. In other words, he thought, someone in the lawyer's office had buggered things up.

'The fact is,' Penrose hurried on, 'we have proceeded to carry out the bequests, which includes the necessity of arranging the sale of various items from the very large antique collections held by the Mannington family for generations. You will see from this sales brochure the range of items that are to be disposed of.' He handed the glossy catalogue to Powell Frinton. 'The auction has been arranged to be held in Newcastle, in two weeks' time.' He hesitated, clearly a little embarrassed. 'The relevant pages of the catalogue are seventeen to thirty-four.'

There was silence as Powell Frinton opened the catalogue and looked at the pages mentioned. After a while he murmured, 'Chinese porcelain.'

Penrose nodded vigorously. 'That is correct. Perhaps I should explain a little further. Lady Mannington made her will shortly after her husband's death. In the intervening years a number of codicils were added, as she determined upon various additional bequests. Then, shortly before she herself died her attention was caught by the activity of your department. In particular, she read an account of your intentions regarding the seventeenth-century wreck of the *Vendela*. A few days later she called for one of our staff to visit her. Business was such, at the time, that, regretfully, a rather junior legal executive was sent to the meeting.' He cleared his throat, unhappy at his own explanation. 'Meetings with Lady Mannington could sometimes be protracted, and difficult . . . However, the young man made no mistakes, drew up the appropriate document, but unfortunately, filed it where it should not have been. Hence the delay.'

Karen shuffled impatiently in her chair. Like Arnold, she had no idea what was going on. Her impatience was communicated to the portly lawyer.

'In short,' he said, 'the codicil in question amends her will in one respect. It makes a bequest, a specific bequest to the Department of Museums and Antiquities. There are certain conditions attached, as one might expect. I have stated these in this letter . . . And I can only apologize for the short notice given to you, with the auction already arranged, and only two weeks away. And, of course, if there is anything we can do to assist you in the decisions to be made you have only to call on our services . . .'

For an appropriate fee, Arnold thought cynically as he received the auctions catalogue from Powell Frinton, and inspected the relevant pages.

After further explanations, Penrose left, and Powell Frinton sat quietly in his chair, lightly drumming his fingers on the desk in front of him. 'I am not sure how you are to handle this, Miss Stannard. You can call upon the services of our own legal department, of course, but I fear there is little assistance they can render.'

Karen frowned. 'I had assumed that this would not be merely a departmental matter.'

Powell Frinton's eyes were slightly glazed. 'I fear I will have to leave it entirely in your hands, Miss Stannard.' He hesitated. 'The fact is, I am about to take leave of absence, and will not be available during the next three or four weeks.' His glance drifted towards Arnold. 'I've no doubt that with the assistance of Mr Landon you can bring this matter to a satisfactory conclusion . . .'

2

'So what's wrong with the Chief Executive?' Portia Tyrrel asked, as she sat with Arnold in Karen Stannard's office.

Karen shrugged. 'There are rumours flying around, but no one seems very sure. You know how close-mouthed and controlled Powell Frinton can be. As far as I can make out he's going into hospital for exploratory surgery, but if he's going to be away for three weeks it must be pretty serious. Still, whatever the problem might be, it's saddled us with the task of dealing with the matter of this bequest from Lady Mannington.'

Portia turned over the pages of the catalogue Arnold had handed to her, and shook her dark head. 'So how come this Lady Mannington decided to be so generous towards us anyway?'

Karen glanced at Arnold in irritation. 'You'd better explain to her. I've got to think things through. The problems we're facing here . . .'

Arnold nodded. 'Lady Mannington read about our plans to establish a learning and educational centre based on the site near where the *Vendela* went down in 1737.'

'So?'

Arnold smiled. 'It wasn't a fact I was aware of previously, but it seems that the Mannington family had an interest in the *Vendela*.'

He leaned back in his chair, recalling the discussion with the lawyer Penrose in Powell Frinton's office.

'There is a common misconception that anything lost at sea is there for the taking,' the lawyer had lectured them pompously, 'but this is not really the case. The legal situation regarding shipwrecks is a complex one: it is necessary to distinguish between the owners of the hull and the owners of the cargo. Fortunately, we are able to say with some assurance that there can be no doubt regarding the items stated in the bequest of Lady Mannington to your department. The articles contained in her bequest were actually salvaged from the wreck of the *Vendela* in 1737, but the family — which was Irish in origin — had already purchased the cargo, and rights of ownership were clearly documented. While the *Vendela* was breaking up on the Black Needles, a number of salvage attempts were made and in particular a large part of the cargo of Chinese porcelain was in fact recovered. The Mannington family has since held those items in a private collection, first in Ireland, and later at Mannington Hall in Northumberland. Now, with the death of Lady Mannington, the collection is to be sold for the benefit of various charities. But be assured. the provenance of the collection is beyond question.'

'Of what does the bequest to the department consist?' the Chief Executive had asked in his usual precise manner.

The lawyer cleared his throat. 'In her will, and the relevant codicil, Lady Mannington states that she wishes her collection, which has been in the family for more than two hundred years, to be kept together as far as this is possible. Naturally, she was aware of the inherent difficulties. After all, the collection may well be valued in excess of five million sterling. The likelihood of public money being raised to purchase the collection, she knew, would be slim. But a sale is necessary: as we know, death duties in this modern world can be crippling to an estate, and there are the charities she wishes to provide for . . .'

He removed his spectacles to peer closely at the document in front of him. 'I have here a complete list of the holdings. As I intimated earlier, the bequest is subject to certain conditions. These conditions are relatively simple. Lady Mannington desired that the Department of Museums and Antiquities should be entrusted with the task of retaining a selection of the items of Chinese porcelain for public display so that some of the collection at least will be retained for the enjoyment of the public. She did not wish all the items to be dispersed to private collections. In recompense for its efforts, and in recognition of the value which she has always attached to the retention by a public body of a display of historical items, Lady Mannington directs that the department shall be entitled to retain thirty items from the collection, to be held on public display in its museum at Morpeth.'

Arnold recalled, in the silence that followed, that Penrose had said the total collection could be worth five million. 'Are the items specified?' Karen asked in a subdued tone.

The solicitor shook his head, replaced his glasses and regarded her owlishly. 'No, the terms of the bequest are clear. Thirty unspecified items. The particular pieces are to be chosen by officers of the department.'

'That's not going to be easy,' Karen muttered, casting a glance at Arnold, 'particularly in view of the short period of time allowed to us. You said the auction is to be held within two weeks.'

'For which, again, I apologize,' Penrose said hurriedly. 'But I need hardly remind you that the selection process will be of considerable importance. A judicious choice could reward the department to the extent of, perhaps, something in excess of a hundred thousand pounds.'

And that would be a conservative estimate, Arnold had guessed. Now, to Portia, he said, 'There's no doubt that in other circumstances Powell Frinton would have taken over, and I suspect the department would have had little say in either the selection or the later display arrangements. Coincidentally, his illness has given us a great opportunity.'

'And a bloody big headache,' Karen argued irritably. 'We've got two weeks to identify the items we want held back from the auction, but what the hell do we know about Chinese porcelain? How can we be sure we'll choose the right items, either for value or historical significance? And there's the balance of the items we choose from the collection — how can we be sure it will make aesthetic sense? I'm telling you, those damned incompetent lawyers have left us with a problem!'

'There may be someone at the university who could help,' Arnold suggested.

Karen snorted. 'I doubt it. A university in the area might have a faculty which teaches Chinese, but that's a far cry from having someone in post who knows enough about such a specialized subject as seventeenth-century Chinese porcelain. I think we're going into this blindfolded. We could be about to make some bad mistakes.'

Silence fell in the room. Karen swung her chair so that she was facing the window. She stared out at a clear blue sky, but Arnold got the impression she was seeing nothing. He could guess what was on her mind: she was a perfectionist, always concerned with maintaining her reputation and professionalism. She would be worried that after the choices had been made, perhaps too haphazardly, there would come a day when, with the chosen items on display, an expert would come along and ridicule the efforts she and her department had made.

Arnold felt helpless. There was little he could suggest, or do to help.

Beside him, Portia Tyrrel closed the catalogue, and tapped it absent-mindedly against the arm of her chair. 'I think . . .'

She paused; there was a brief silence and then Karen swung around in her chair to face her. 'You said?'

Portia had a gleam of excitement in her eyes. 'I think . . . maybe . . . I'm not sure, but it's possible I can find someone who'll be able to help . . .'

* * *

The building had gone through various regenerative phases. It had been built in the early 1800s as a Primitive Methodist chapel, stolidly facing the terraces of cottages built for miners, for whom the chapel was intended to provide uplifting experiences, closer to God than the Baptist chapel that already occupied the area close to the main road to South Shields. Within thirty years the congregation had dispersed — if it had ever arrived — and the building had been occupied as a Miners Institute until a new one was built by public subscription, after which it had gone through numerous change of use: a sanctuary for fallen women, a scout base, in the 1940s a cinema and some twenty years ago a billiard and pool hall. The old, dilapidated cottages had been converted, modernized or pulled down; featureless bungalows had been constructed in the vicinity, and a small industrial estate had sprung up just half a mile away. When Portia pulled into the parking area in front of the solid, grey stone building, among ten or more other cars, Arnold looked at her askance. It hardly seemed the kind of place where their search for esoteric advice on ancient Chinese porcelain would be successful.

As they got out of the car Arnold glanced up to the freshly painted board above the entrance. It partly covered the stone carved identity of the original building: Primitive Methodist Chapel 1850. The new sign stated the building was now in use as a Martial Arts and Community Centre. Arnold raised his eyebrows in doubt. Portia, locking the car, snorted indignantly. 'Trust me,' she snapped.

They walked into the reception area where Portia spoke to the blonde, comfortably middle-aged receptionist and explained they had arranged to meet someone at the centre. In a broad Northumberland accent she suggested they went through to the coffee bar on the first floor while she paged the person they were to meet. As they walked up the stairs, Arnold asked, 'Just who are we meeting anyway?'

Portia wrinkled her nose and moved through the swing door as he held it open for her. 'It's just a guy I went out with for a while, last year. It's something he told me once about an uncle of his. He was trying to impress me, you know how it is. But he said his uncle was rich. Said he was big in antique collections. So, I thought it might be useful if we met him, and had a chat.'

'Sounds all a bit vague to me,' Arnold remarked. 'This boyfriend of yours—'

'Not a boyfriend. Not now,' she snapped. 'I dumped him.'

Arnold raised an eyebrow. He knew the feeling.

They sat down at a table near the door; there was no one else in the room apart from the girl behind the counter. 'Looks Malaysian to me,' Portia muttered when she caught Arnold observing the waitress.

'So what is this place?' Arnold wondered.

'You saw the sign at the entrance.'

'But what kind of community? I wouldn't have thought Geordies were heavily into martial arts.'

Portia looked at him; he caught the stain of contemptuous amusement in her eyes. 'You don't get around much, do you? There's quite a gathering of Chinese in the northeast and Tyneside in particular, you know. A lot of them are in the restaurant trade, as you might expect, but there are plenty working in other industries too. All right, I'll agree they don't show up very prominently, not the way you find groups of Indians or Pakistanis congregating in areas like Bradford, but that's because the Chinese in particular like to keep themselves to themselves, adopt a low profile, don't get involved much in society beyond their own families and business connections. But believe me, there's plenty of them around.'

She turned her head as the swing doors opened. Two young men entered, dressed in identical black leotards, and wearing red bands across their foreheads. At sight of Portia one of them smiled, came forward hurriedly, extending a hand. 'Portia! It's good to see you!'

He was in his mid-twenties, Arnold guessed. He was Chinese in origin, of middle height with close-cropped

25

black hair, and his body was lean and smoothly-muscled. He exuded a sense of controlled power, his glance was searching as it swept past Portia to take a quick impression of Arnold, and then the man was holding Portia's hands in his, but not stepping too close, admiring her with sharp, snapping black eyes. 'You're looking good, Portia, it's been too long! But I won't come too close: we've been having a heavy workout and I need a shower.'

Arnold gained the impression that Portia preferred it that way, a measure of distance between them. He recalled her comment, that she had dumped this man. She was smiling, nevertheless, as she turned towards Arnold. 'This is a colleague of mine, Arnold Landon. He works in the department with me, and is a kind of elder statesman.'

'But not really that old,' Arnold smiled, and held out his hand. The grip he met was firm and competitive; the glance that met his was appraising and hard. Arnold guessed this man would have depths of commitment that were belied by his easy manner. 'Portia was never all that great on introductions,' the Chinese man averred. 'My name's Jeremy Tan.'

Portia tapped him on his muscled arm. 'Will your uncle be coming to meet us here?'

Her ex-boyfriend released Arnold's hand and turned back to her. 'I spoke to Uncle Henry and told him what you'd asked about and he said he'd be only too pleased to meet you, to discuss matters. He's got business interests in the area — you know that property development on the north shore? Anyway, he said it suited him to call in here, so that's why I suggested the centre. You've not been here before?'

'I'm not into martial arts.'

'No,' Jeremy Tan grinned. 'You always liked other kinds of games, as I recall. Anyway, look, I need to get a shower and — oh, I'm sorry, I should have introduced my friend here. Portia, Mr Landon, this is Steven Sullivan.'

Sullivan came forward, a towel slung loosely about his broad shoulders, taller than Jeremy, also black-haired but with startling blue eyes. Like Portia, he showed traces of

Asian heritage in his features: high cheekbones, an olive skin, and he moved with an easy grace, almost panther-like in his stride. He nodded to Arnold and shook hands; his glance rested rather longer on Portia as he took her hand. 'I've heard of you from Jeremy.'

'Not a lot, I swear, Portia,' Jeremy Tan said and guffawed. 'I was never a kiss-and-tell man!'

Arnold could see that she was slightly irritated; he also became aware that she had been immediately attracted to the man who was holding her hand. There was something about the way she held herself, the way she raised her head to hold the man's glance. She had a way of showing a man she liked him: Arnold had once experienced it.

'Anyway,' Jeremy Tan was saying, apparently oblivious to the slight tension that had arisen in the small group, 'like I said, Steve and I need to clean up. I would guess Uncle Henry will be along in a little while, so while we go off to the showers maybe you could get yourselves a cup of coffee. We'll be back shortly.'

The two men turned and made their way back through the swing doors. Portia watched them go. A feline smile touched her red lips, as her eyes dwelled on the man walking out behind Jeremy Tan. 'Dishy . . .' she murmured.

Arnold left her to her dreams and went across to the counter to obtain two coffees. When he came back and sat down beside her, he asked her, 'So where did you meet Jeremy Tan?'

She shrugged diffidently. 'Oh, it was the usual kind of contact. I was in a nightclub with a few friends — no one you'd know, Arnold — and he was there with some other guys. We got to talking — he knows Singapore well, and he's travelled quite a bit in Southeast Asia, so it was a point of contact. He asked me out, we had a thing going for a while, but, well, these Chinese guys, you know they have a kind of different view about women than we usually see in the West. I didn't care for some of his attitudes, so, in the end I dumped him.'

'Amicably enough, it seems,' Arnold observed.

Portia humphed in disagreement. 'I wouldn't count on that. Jeremy . . . he can be a hard man. But, well, yes, I suppose there's not been any bad blood. Or if there was, he got over it.'

'What's he do?'

She wrinkled her brow, and shrugged. 'I'm not really sure, to tell the truth. He works in Leeds, sometimes, and Manchester — I know that. He's got a base in Newcastle, though, and I think all he ever told me was that it was a kind of import-export business. He did tell me once his boss was a man called Freddie Cheung, but what he does I really don't know.'

'And he's got an Uncle Henry,' Arnold murmured as he sipped his coffee.

'Henry Wong.' Portia was silent for a little while. 'I didn't say too much about it, because I had to contact Jeremy and make sure that I was getting things right. But when I rang him Jeremy confirmed that his uncle is a bit of a collector of antiques and should certainly know a great deal about Chinese porcelain. Mr Wong has his fingers in a number of pies, it would seem. I looked him up in *Northern Who's Who* and it seems he's on the board of a number of companies here in the north, well respected, wealthy, been honoured by a couple of universities, that sort of thing.'

Arnold removed the auction catalogue from his briefcase and opened it, flicking through the pages ruminatively. 'Well, let's hope he can help us identify the best pieces here.'

They sat in silence for a little while, until the swing doors opened again. Arnold looked up to see Steven Sullivan entering. He was dressed casually in a roll-neck sweater and dark trousers; his dark hair was swept back damply, and his blue eyes were fixed on Portia as he came forward. 'Jeremy won't be long; he's on his way.'

Arnold wondered whether the man had deliberately hurried his shower to get here before his companion; certainly he took the chair next to Portia with alacrity when she offered it to him. He signalled to the waitress to bring him a coffee: clearly, he was a regular here at the centre.

'So,' Portia murmured appreciatively, 'martial arts. Bit dangerous, isn't it?'

Steven Sullivan grinned; his teeth were even and white. 'Not really. More like ballet, in fact.'

She snorted. 'Kicking the hell out of each other? Come off it!'

'It's a discipline,' he argued. 'Yes, it's possible to maim or even kill by using hands and feet but the objective is to strengthen one's focus, sharpen physical reflexes, control the mind and the emotions. Not to injure anyone.' His gaze held hers and Arnold felt vaguely uncomfortable. There had been an immediate and very real attraction between these two and he felt very much on the edge of things.

'So, do you work with Jeremy?' he asked.

'Me? No,' Sullivan said quickly. 'In fact we only met because of our mutual interest in martial arts. It's at this centre that we first made each other's acquaintance. No, I'm afraid I'm a rather boring accountant of a kind. I work in Newcastle with a big auditing firm. Carling and Chataway. You might have heard of them.'

A big firm indeed. 'Do I detect a certain transatlantic element in your voice?' Arnold asked.

Sullivan laughed. 'It's one of those things that always seem most difficult to suppress. I had an Irish mother, so you'd think there'd be something of the Old Country in my accent, but in fact I've spent the last fifteen years in the States. My mother did right by me: she managed to get me a good education. MIT for my degree in Maths and Computer Science; Yale for my MBA. Then Anderson's, before they blew up as an accountancy firm, after which I came to the UK when I got a good offer from Carling and Chataway.'

Arnold guessed the brief history was for Portia's benefit, not his. She was smiling at Sullivan. 'Your mother must be proud of you.'

He shook his head. 'She never really saw it happen. She died five years ago.'

Portia reached out a hand and touched his. 'I'm sorry,' she said softly, sympathy swimming in her dark eyes. Arnold shuffled in his seat, wishing he was somewhere else.

'Is your father still alive?' he asked.

Steven Sullivan glanced at Arnold, shook his head quickly. 'No. He died before I went to the States. Ah . . .' As the door behind them swung open he turned his head, rose quickly to his feet. 'Here's Jeremy.'

Jeremy Tan was standing in the doorway, holding open the swing doors. The man who entered behind him, leaning slightly on a stick, was dressed in a dark, well-cut business suit. He was perhaps approaching sixty years of age, and was portly in build. His head was hairless, his face almost cherubic: piggy eyes twinkled happily behind dark-rimmed spectacles as he advanced towards them, and his smile was wide and welcoming. He was quite short, perhaps five feet five in height, but he exuded a confidence that was unassumed. Arnold guessed he was a successful businessman who was used to getting on with people: he would be the kind of man who would find a solution in the most difficult of circumstances, who knew that he could charm, manipulate and persuade the most recalcitrant of colleagues. 'Henry Wong,' he stated, with chubby hand extended.

Jeremy quickly made the introductions. They sat down, and Henry Wong looked around him with a smile. 'Methodist chapel turned into martial arts centre. It is one of the very few ways in which the East conquers the West. For me, however, martial arts are a closed book. There are different battles to be fought in board rooms!' He chuckled infectiously, as he looked at Arnold. 'So you and the young lady here want to talk to me about Chinese porcelain. You will forgive me coming straight to the point, but I have a meeting to attend in half an hour, and in any case I have a great passion for antiques and am at my happiest talking of such things.'

'Which means, Uncle Henry, that I ought to excuse myself,' Jeremy Tan observed. 'I need to get back to my office.'

'And you have no interest in antiques.' Wong smiled indulgently.

Steven Sullivan also rose to his feet. 'I also should leave. It's been a pleasure to meet you, Mr Wong . . . Mr Landon.' He turned to Portia and smiled. She glanced at Arnold and he thought he caught a hint of panic in her eyes. Jeremy Tan was already heading for the door and Sullivan was about to follow him. Her glance slipped from Arnold to Wong and back again. 'Er . . . would you mind, Arnold, perhaps you could talk to Mr Wong about this business? Steven, could I have a quick word with you?'

Sullivan was clearly more than happy to have an opportunity for a private conversation with her. He glanced at Jeremy Tan, who hesitated, then nodded, and when Henry Wong's nephew had left Portia rose. With Steven Sullivan she moved towards the coffee counter; Henry Wong watched them go. The gleam in his eyes suggested to Arnold that he could guess what was happening. 'Young people,' he murmured, 'they can be so . . . impatient.' He sighed theatrically. 'At my age, one is left only with old things, the smoothness of ancient oak, the glint of gold from another age, the perfection of porcelain . . .' His wise old eyes turned back to Arnold. 'So, perhaps you and I, we can have a conversation untouched by unfulfilled desires . . . ?'

Arnold handed the auction catalogue to him, and explained the situation regarding the bequest. 'Portia contacted your nephew, he put us in touch, and we've been hoping you can help us identify the most appropriate pieces for retention by the Department of Museums and Antiquities.'

'This Lady Mannington,' the older man murmured. 'She was a great philanthropist . . .'

He fell silent for several minutes as he examined the catalogue, peering at each item with care, clucking his tongue in delight from time to time, caressing the glossy pages of the booklet when he found a piece that particularly attracted his attention. Finally, he checked the date of the auction and nodded. 'Interesting . . . I think that I shall be attending this sale. There are a number of pieces . . . In reality, Mr Landon, I find myself in something of a quandary. There are things here I desire. I would pay much for them. But some of these would be items I would advise you to retain, for their beauty, their intrinsic value, and for their relationship with other pieces in the collection.' His eyes widened thoughtfully behind his glasses. 'A dilemma, certainly. But . . . I am known as a man of probity. I have a reputation to uphold in the community. I will not cheat you, Mr Landon.'

'I would be the last to suggest—' Arnold began hastily.

Henry Wong smiled broadly, and held up a fleshy, beringed hand. 'Please, do not protest. I tease you. Mr Landon, I will be happy to advise you. I will need some days to make some enquiries, check some sources . . . but I will suggest a list of items to you. Meanwhile, it would be useful if you explained to me the provenance of Lady Mannington's collection.'

Arnold leaned forward. 'I imagine you'll be aware that the East India Companies were formed in the early seventeenth century to develop the trade between Europe and the Orient. The English company was formed in 1600; the Dutch in 1602, with French, Swedish, Portuguese and Danish companies starting a little later. They all used large ships known as East Indiamen to carry immensely rich cargoes — gold and silver on the way out, spices, pepper, cinnamon, cloves, balsam, silks and perfumes on their return.'

Henry Wong nodded sagely. 'Yes . . . I understand the tea trade started a little later, but I am also aware that another of the important items the East Indiamen carried was Chinese porcelain.'

'That's certainly so,' Arnold agreed. 'The outward route for the East Indiamen took advantage of the north-east trade winds to head for China; on their return the ships followed the south-east trade winds up the Atlantic. The *Vendela* was a Danish company ship. In 1736 it began its return journey from Formosa with a cargo of Chinese porcelain, through the South China Sea into the Indian Ocean. Extant documents demonstrate that it added to its cargo en route, taking pepper on board at Calcutta, before picking up a cargo of cinnamon in Sri Lanka, or Ceylon as it was then called. From there the *Vendela* drove south, rounding the Horn and running north into the South Atlantic. The south-east trades took the *Vendela* up beyond Cape Verde, past the coasts of Portugal and France before it entered the Channel and berthed in Amsterdam.'

'This would have been its main destination?'

'It would seem so, as far as most of its cargo was concerned. At Amsterdam it offloaded its spice cargo, and took on silver coin and bullion. But from the accounts of the company it seems that part of the *Vendela*'s cargo of Chinese porcelain was destined for Dublin. Now, it could have offloaded that part of the cargo while driving north for Amsterdam, but probably because of adverse weather conditions the owners agreed with the captain's decision to land the porcelain in Dublin on the new, outward journey back to the Indian Ocean. The *Vendela*, now with silver coin, bullion and the remnants of the Chinese porcelain, set out for China in September 1737. It was quickly in trouble.'

'In order to pick up the north-east trade winds where would it head?' Henry Wong asked curiously.

Arnold traced a route on the table in front of him, using the coffee cups to illustrate the problem. 'From Amsterdam, the *Vendela* would have had to head northwards, to round the Shetland Islands and then skirt Ireland, calling in at Dublin before beginning its run south back into the Atlantic. Unfortunately, the East Indiaman never even reached the Shetlands. A storm blew up, strong gales drove them west, the Indiaman was dismasted, and the ship went aground on the north-east coast of England.'

'Much of the cargo was lost?' Wong queried.

Arnold shook his head. 'No, not really. Salvage operations were undertaken immediately the storm blew itself out. The silver coin and most of the bullion were taken off successfully. The *Vendela* was a large vessel; it took a pounding on the Black Needles but it held up well for almost five days.' Arnold extracted a slim file from his briefcase. 'Salvage vessels clustered around her — look, there's an old etching here of the scene taken from a contemporary account — and they were all hurrying to take off the silver and gold. But the luck of the salvors finally ran out: another storm blew up, the ship broke her back, and she sank.'

'Taking the porcelain with her,' Henry Wong mused.

Arnold nodded. 'Not all of it, as we know. Some had already been taken off and was claimed by the Mannington family. And then, there was another salvage operation some twenty years ago. The location of the wreck was well enough documented, and held by the Manningtons, so with the new technology available, further items were recovered. They all formed part of the private collection held eventually by Lady Mannington.'

'Which is now up for sale, after the death of the elderly lady,' Henry Wong murmured, turning over the pages of the catalogue once again.

Arnold was silent for a while as he watched the Chinese businessman pore over the glossy photographs in the auction brochure. 'The bequest by Lady Mannington includes that part of the porcelain which was salvaged; the rest remains in the wreck of the *Vendela*. What we've been trying to do in the department is to mount an exhibition and create an observation point where we can inform the public at large of the history of the *Vendela* and, perhaps, in due course interest someone in conducting a new undersea search. But that is unlikely. The last information we have dates from the eighties, when a dive was carried out and soundings taken. They weren't all that successful, but in any case we at the department feel this is all part of our heritage, and should be preserved.'

'And this project was what drew Lady Mannington's attention to your department?'

'That's so. And it resulted in the bequest,' Arnold confirmed.

'Everything all right?' Portia Tyrrel asked, approaching the table. Startled, Arnold looked up. Her eyes were gleaming, and there was a slight flush to her cheek. Beyond her he saw Steven Sullivan walking towards the back door of the café. He raised a hand in farewell.

Henry Wong was amused. He nodded to her, smiled knowingly at Arnold. 'Everything is fine,' he asserted. 'We've managed well without you. Mr Landon has explained all to me. And I think I will be able — indeed, happy — to assist you. May I keep the catalogue?'

'By all means,' Arnold replied as Henry Wong rose, shook hands with Arnold, and patted Portia's between his own, in an avuncular fashion.

'I will be in contact very soon,' Henry Wong assured them, and made his way towards the door, leaning slightly on his gold-headed walking stick.

After he had left, Arnold looked at Portia. 'I thought you were supposed to be here on business. What was all that with Steven Sullivan?'

She laughed. 'Hey Arnold, ain't I entitled to a life?'

3

With the Chief Executive ill in hospital, administrative matters in the offices were somewhat disarranged. Committee meetings were rescheduled as the Deputy Chief Executive, close to retirement and never known for decisive decision making, found himself forced to undertake responsibilities he had managed to avoid most of his working career. His response to the unwelcome burden was to delegate duties left right and centre, and for a few days Karen Stannard was unable to devote much attention to her department as she was called away to stand in by way of support at various finance and budgeting meetings of the general council. It made no difference to the *Vendela* decision. The project was shelved.

On the other hand Arnold, in Karen's absence, managed to clear his own desk of a number of files that had been clogging up the system. He remained more desk-bound than he desired, but at least he caught up with a considerable backlog of work. Yet at the back of his mind was the ever-present query whether Henry Wong would be able to help them in the matter of the Mannington bequest. They had no other avenue to explore. They had tried the universities, and other museum departments in the north-east, and there were no experts on Chinese porcelain to be found. Moreover, there was no assistance to be obtained centrally: time simply did not permit the gathering of advice from auction houses and other experts in London.

Happily, Henry Wong proved as good as his word. He was on the telephone to Arnold at the end of the week. Aware that the date for the auction was looming, he had undertaken the research he needed to make as a matter of urgency.

'I shall come up from Manchester to be present at the auction myself,' he explained. 'There are a number of items in the sale which are of considerable interest to me. For example, listed are some coins from the reign of the Chinese Emperor Kangxi — they would be dated between 1662 and 1722. I am most interested in them. But of course, the major interest lies in Lady Mannington's collection. I have now had time to consider the matter carefully, and I have discussed the items in the collection with some friends and colleagues of mine who hold similar interests . . .'

Arnold arranged a meeting with Karen Stannard to report on the conversation. He took with him another copy of the auction catalogue. She was a little late for the meeting; she entered in a somewhat flustered state, muttering about incompetent hack politicians, and when she saw him waiting in her office she dumped her files on the desk and immediately picked up her phone. 'Portia? I think you'd better sit in on this, since you were involved in the earlier meeting with Mr Wong.'

Portia had arranged the meeting with the Chinese businessman, Arnold agreed mentally, but she had hardly been involved.

Portia smiled sweetly at him when she entered the room. She was wearing a tightly fitting dark blue dress, high at the neck, emphasizing the slimness of her figure. She had a confident, self-satisfied air and the glance she sent in his direction, raising one eyebrow, was provocative. Rumours were already circulating among the gossips in the department: Portia Tyrrel had found herself a new man. Arnold had a pretty good idea of the man's identity. A half-Chinese martial arts enthusiast called Steven Sullivan.

Karen Stannard looked Portia up and down inquisitively, seemed to be about to ask a question then thought better of it. She settled back in her chair, raised her chin and suggested, 'So let's not waste any time. What's the news?'

'Mr Wong's been in touch,' Arnold explained, 'and he advises that the auction house should now be informed that the following items marked in the brochure be withdrawn from the sale, as they should be included among the thirty items that the department is entitled to claim under the bequest Lady Mannington made.' He handed the catalogue across the desk to Karen, open at the relevant page. 'Wong advises we should make a choice as marked in the brochure: this set of blue and white goblets, shown on that page, then those teapots on the following page. He also suggests we should acquire these mustard pots, pillboxes and tea bowls.'

'You've also got marked some small *blanc-de-chine* figures,' Karen murmured, after a short silence as she inspected the objects identified.

'That's right. And also those bowls and soup spoons. Mr Wong explained that they were popular because of the seventeenth-century craze for oriental porcelain. He tells me Daniel Defoe referred to it as Chinamania, describing it rather scathingly as "the Custom or humour, as I may call it, of furnishing houses with China-ware".'

'Mr Wong sounds like an erudite individual,' Karen observed, studying closely *blanc-de-chine* figurines.

'He's quite a charming old man,' Portia enthused. Arnold glanced at her. She had barely made Wong's acquaintance, he recalled irritably.

'Henry Wong made the point to me on the phone,' Arnold continued, 'that the collection is very valuable for its rarity: he's ascertained that the porcelain comes from the kilns at Fowliang, which had only just started production again in the 1680s, after decades of disruption caused by the Manchu invasion from the north of the Ming Empire.'

'So the estimate made by the executors to the Mannington estate may not be far out,' Karen suggested, with a calculating glance at Arnold.

He shrugged. 'Penrose thought a hundred thousand. I suspect it could be more. Certainly, Henry Wong is excited about the collection. He intends bidding himself for several pieces. But the value of the items will only add to our problem.'

'What particular problem is that?' Karen enquired.

'As you know, the purpose behind the bequest is that the items we choose shall be put on display for the benefit of the public at large. That's going to be difficult, for security reasons. It's a pity, of course, that we won't be going ahead with the *Vendela* project, because that would have been an ideal setting to draw attention to the items, and even have occasional display of the bequest. The publicity, the tourist potential—'

'We've been over all this before,' Karen interrupted testily. 'No point in discussing it again. The *Vendela* project is suspended at best; my opinion is it's dead. But that doesn't mean we shouldn't put our heads together to plan how best to take advantage of this bequest, and ensure that Lady Mannington's wishes are carried out.' She was silent for a little while, staring at the marked items in the catalogue, tapping her slim fingers on the photographs. 'We haven't even seen the things at first-hand yet. When is the auction?'

'Tuesday,' Arnold replied.

'What are your diaries like?' Karen asked after a short pause. 'I think maybe we should take some time out of the office and attend the auction, get a feeling for the kind of things we're taking on.'

Without the Chief Executive breathing down their necks, Arnold thought, and questioning whether the department could afford to have its three senior staff off on a jaunt to the auction rooms. He wondered, nevertheless, why Portia seemed to have brightened up even further at Karen's suggestion.

* * *

The answer came when they walked into the auction room. It had been decided to hold it in a disused showroom at Jesmond, which had been specially hired for the purpose.

The sale had attracted a great deal of interest and the room was packed. The artefacts claimed by the department had been removed from the catalogue but there was still a sufficiently large number of items to bring in dealers from London, Liverpool, Manchester and Leeds, as well as members of the general public locally. There was a considerable buzz of excitement as the auctioneer began the sale, after stating its provenance. Arnold kept his eye on Henry Wong, seated near the front of the high-ceilinged hall. The plump Chinese businessman, looking around, had seen their group when they had entered and taken the seats they had reserved, and he had raised a hand in acknowledgement. Arnold had already thanked him over the telephone for his assistance, but Wong had dismissed the matter gracefully, stating he had felt honoured to have been asked. Now, Arnold watched Wong as the sale proceeded: the businessman sat placidly, waiting for the items in which he was interested.

When Karen had led the group to their seats Portia had been looking around with a certain anxiety, and Arnold soon realized why. Shortly before the sale commenced Portia raised a hand, Arnold followed her glance, and saw that standing near the door was Steven Sullivan. Portia gestured to him to join them: surreptitiously she had managed to keep a seat empty beside her. Karen Stannard looked surprised when the tall young man joined them. Portia quickly made the introductions.

'I'm surprised to see you here,' Arnold observed. 'I didn't know you were a collector.'

Sullivan smiled, glanced at Portia and shook his head. 'I'm certainly not a collector, but Portia told me about the auction, and since I'm working on an assignment here in Jesmond for a few weeks I thought I'd come along to see the fun.'

'Mr Wong's seated down the front,' Portia remarked as she patted the seat beside her. 'Sit down here, and you can say hello to him later.'

Steven Sullivan did as she suggested and shook his head again. 'I don't really know Mr Wong. All I know is he's Jeremy

Tan's uncle. The only time I've met him was at the martial arts centre that day.'

'Well, it seems he'll be bidding today, for some of the porcelain items,' Arnold remarked.

The group settled down as the auction commenced. It was the first time Arnold had attended such a large sale and he was interested to note how the bow-tied, bald-headed auctioneer used a practised eye to pick out the bidders unerringly. He realized there were some determined collectors in the room, and the general air of excitement rose as the bids for some of the items began to rise dramatically. But he was unprepared for the stir of excitement that was generated when the Mannington items finally came up for sale.

Beside him he could almost feel the tension in Karen Stannard's body. She was leaning forward slightly, concentrating, her lips parted, eyes gleaming. He guessed she appreciated the controlled urgency that lay behind the bids, understood the almost animal, hunting instincts that some of the purchasers were gripped by, and when a group of blue porcelain bowls went for almost fifty thousand pounds she turned to him, gripping his arm in excitement. 'I think that damned estimate of Penrose's is going to be far too low.'

Arnold was not taken with a similar enthusiasm. Instead, he was interested to observe how patterns of activity emerged: he soon identified some seven people in the room who seemed to be engaged in a contest. Three men to his left were very active. They were probably dealers, he guessed, known to each other, and rivals for the better pieces. But two other men were also worth watching: one of them was Henry Wong, who sat almost complacently in his seat but to whom the auctioneer turned his glance regularly. The other was another Chinese bidder, seated two rows back from Wong. He was of much the same age, heavily built, his grey hair cropped almost to his skull. He was less impassive than Wong, and took his defeats with less equanimity; from time to time he glanced at the Chinese businessman almost aggressively, and when he outbid Wong a small spasm of pleasure touched his features. Arnold smiled: it was clear that the two Chinese bidders were known to each other, and were locked in rivalry. With one particular piece the price rose rapidly and other bidders soon dropped out while the contest raged between the two men. It was finally knocked down to Wong's rival: Arnold heard the auctioneer say, 'The bid is with Mr Cheung.' When the hammer fell, Henry Wong looked back to his rival. He inclined his head graciously in defeat; Cheung made no secret of his triumphant pleasure.

'That's the guy Jeremy works for,' Arnold heard Steven Sullivan murmur to Portia.

The auction continued until late afternoon. At its conclusion, as the crowd filtered out of the showroom to return to their cars Karen Stannard exclaimed in delight. 'I've been keeping a rough count. Have you any idea how much those pieces in the collection went for?'

Portia linked an arm into Steven Sullivan's. 'How much?'

'It's unbelievable. By this calculation, the whole collection is worth nearly seven million! And the items Mr Wong chose for us — all I can say is they must be valued at something like three hundred thousand!'

A quiet voice murmured at her elbow. 'That would be a conservative estimate. You would be Miss Stannard, I presume.'

Karen turned quickly to see the portly Chinese businessman at her elbow. There was a slight smile on Henry Wong's chubby features as he took her hand and bowed over it in an old-world manner. Arnold hastened to confirm the introduction, and Karen was quick both to offer her congratulations to Henry Wong on his own purchases, and to thank him effusively for the assistance he had provided the department in selecting the items held back from the auction. He waved a deprecating hand. 'Believe me, it was more than a pleasure. It was a privilege to be able to inspect the collection so closely before it went into the auction. It gave me some advantage over my rivals.'

'Mr Cheung, you mean?' Arnold ventured.

Wong flicked a shrewd, calculating glance at Arnold, hesitated, then smiled broadly. 'Ah, you noticed. Mr Cheung is well known to me: we have interests in common, and he is a collector like myself. I fear we were guilty, between us, of inflating certain prices merely because of our long-seated rivalry.' He nodded to Karen. 'But I detain you. I trust that we shall meet again.' He smiled at Arnold and Portia, then glanced at Steven Sullivan. Surprisingly to Arnold, there was no hint of recognition in his eyes. But then, it had been merely a brief meeting at the martial arts centre.

Arnold watched the Chinese man as he left, limping slightly, leaning on his cane. As he neared the exit from the showroom Arnold saw him exchange a few words with his crop-haired, Chinese rival. They were both smiling; perhaps they both had reason to do so, since Arnold calculated they had probably broken even in their contest to obtain items from the Mannington collection.

Karen Stannard let out an explosive sigh of pleasure. Excitement still glittered in her eyes. She was in an unusually expansive mood. Triumphantly, she looked at Arnold. 'It's been a good day! I don't think we should really let it end here. Why don't we go somewhere for a meal?'

Arnold glanced at his watch. 'It's six o'clock. Bit early, but if we get out of town, maybe try one of the country pubs up around Morpeth way—'

Steven Sullivan intervened. He glanced at Portia, then said, 'Er . . . if you would excuse me. Perhaps I could make a suggestion . . .'

Karen hesitated, frowned slightly; perhaps she had not contemplated his joining them in what would have been a departmental celebration. But after a brief glance towards Portia she looked back to the young accountant. She eyed him approvingly, and Arnold could guess what she was thinking: a well-set-up, good-looking young man, and if he was a friend of Portia's it might be amusing to gatecrash a budding friendship. 'Somewhere here in Newcastle, are you suggesting?' she enquired.

Steven Sullivan smiled. His teeth were white and even, his smile attractive, and his blue eyes, fixed on Karen, really were quite startling. His Irish heritage, Arnold thought. 'We could go out to Tynemouth,' Sullivan suggested. 'It's not far, and I know quite an interesting place, which I'm pretty sure opens early in the evening . . .'

Portia Tyrrel frowned, seemed a little hesitant, but that would be due to Karen's sudden interest in her acquaintance. But she was in no position to argue as Karen said firmly, 'Well, then, why not? Lead on, and we'll follow! Or better still,' she offered, as she linked an arm in his, drawing him away from Portia, 'why don't I go with you in your car, and Arnold and Portia can come along in his?'

Arnold was amused. He noted Portia's disgruntlement as they made their way out to the car park, Karen still in deep conversation with Sullivan. She settled comfortably into the grey Mercedes that Sullivan drove; Portia slammed the passenger door in Arnold's car in annoyance. Traffic was fairly heavy as they made their way out of town on the coast road and Portia remained hunched in the passenger seat, glowering her displeasure. Arnold heard her mutter to herself, 'That bloody woman . . .'

They followed the Mercedes the short distance to Tynemouth and Arnold pulled in beside it when it parked near the rocky headland occupied by the priory and castle built by Robert de Mowbray, the Norman earl of Northumberland. There was a hint of rain in the air and the sky had darkened as the small group walked down the street towards the restaurant recommended by Steven Sullivan. Karen was at her most flirtatious, animated and charming, out to impress, determined to irritate her junior colleague. It was the way she operated, Arnold knew, and Portia herself ought to be well enough aware that it was Karen's way of demonstrating her power and position.

The restaurant, named the Golden Palace, was decorated in traditional red and gold. They entered the narrow doorway into a small seating area: from behind a frieze screen of a prancing golden dragon, a black-waistcoated waiter came hurrying forward to welcome them. They took seats and accepted menus: Sullivan ordered a round of drinks. After a brief glance at the menu Karen played the role of the helpless unsophisticate, suggesting that since he knew the restaurant perhaps Sullivan should order for them all. Portia opened her mouth to protest but thought better of it as Sullivan caught her glance and raised an eyebrow. Arnold smiled: Sullivan was clearly aware of the game Karen was playing.

Karen still dominated the conversation during the next ten minutes, enthusing about the porcelain, flirting outrageously with Sullivan, and enjoying Portia's clear discomfiture. Sullivan had ordered some wine: it was waiting for them on their table in the main dining area. It was getting dark in the street outside but it was still early for diners and there was only one other person in the room, seated at a table near the kitchen entrance, engrossed in his meal. Arnold paid little attention to him, other than to note he was dark-suited, heavy-set, perhaps in his mid-thirties, with fair hair and gold-rimmed spectacles. He glanced up as they entered, but then returned to his food. Arnold took a seat beside Portia, with his back to the kitchen; Karen was already seating herself beside Sullivan.

'So, Steven, what exactly is it that you do?' she asked, fixing him with eyes widely innocent, leaning forward as though hanging on his every word.

It was to be the pattern for the next ten minutes, while they sipped their drinks and waited for the arrival of the food Sullivan had ordered. He explained he was a corporate accountant; she asked him about his work and the firm he was employed by. She drew from him an account of his time at Massachusetts Institute of Technology, and discussed with him the content of his course at Yale for the MBA. He had ordered a combination dish for them to begin, but Karen paid little attention to it as she continued to monopolize Sullivan's attention, to the considerable annoyance of Portia. She was glowering sullenly at the spare rib on her plate as though she was tempted to throw it at Karen's head. Steven Sullivan was relaxed and, Arnold guessed, somewhat amused.

'And your mother was Irish?' Karen asked.

The waiter came forward, asking whether the combination was to their taste. When Sullivan said something clearly complimentary in Cantonese he ducked his head, smiled and walked away. Sullivan turned back to Karen.

'That's right. She was from Dublin, originally. She came to England to attend Manchester University, then got a job as a teacher in a college in Stockport for a while. Linguistics. But she came into a certain amount of money and I think she considered my prospects would be better in the States. I was in my early teens. We went to New York, first of all.'

Karen was slightly puzzled. 'And your father . . . ?'

Steven Sullivan sipped his drink. There was an amused glint in his eyes. 'He was Chinese.'

'Well, yes, I suppose I realized . . .' Karen was suddenly floundering. Portia raised her head, a malicious gleam in her eyes. Karen had backed herself into a corner suddenly, and a social gaffe was on its way. She was unable to resist it. 'But your surname . . .'

Portia shifted in her seat; her thigh struck Arnold's and he glanced at her. She was alight with muffled pleasure. But Steven Sullivan was in no manner disturbed. He smiled broadly as he reached out with his chopsticks and picked up some dried seaweed to transfer to his plate. He followed it with a portion of prawn. 'You know, it's interesting that, oddly enough, modern attitudes to marriage among young people in England are merely an echo of Chinese practices for centuries. Chinese men married, of course, but such marriages were in many instances for reasons of convenience, status, or the acquisition of wealth. Thereafter, men often acquired mistresses, for purposes of sexual pleasure, social activities, a whole raft of reasons. But the reality in Chinese society was that concubinage was never looked down on. It was an accepted part of life in China. And the status of a favoured concubine could be significant.'

Karen's glance dropped. A slight tinge of colour had crept into her cheek. She hesitated. 'I didn't mean to suggest—'

'Please, don't be embarrassed.' He was grinning. His glance rose, to look past Arnold's shoulder as the doors to the kitchen opened. 'The fact is my parents weren't married. That's why I use my mother's maiden name. It's the way I was brought up in the States. But that's not unusual in this day and age, is it? As for my father—'

He broke off suddenly, his blue eyes widening, and he straightened in his seat. Arnold stared at him. Sullivan laid down his chopsticks, his attention riveted on something behind Arnold. Then there was a sudden cry, a sharp, cracking, explosive sound, followed by a crashing, as a chair went over backwards. Arnold turned his head, looking behind him. The fair-haired man he had noticed earlier was thrashing on his back, his foot drumming against the table, while the chair he had been seated on was skidding across the floor. The white tablecloth was disarranged, with dishes sliding off the table, crashing to the carpet. From the corner of his eye Arnold caught further movements, the figure of a man, dark-clothed, pushing his way hurriedly through the swinging door of the kitchen, and then for one long moment everything seemed to stand still, Karen, Portia, himself and Sullivan seated in a horrified group as the man behind them pulsed his life on to the reddening carpet.

It was Steven Sullivan who was the first to move. 'Wait here!'

His chair crashed backwards as he lurched to his feet. Arnold became aware of the lithe muscularity of the man as he leaped away from the table, sending dishes flying, and ran towards the kitchen doors. He hesitated briefly to give only a cursory glance at the fair-haired man who lay dying beneath his table, before he thrust his way through the swinging door. There were sounds of panic in the kitchen, frightened cries, the clatter of pans and dishes. Arnold was on his feet also, tardily, as Sullivan disappeared, Portia was white-faced, panic-stricken, and Karen was grabbing at Arnold's arm, as though to detain him. He thrust her away and ran across the room, to kneel beside the dying man on the floor. He saw the wound in the man's throat, the blood pulsing out in a regular flow, and he became aware of the glazing of the man's brown eyes, a gurgling rattle in his throat. The gold-rimmed spectacles lay twisted and broken on the carpet beside his head.

Arnold swung around, shouting at Karen. 'The phone! Call an ambulance!'

Portia seemed incapable of movement; shocked, her mouth was open in a silent scream. Shaken, but more self-possessed than her colleague, Karen took a mobile phone out of her handbag and pressed the buttons. White-faced, eyes fixed on Arnold, she began to make the call.

Arnold felt helpless. He stared at the dying man. He didn't know what to do. Then further sounds of panic from the kitchen drew his attention. With a quick glance at the two women, Arnold rose from his knees and ran towards the kitchen. Within the area was a scene of confusion. There were three Chinese men there, the waiter and two others dressed in stained aprons. They stood against the wall, terrified, shaking. One, the youngest, was bleeding from the nose. The kitchen itself was in chaos, with cooking utensils scattered about, rice and meat scattered on the tiled floor. The tiles were slippery with brown-coloured sauce. There was no sign of Sullivan.

'What's happened?' Arnold demanded. 'Where's the man who came in here?'

They stared at him as though uncomprehending, made no reply. Arnold shouted at them again, then grabbed the arm of one of the scared cooks and shook him. The man's eyes were wide in panic but he turned his head, gestured towards the back of the kitchen. Arnold ran forward, skidding on the greasy floor, kicking aside pans and plates under foot. At the far end of the narrow room that served as the kitchen there was a door, half-open. He dragged at it: he found himself in a small vestibule, a store room containing boxes and bags of varied provisions. The door at the exit from the store room was closed. Arnold grabbed the handle, pulled open the door.

A pile of black plastic bags lay at his feet. There was a strong, pungent smell of decaying refuse in his nostrils as he stepped over one of the bags, which had burst open.

He was in a narrow dark alleyway, lined with dustbins. The light was fading, the alley seemed deserted. At the far end, where the alley gave way to the street, he caught sight of movement as a black cat began to cross; it paused, staring down towards Arnold, one paw raised, still, tense with suspicion.

Then Arnold heard a groan, a stirring close by. Two of the bins had been knocked over. They lay on their sides. Arnold saw a hand, fingers curling. The cat watched impassively as Arnold stepped over the bins and knelt down. Beside the bins in the dark alley he could make out the body of Steven Sullivan, lying on his side, an arm flung over his face. The groan came again, and Arnold reached out, moved Sullivan's arm. The young man's eyes opened, the lids flickering. There was a dark stain on one side of his head, just above the left ear.

The black cat had seen enough. Losing interest, it moved across the alleyway opening, unhurried, and was lost to sight.

CHAPTER TWO

1

The Chief Constable was not a man addicted to his desk. He enjoyed his status and position, but felt that an important element of his role lay in what he described as 'networking'. It meant spending time with politicians and wealthy businessmen, attending professional dinners, giving speeches locally and, when called upon, elsewhere in the country. And if there was a conference called on police matters, he was inclined to attend personally. Not that such attendance meant necessarily attending all the sessions of the conference: there was always more networking to undertake. So when he went to a conference, he usually insisted upon a senior police officer — senior but not too senior — to accompany him, make notes, prepare a report and attend all the sessions the Chief Constable could not.

This was an occasion when Detective Chief Inspector Jack O'Connor had been called upon to carry out the necessary dogsbodying.

Not that O'Connor minded too much. It got him away from the daily grind of office work back at headquarters, gave him some more interesting surroundings to visit, and played a part in dragging him away from the preoccupations that had been spiralling him down into depression lately.

There was his father, in a York nursing home, stricken with Alzheimer's and recognizing no one. And there was the woman for whom he still yearned, the woman who touched him in his dreams, the woman who was still out there, but unavailable as far as he was concerned because she had almost brought his career crashing down about his ears, as she could yet do if he attempted to renew their dangerous relationship.

And Padua, the city of St Anthony, gave him the opportunity to clear his mind of the woman, and the job, and thoughts of his dying father. The Chief Constable had decided they should arrive a day before the conference began, so while his superior officer networked with important people attending the meeting, O'Connor was free to stroll along the Corso del Populo and through the Piazza delle Erba into the lively heart of the old city. He was not interested in the usual tourist opportunities such as the fourteenth-century Augustinian church, painstakingly rebuilt after being bombed in the Second World War, or the Palazzo del Capitanio, the former residence of the city's ruler. He was content that first afternoon and evening to enjoy a solitary cappuccino in viewing distance of Donatello's magnificent *Gattamelata* equestrian statue, and later a quiet dinner of *ravioloni di agro* — a light ravioli in butter and sage sauce — in the courtyard of a small restaurant where posters on the walls explained to him that jazz groups performed on Saturday nights.

The wine was light, but good. The evening was warm. The courtyard was busy with diners, but most seemed to be couples. It was difficult not to remember Isabella . . . as he sat here, alone, in Italy.

Back at the hotel he spent a sleepless night, plagued by memories and recollections of the softness of her, the love-making on shuttered afternoons. Until the horrific, explosive ending to their affair.

It was something of a relief next morning to be forced to listen, in the conference room in the Oratorio di San Giorgio, which had been hired for the occasion, to the conference speakers, and try to wash his mind clear of his problems. The

Chief Constable, seated three rows in front of O'Connor with other senior officers, would expect O'Connor to produce a full report of the proceedings: it would be a report that the Chief Constable himself would later present to the politicians and senior officers back in the north-east.

On the platform facing the delegates the chairman, a light-suited, sallow-featured man with an inquisitive nose, introduced himself as an official of the recently formed sub-committee of Europol dealing with organized crime developments within the European Union. He was French, spoke excellent, unaccented English, and began by introducing the two speakers on the platform beside him.

'This conference,' he explained, 'is being held to discuss the actions we might all take in our respective countries represented here to recognize and counter the growing international menace of organized criminal groups within the European zone of activity. We have with us Signor Bettani from Europol . . .' On his left, the plump, balding man with the self-satisfied air leaned forward slightly and nodded. 'From the UK Home Office, we have Mr Franklin,' the chairman continued, and gestured to the heavy-set man in the pinstripe suit on his right, 'and from the USA, Mr Garland, who works for the Federal Bureau of Narcotics and Dangerous Drugs, or FBNDD.'

O'Connor observed the American with interest. He was leaning back almost casually in his chair, arms folded over his broad chest. He was heavily built, perhaps fifty years of age, with dark hair thinning at the temples, and eyes that seemed heavy-lidded, sleepy in appearance. Yet there was something in the way he glanced around that made O'Connor suspect that this man was more aware than he wished to appear: a coiled serpent, dangerous to approach.

'This is scheduled to be the first of a number of meetings we're holding in Europe,' the chairman was saying, 'to bring everyone up to date with what the United Nations Committee has described as a growing menace within our borders.' He paused, looked up from his notes, and then turned to the man from the Home Office, seated on his right. 'Mr Franklin, perhaps you'd like to begin?'

Franklin hunched his heavy shoulders, and nodded ponderously. He wasn't exactly O'Connor's idea of a British civil servant, apart from the usual air of assumed superiority. 'The groups we shall concentrate upon are Chinese in origin. I should begin by pointing out that for the last three centuries, to whatever part of the world Chinese men have emigrated, they have taken with them their secret brotherhoods. At first these groups were little more than mutual self-interest societies, but they have since evolved into the most efficient, ruthless and international of criminal fraternities.' He straightened, raising his chin, almost glaring a challenge at the assembled police officers in the room. 'We are here to talk about the Triad organizations.'

O'Connor saw the Chief Constable lean sideways to whisper something in the ear of the man on his right. He was smiling. O'Connor could guess what the message would be: we don't get Chinese trouble on our patch. But then, the Chief Constable had always believed what he wanted to believe.

'It's certainly true,' Franklin was continuing, 'that Triad societies were first founded for various reasons: patriotism, fraternity, political agitation or social conscience. But let's be clear: nowadays, in essence, Triad societies exist merely to make money for their members.' He paused, swept the group of delegates with a grim glance. 'That money is mainly made through crime. The activists work at various levels. The lowest form of crime — the street-crime business — is carried out by what are known as the *hung kwan*, or Red Poles, and the *sze kau*, what we might describe as foot soldiers. Their work will be familiar to many of us: narcotics trading on the street, pick-pocketing, or armed robberies, often of gold or jewellers' shops. Larger criminal enterprises are carried out by middle-rank Triad members, backed by Red Poles and *sze kau*: kidnapping, or loan-sharking. The most senior officials are responsible for what may be described as corporate crime — supported, of course, by underlings with specific skills.' He gestured towards the document file in front of him. 'In your files, you'll find details of the Triad structures I'm talking about.'

O'Connor glanced at the closely typed notes. In the notes the *sze kau* were described as street thugs whose favourite weapons were the razor-sharp cleaver, or the throwing star fashioned from thin steel. Promotion to become a Red Pole depended upon expertise, ability and commitment.

Franklin cleared his throat. 'We must all also be aware of what now amounts to a much more important activity, the smuggling of illegal immigrants. In Triad jargon they are known as *tou du ju jia*, or little smuggled pigs. The immigrants are often sent from central China into Turkey, then on to Bulgaria and then by various routes into Western Europe. We believe the Triads have linked with Italian Mafiosi to run immigrants through Albania, the Czech Republic and St Petersburg.' He glanced sideways: Signor Bettani was nodding vigorously in agreement. 'Where the immigrants are smuggled in ships the operation will be organized by a *sh'e tau*, or snake-head.'

Franklin lacked a mesmerizing tone: his voice was flat, dry, and he placed little emphasis upon individual words or phrases. He clearly knew what he was talking about, but as he launched into a mass of statistical information he began to lose his audience. O'Connor wondered how long he'd be droning on. Matters began to improve, however, when Franklin turned to detail regarding Triad criminality.

'One of the more traditional Triad operations consists of the organized vice rings, which are international: brothels exist in every country where there is a Chinese presence.' Franklin raised a hand, scratched his cheek and frowned, as though even discussing the trade offended him. 'A hundred and fifty years ago they were designed for expatriate Chinese workers, men living far from their homes. The girls were purchased from poor families. In modern times this has changed: now, they are enticed abroad with the promise of work and a better life. These girls then find themselves trapped in a foreign land, without travel documents, unable to speak the language, and inculcated with an in-built dread of coming across law enforcement officers.'

Perhaps, like the audience, the FBNDD officer had become a little bored by the droning sound of Franklin's voice. Clearly reluctant to listen to a long-winded history lesson, the American official cut in: 'We're not now speaking of a Chinese market, of course.'

Franklin scowled: he did not appreciate the interruption but he nodded, nevertheless. 'Nowadays the clients are mainly Westerners, looking for Asian women who they are led to believe are more sexually dextrous than Western women. It is a myth, of course.' He permitted himself a thin, humourless smile. 'Or so I understand. The women are also not necessarily Chinese: also entrapped are Filipinas, Thais, Cambodians, Vietnamese, and to a lesser extent Malaysians and Indonesians. The Triads operate them on a circuit, moving them from one brothel to another.'

Signor Bettani, nodding, leaned forward to add his own point. 'The success of a vice establishment lies not only in beautiful women, of course, but turnover of faces and flesh. The rotation system works on a three-month basis. Some are exported to North America, after a run in Europe.'

He leaned back, folded his arms. Franklin, irritated, flicked over a page in the notes in front of him. 'The Triads also operate other forms of prostitution, of course: gay liaisons, massage parlours, sex with minors through the *hong lok chung sum*, what we call health or recreation clubs. But let's be clear: not all Triad sex trade is seedy and downmarket. They also run Western-style nightclubs, and escort agencies employing foreign prostitutes. And alongside prostitution the Triads have created a virtual monopoly for themselves over pornography in Southeast Asia. They started with pornographic books, moved on to 8 mm cine films, and then videotape. Inevitably, CD-ROMs with higher technical standards was the next step: they now command a large market in sex films on such CD-ROMs.'

Bettani leaned forward again, spreading his hands wide. 'We have noted a different problem in our area, of course. The locals won't talk, but we know that in Italy there is a growing problem over the calling in of gambling debts.'

Franklin glanced at him, showed his teeth in an odd grimace, and cleared his throat. 'Yes, this is another long-standing Triad activity. Loan-sharking. This often arises out of the settlement of gambling debts: as is well known, gambling is a major Chinese vice. On occasions, loan-sharking leads to kidnapping — if repayments fall too far behind, the debtor is abducted and held until the family pay up. During the abduction, the prisoner is often beaten up, raped, photographed naked in sexually compromising situations, or in apparent homosexual unions. And then, in addition there are huge profits made from horse racing and casinos . . .'

Franklin went on to outline the links that had been established between Mafia and Vietnamese organizations with the Triads. He explained that international narcotics smuggling was the biggest Triad enterprise. 'Most of the Triad heroin comes from the Golden Triangle. Profits are beyond estimate, and the trade is sourced by the *Teochui* Triads who have their own global underground banking system based upon the *guanxi*, or money launderers. Proceeds are partially invested in vice but most is laundered into legitimate businesses: hotels, restaurants, cinemas, nightclubs, casinos. But they put money into finance, construction, transportation, the media, sports promotion and housing. Trained *sze kau* work as street-corner pushers, heroin being sold in two-centimetre-long heat-sealed plastic drinking straws which can be concealed in the hand, or flicked away at signs of danger. Telephone ordering systems are also in place . . .'

O'Connor watched Garland: the American official seemed to have fallen asleep.

'I would now like to turn specifically to the United Kingdom,' Franklin went on. 'In the sixties, the influx of Hong Kong Chinese into Britain increased sharply. With them came the Triad organizations: they set up three power bases in London, Liverpool and Bristol. Subsidiary centres were later established in Manchester and Southampton. Each centre was autonomous and to a certain extent they were rivals. Any relationship between them was not fraternal, but merely based on a business contract.' He sniffed, wrinkled his nose and looked around the room at the silent officers facing him.

'The police weren't prepared, naturally enough, because it was a new phenomenon. Warnings came from the USA, by way of the Federal Bureau of Narcotics and Dangerous Drugs and the FBI. Indeed, the US Embassy in London even maintained a resident officer who gathered intelligence on drug traffickers, infiltrated operations and identified couriers.' He paused, uncertain what next to say, in view of the man seated beside him. 'While that officer worked hand in glove with the British authorities there was a . . . er . . . certain falling out. We could not countenance some of the methods used.'

Garland, the FBNDD man, opened his heavy-lidded eyes, raised an eyebrow, then tilted his head back, regarding the ceiling and smiling slightly. Franklin was about to continue, when Garland broke in, his tone lazy and slow.

'We were dealing with narcotic operations, but as Mr Franklin has already noted, the reality was that the British police weren't yet alive to the gravity of the situation. You've all heard of the French Connection: it was busted in 1972. After that, the Turkish government banned opium-poppy farming which was producing almost forty per cent of Europe's supply. A man called Chung Mon responded by organizing supplies from Vietnam. In 1975 he started exporting to the USA and set up in Amsterdam. When other Triads followed his example and set up in Rotterdam it all broke out into open warfare, with sawn-off shotguns. We warned the British police. It would only be a matter of time before the whole scene shifted to the UK.'

Franklin was not pleased. He grimaced, cleared his throat. 'By that point, emphasized by Mr Garland, the

Dutch police had had enough and they clamped down on the Amsterdam Triads. The consequence was they moved to Germany, back to the Far East and elsewhere—'

'But several Triad societies moved to Britain,' Garland interrupted. 'We received information that they were setting up in London, Birmingham, Liverpool and Manchester. Roots were put down, businesses established.'

'*Quite.*' Franklin almost bit out the word. 'We received intelligence from your people, but at that stage there had been no outbreak of violence, and in the view of the Home Office the matter was being contained—'

'Contained? Ignored, more like,' Garland murmured audibly.

Colour flooded into the Home Office man's cheeks. 'The matter was being contained, people were under surveillance, and—'

'And as long as the media didn't get hold of the problem, you swept it under the carpet,' Garland announced casually.

Things were getting out of hand. Franklin, puce-faced, was about to make an angry retort, when the chairman intervened anxiously.

'I don't think these are issues which we need to be addressing at this point of time. I am of the opinion that—'

'You're right,' Garland said easily, but with an underlying note of steel in his voice. 'We shouldn't be dwelling on mistakes, or failures of communications—'

'Or illegal methods,' Franklin spat angrily.

'—or problems of the past,' Garland went on, ignoring the Home Office man. 'But we should be aware, and concentrate on the fact, that things move on. The trade in narcotics is well enough documented, and measures are in place to deal with it — even in the UK.'

Franklin sputtered, raised his hand, but Garland ploughed on relentlessly. 'What is of great concern at the moment is that too little attention is being paid to more recent developments. I speak in particular of counterfeiting. The counterfeiting trade is important to the Triads because it is an efficient method of laundering money. They started their operations with dealings in currency, moved on to expensive textbooks, and then launched into the luxury goods market: wristwatches, designer clothing with fake labels, handbags, and finally computer software. And that's where it became big. Software protection is bypassed by Triad hackers, and production is undertaken in CD-ROM factories in southern China, the Philippines and Thailand. Anything you want, they can produce. Movies on video are copied, as are music CDs. But the trade isn't limited to manufacturing items for sale.'

Franklin slammed a hand on the table in front of him. Viciously, he snarled, 'We are well aware of the problem. After all it started in Hong Kong, when we were still in control of that area.'

'Which tells its own story,' Garland countered easily. 'But you don't seem to be doing much about what's resulted. We've taken action in the States. We've established a special agency: FinCen, the Financial Crimes Enforcement Agency, just to deal with this kind of criminal activity. The Triads now also produce fake bond or share certificates, passports, travel documents and, of course, gold and platinum credit cards with high credit level—'

'And what country was really responsible for this upsurge,' Franklin sneered, 'for the development of the whole must-have-it-now ethos?'

The chairman had had enough. He looked pointedly at his watch, raised a hand, and announced, 'I think we'll take an adjournment at this point. Coffee is served in the next room.'

Franklin rose immediately, stony-faced. Garland was smiling slightly, O'Connor noted, obviously pleased at having got under the Home Office man's skin. As O'Connor moved into the coffee room with the other delegates he caught sight of the Chief Constable, engaged in conversation with a uniformed employee of the Oratorio di San Giorgio. He was staring at a piece of paper in his hand. O'Connor obtained a cup of coffee for himself and moved to a corner of the room. He noted that while the platform party had gathered together, Garland was somewhat isolated. If he was being ostracized, it appeared to affect him little. He turned his head, caught O'Connor's glance, and after a moment moved across to join him where he leant against the wall.

'So, where do you hail from?' he asked.

'Britain.'

Garland grinned. 'One of the cops I been complaining about up there.'

'Decisions aren't taken at my level. But I was interested to hear what you had to say about financial crime.'

'The FinCen deal?' Garland nodded. 'In fact, that's what I'm mainly concerned with these days. We have problems in the UK of course, with people not approving of our methods, but with support in the Home Office—'

As the American spoke, O'Connor, glancing around, saw the Chief Constable staring at him. He raised a hand, beckoned.

'I'm sorry, you have to excuse me,' O'Connor said. 'My Chief Constable wants me to join him.'

'Maybe he doesn't approve of the company you keep,' Garland suggested sardonically.

O'Connor moved across the room towards his senior officer. 'A lively debate, sir,' he suggested as he reached the Chief Constable.

'The rest of which I'm afraid you'll have to miss, DCI.'

'Sir?'

The Chief Constable handed him the note he held in his hand. 'I've just received this. It seems we have a killing on our hands. You'll need to get back to Newcastle.' Disgruntled, he glanced sourly across the room, scowling at the American who had raised the temperature among the platform party. 'Saw you talking with Garland. His people caused a lot of trouble a few years back, by using methods that were more suited to Chicago hoodlums than good policing. They had to be told at the time that it wasn't the way things were done in

England.' He snorted contemptuously. 'It's interesting, isn't it, that these Americans always want to make out that the rest of us are incompetents? I'm tempted to walk away from this conference myself, and come back with you.'

And escape the drudgery of making your own report, O'Connor thought cynically.

The Chief Constable sighed. 'But, I suppose, duty calls . . .'

'I'll get back to Newcastle at once, sir,' O'Connor assured him. He didn't even wait to finish his coffee.

2

The interview room was almost bare of furniture: a desk, three chairs — one of which was occupied by Arnold Landon — and, incongruously enough, a standard lamp in the corner. A narrow window looked out on to a strip of lawn in front of a car park. Arnold wondered vaguely whether anyone had ever tried to squeeze through that window and make a run for it to avoid police interrogation.

The door opened behind him, and two men came into the room. Arnold turned his head. He recognized both men. The first to enter, tall, lean, slightly greying at the temples, carrying a manila folder in his hand, was DCI Jack O'Connor. Behind him Arnold saw the saturnine features of DI Farnsby, who had already interviewed Arnold over the killing in the Golden Palace.

O'Connor thrust out a hand, and Arnold took it reluctantly. The DCI took a seat opposite Arnold, and Farnsby sat down beside him. 'I'm sorry to drag you in again like this, Mr Landon,' O'Connor remarked apologetically. 'I was out of the country when this business blew up, and now I've taken over I thought it would be useful if we had a chat about it all.'

Arnold caught the flicker of annoyance that shone in Farnsby's cold eyes as O'Connor spoke. He wondered whether the irritation was caused by O'Connor's taking responsibility from Farnsby, or whether it rose from darker depths. Arnold shifted uneasily in his seat. 'I've already told DI Farnsby everything I know,' he complained.

'Well, yes, that's probably so,' O'Connor replied, 'but I need to get my own handle on this case. I've read the notes on what you, Miss Stannard and Miss Tyrrel had to say about the events of that evening, checked your statements, but I'd like to get confirmation regarding some of the comments you made. Not least, I'd like to get clear the part played by Mr Sullivan.'

'Have you spoken with him yet?' Arnold asked. 'I understand he was taken to hospital with concussion.'

Farnsby raised his head, nostrils dilating as though sniffing at the wind. 'Suspected concussion,' he corrected. 'But he was all right. We took a statement from him at the hospital, but he's agreed to come in this morning to be interviewed.' He hesitated, flicking a sharp glance at his companion. 'DCI O'Connor will conduct the interview.'

Arnold shrugged. 'Well, how can I help?'

O'Connor consulted the notes in front of him. 'According to this, you at no time had a good look at the man who fired the handgun.'

Arnold nodded. 'That's right. I had my back to the kitchen. So did Miss Tyrrel, who was sitting beside me. I was startled by the sound of the shot and only then turned around, as a chair went flying. After that . . . well, I was sort of stuck there, paralysed, if you like, for a few moments.'

'So the killer came in through the kitchen?' O'Connor asked.

'I presume so. No one came into the restaurant through the main entrance after we arrived. But I didn't *see* him come through the kitchen doors.'

O'Connor stared at him reflectively for a few moments, then nodded. 'Of course. You had your back to the kitchen. But in your statement you say that you saw the man after the shot was fired.'

Arnold wriggled uncomfortably. 'Not enough to be able to identify him. I caught a quick glimpse of him. I mean, it was all very confusing, you'll appreciate. My immediate attention was drawn to the man on the floor. His attacker . . . well, all I really saw was someone in dark clothes rushing towards the kitchen.'

'You didn't see his face?' O'Connor demanded.

'It was all so quick,' Arnold ruminated doubtfully. 'No, I didn't really see his face or—'

'Was he bare-headed? How tall was he? What kind of build? What was he wearing?' There was a hint of impatience in O'Connor's tone.

Arnold shook his head. 'I can't help you. I'm sorry, but all I received was a quick impression.'

'Pity . . .' O'Connor murmured. 'We've had the same kind of story from Miss Tyrrel, who also had her back to the kitchen. And Miss Stannard seems to have seen very little that registered with her either.' He glanced at Farnsby, impassive at his side. 'All right, Mr Landon, let's move on. Your reaction was to go to the dying man . . .'

'There was nothing I could do, really. I asked Karen Stannard to phone for an ambulance, and then I went after Steven Sullivan.'

'Why did you do that?'

'I don't know. There was noise, confusion . . .'

'Sullivan had already run after the killer. You didn't react as quickly as he did.'

Arnold was aware of a slight flush to his cheeks. He stared levelly at O'Connor. 'Mr Sullivan is younger, fitter — and perhaps rather more impulsive than I. He reacted very quickly, and chased the gunman. I hesitated beside the dying man to see what I could do. Then, when I heard the clattering and shouting, I ran after Sullivan.'

O'Connor nodded, staring at the notes. 'And you found Sullivan injured in the alleyway.' He paused, thinking. 'You went through the kitchen. According to your statement you saw three men there. One was bleeding about the face. Tell

66

me, what impressions did you receive? What do you think happened in that kitchen?'

'After the shot was fired?' Arnold hesitated. He had naturally thought a great deal about the events of that evening, had discussed them with both Portia and Karen, and while they were in broad agreement they each had received different impressions, perhaps inevitably. On small matters only. He shrugged. 'I can't say what happened, of course, but the impression I got was that maybe there had been a struggle in the kitchen. It's possible one of the cooks tried to stop the man with the gun, delayed him somewhat before Sullivan entered the kitchen. But no doubt the cook himself will be able to tell you what happened.'

A hint of cynical amusement touched Farnsby's thin lips, but he said nothing. 'We'd still like to hear what you think might have happened,' O'Connor said.

Arnold took a deep breath. 'My guess, and it can only be a guess, is that when the killer burst into the kitchen after firing at his victim he was impeded by the young cook. That delayed the killer, so that when Steven Sullivan came after him he had to deal with Sullivan also. The killer ran through the store room, Sullivan after him. They tangled in the alley. It seems that the killer hit Sullivan, stunned him. That's where I found Steven, in the alleyway, groaning. But beyond that . . .'

'How do you think the gunman entered the restaurant?' Farnsby spoke for the first time.

Arnold shook his head. 'It's possible he was already in the restaurant, though I didn't see him. I presume he came from upstairs, but I don't know.'

'Not through the kitchen, in the first instance?'

Arnold stared at O'Connor, puzzled. 'Wouldn't the cooks have tried to stop him, a stranger, at that point? I mean, if they tried to stop him leaving . . .'

'Perhaps they didn't pay too much attention when he arrived,' O'Connor suggested, 'but after hearing the gunshot, one of them, at least, tried to prevent his escaping that way. You think that's the way it might have been?'

Arnold shook his head. 'I can't really say what actually happened. Sullivan's the man to ask.'

* * *

After Arnold Landon had gone, Jack O'Connor walked out into the corridor, and obtained a carton of coffee from the dispensing machine near the swing doors. A few moments later Farnsby joined him, leaning with his elbows on the window sill, staring out across the lawn to the former college administrative block, now converted to police cadet accommodation. O'Connor sipped his coffee, studying the younger man. He had an uneasy relationship with DI Farnsby. The fact that O'Connor had joined the force upon the retirement of DCI Culpeper, and had been appointed in Culpeper's place, had given rise to a degree of resentment in Farnsby: he had been expecting promotion. His expectations had been high; rumour had it that he had been the blue-eyed boy of the previous Chief Constable, but when the Chief had departed under a cloud, taking early retirement 'to spend more time with his family', Farnsby's expectations had not been realized. The new Chief Constable had brought in new blood — O'Connor — and Farnsby had been sidelined, as he saw it. It had caused friction between the two men. It remained a source of resentment.

'So do you think the cooks tried to stop this man entering the kitchen?' O'Connor asked quietly.

Farnsby shifted irritably. 'Not if they recognized him. But we're not going to find out, are we? Two of them deny having seen anything, and the third man — the one who got the bloody nose — he's disappeared.'

'You think he was an illegal?'

'I'd put my shirt on it. My bet is the other two maybe knew the killer. The young one didn't, and after the killing he tried to stop the man. But after the event, there was no way he was going to hang around to be interrogated by us if he had entered the country illegally. And we all know that half the restaurants and hotels in this area are making money by using poorly paid illegal immigrants in their kitchens.'

It was a moot point. From the notes compiled by Farnsby it seemed that neither of the two remaining kitchen workers claimed to have noticed the gunman entering the kitchen. One explained he had been too busy preparing the food, the other stated he had slipped outside for a smoke but had seen no one enter. They had no information regarding the missing cook — they claimed he was new, had recently joined the restaurant, and they suffered considerable memory loss as to what had actually happened that night. O'Connor finished his coffee in silence. He had come across this kind of thing before. Within Chinese communities there was a reluctance to deal with authority. They closed ranks, out of fear. But as to what they feared . . .

A uniformed police constable opened the swing doors, and called to O'Connor. 'Sullivan's arrived, sir.'

'Send him to the interview room.' O'Connor tossed his paper cup into the waste bin and strode ahead of Farnsby to the room they had just left. A few minutes later Steven Sullivan was shown in, and he took the seat that Arnold Landon had vacated.

O'Connor observed the man in front of him with interest. He was perhaps thirty years of age, his dark hair recently cropped, presumably because of the head injury he had received. A dressing had been applied just above his left ear, but Sullivan's eyes were bright and he seemed to have suffered no significant ill effects from the blow he had received. He had a broad, intelligent forehead, O'Connor thought, straight nose, Asian cast of features, but intensely blue eyes. He had a direct manner of looking at someone which denoted a degree of confidence. His body was lean, lithe, and he moved with grace.

'Thanks for coming in, Mr Sullivan. How are you feeling?' O'Connor enquired solicitously.

'I've got a thick skull, it seems,' Sullivan replied with a flash of white teeth. 'The gift of my Irish ancestors, I suspect.'

'You've had concussion.'

Sullivan shrugged. 'They kept me in hospital under observation.' His hand strayed up to the dressing above his ear. 'It's not a deep cut, and I had headaches for a couple of days, but it turns out it wasn't a big deal.'

'I suppose it helps,' O'Connor said carefully, 'if you keep yourself fit.'

'I work out,' Sullivan admitted. 'Martial arts. It's a bit of a hobby.'

O'Connor observed him quizzically. 'Martial arts . . . Is that why you chased after the gunman in the restaurant?'

'How do you mean?'

'Confident in your strength. Used to swift reaction. Always ready to get into a rough and tumble.'

The clear blue eyes stared at O'Connor unblinkingly. 'It wasn't really like that. I didn't think about it. I saw the gunman hit his victim. I just . . . reacted.'

'And when you struggled with the gunman in the alley,' O'Connor asked casually, 'did you find you were unmatched?'

The blue eyes were calm. 'I don't follow you.'

O'Connor shrugged. 'You're skilled in martial arts. You're fit. You caught this man in the alley. Was he stronger than you? Bigger? What was he like, Mr Sullivan?'

Steven Sullivan glanced at DI Farnsby. 'I gave a statement when I was in hospital.'

'That's right, you did,' O'Connor replied gently. 'But it sort of lacked detail. Probably because you were still suffering the effects of the blow to the head. Or maybe drugs administered to you. The thing is, it's all a bit vague. That's why we asked you to come in. To see if your recollections are a bit clearer now.'

Sullivan hesitated. He frowned. 'I suppose I was still a bit woozy, when I was interviewed in the hospital. Things are a bit clearer, but the truth is, it was all pretty rushed, it was chaos, there wasn't time to think. It all happened so quickly.'

'Well, maybe we could go over the ground again, Mr Sullivan,' O'Connor suggested.

Sullivan nodded in compliance. 'That's fine by me. Where do you want me to start?'

'Your first sight of the gunman.'

'Right . . . Well, we were at the table, and we were talking, and I don't know what first caught my attention, but there was movement over at the other table in front of the kitchen. I saw this man—'

'Whom you haven't really described,' Farnsby interjected coolly.

'Well, no, but at first I paid little attention, was simply aware of him in a vague kind of way, that's all, until the gun went off, and by then the guy was haring back to the kitchen, and I just followed, almost instinctively.'

'So what did he look like?' O'Connor insisted. 'Are you able to provide us with a description now?'

Sullivan frowned again, recollecting. 'Medium height, I guess. Dark clothes: roll-neck sweater, I think, dark blue pants. Black hair. But that's about it, really.'

'Caucasian?' O'Connor asked quietly.

There was a short pause, a hesitation, before Sullivan replied. He shook his head slowly. 'No. I think he was Chinese.'

O'Connor stared at the notes in front of him. 'All right. So what happened then?'

'I heard the shot, saw the man fall backwards — the victim, that is — and the chair went over with a crash. There was only the one shot, I think, and this guy was running for the kitchen. I paused beside the man on the floor, but Mr Landon was following me, and I heard a ruckus in the kitchen so I just followed, like I said, not thinking about it, and when I reached the kitchen there was a sort of struggle going on.'

'Who was involved?' O'Connor asked. 'Describe what was happening.'

Sullivan shrugged. 'It's as I said in the statement, it was all kind of chaotic in there. Everything happening too quickly for things to properly register. There were two guys standing against the wall, scared as hell as far as I could see. Then there was another, a young Chinese guy, he was sort of barring the way to the exit, grabbing at this man in the dark clothes, but it was all over in seconds. Before I could get there, the Chinese kitchen worker got slammed in the face, he fell backwards, and the guy I was chasing headed for the exit at the back, through the store room.'

'So you didn't reach him while he was struggling with the kitchen hand?' O'Connor asked.

Sullivan shook his head. 'No chance. He hit the young guy, he went down and it sort of impeded me as I ran forward. And the floor, it was greasy: I skidded on the tiles, clambered over the guy bleeding on the floor and headed out after the gunman.' He paused, frowning slightly.

'So what happened then?' O'Connor queried.

Sullivan grimaced, baring his teeth thoughtfully. 'I don't really know . . . I remember scrambling past some stuff in the store room, and the door to the alley was open. I ran forward, came out into the alley, and it was dark, unlit. Then everything sort of exploded. I saw stars. Next thing I was aware of was Mr Landon, helping me to my feet. I was real groggy, I tell you.'

There was a brief silence. O'Connor leaned back in his chair, folded his arms and regarded the man in front of him with eyes that gave nothing away of his feelings. 'So you didn't really get into a fight with this man you were chasing. And you didn't even see him in the alley.'

'It's why I can't give you much of a description. About his size, and that sort of thing,' Sullivan confessed. 'I ran into the alley and he must have been waiting for me.'

'Why would he do that?' O'Connor mused. 'If he was running away, why would he take such a chance, and wait for you?'

Steven Sullivan shook his head. 'I can only assume, when he saw me coming into the kitchen while he was tussling with that young guy, he'd not have much chance to get away without dealing with me the way he did. He stopped in the alley, waited for me to come through the door, then hit me from behind.' He paused. 'That's my guess what happened, anyway.'

The silence grew around them. Steven Sullivan waited, seemingly at ease.

'If you had caught him,' O'Connor suggested, 'do you think your skills would have allowed you to subdue him?'

Sullivan hesitated, smiling ruefully. 'That depends, doesn't it? I mean, depends on how tough he was. And he had a weapon.'

'I wonder why he didn't use it, as he'd done inside the restaurant,' O'Connor considered. 'He clubbed you instead.'

'That's something you'll have to ask him, I'm afraid,' Sullivan replied, with a slight smile. 'When you catch him . . . What happened to that young kid in the kitchen, by the way? The one I saw struggling with the gunman.'

'He's disappeared,' Farnsby replied in a cold voice. 'He's vanished, and the other two men who were present, it's as though they were blind and deaf.'

Silence fell. O'Connor regarded the man seated in front of him for a little while. Sullivan's face was expressionless; he seemed happy enough to sit there and wait. O'Connor clucked his tongue and closed the file in front of him. 'So there's nothing more that you feel you can add. A better description of the killer, perhaps or—'

'I've given you all I can remember,' Sullivan replied, wrinkling his brow. 'But of course, if anything else occurs to me I'll certainly get in touch.'

O'Connor rose, extended his hand. 'We're very grateful, Mr Sullivan. You displayed considerable courage going after a man with a gun in his hand.'

'Foolhardiness, Portia Tyrrel suggests,' Sullivan demurred, shaking O'Connor's hand. 'She's taken me to task about it.'

'You're close friends?'

Sullivan grinned. 'I suppose you could say that. And she's played hell with me for what she reckons was recklessness.

But she doesn't have much recollection of what happened that evening, though.'

'Worrying about you?' O'Connor asked.

'I guess so.'

After Steven Sullivan had been escorted from the building O'Connor turned to look at Farnsby. 'So, what do you think?'

'I don't know,' Farnsby replied stolidly.

O'Connor grimaced. 'I'm in the same boat. But I get the feeling there's something missing in all this. Somehow or other, what we've heard from our muscular young accountant, there's something missing, something not quite straight . . . We need to find that young cook who tried to prevent the gunman leaving.'

'Fat chance, in my view,' Farnsby replied. 'Anyway, it seems Assistant Chief Constable Cathery wants to see us when we're through here.'

'What the hell does he want?'

Farnsby's eyes held more than a trace of resentment. 'The ACC doesn't normally take me into his confidence.'

* * *

Sid Cathery had used his shoulders and bull neck to good effect when he had played in the front row for Somerset Police. He had gained a reputation as a player who would kick anything that moved above the grass, and had never been averse to the odd bit of ear-chewing in the West Country scrums where thuggery was all part of the game. He had brought some of those attitudes to his job in the police: having risen to the exalted rank of Assistant Chief Constable, he deemed that his methods were approved by those in more senior positions. He detested sloppiness and caution. He approved of direct force. And he demanded quick results from the men reporting to him.

'So where are we with this bloody investigation?' he snapped, as Farnsby and O'Connor entered his office. 'You get anything more out of our hero, that accountant feller?'

'Nothing of significance,' O'Connor suggested.

'Pity he didn't get the chance to really get hold of that gunman,' Cathery remarked, his grim mouth twitching into a grimace. 'Bet he'd have taken the guy apart. He's the only one who seems to have done something so far, chasing that killer. Got guts, that lad. Never was into martial arts meself, but I hear they're pretty violent guys.'

It was clear he approved of such skills. 'Anyway,' he barked, eyeing O'Connor with subdued malevolence, 'you managed to get up to speed with this investigation after your little Italian jaunt with the Chief Constable?'

O'Connor ignored the jibe. 'DI Farnsby's given me the files and—'

'So what more have we got on the dead man?' Cathery interrupted.

Farnsby coughed lightly, and clasped his hands behind his back. 'We have very little on him, sir. From the credit cards found on his body it seems his name was Charles de Vriess. Probably of Dutch origin. And with a sound line of credit. We've been in touch with the credit card companies and he had a credit level of more than forty thousand: his bank accounts have been checked, and there's been considerable sums going through his accounts.'

'So what the hell did he do for a living?' Cathery growled.

Stiffly, DI Farnsby replied, 'We found in his wallet a card identifying him as a pharmaceutical representative, employed by a conglomerate based in Amsterdam. However, when we attempted to get in touch with representatives of this company we learned that the company does not in fact exist. At the moment we are concentrating on trying to determine how long he has been in this country, where he's been residing, what point of entry he made . . . In other words, we're checking hotels, airport records, leases, the usual stuff. But so far, there's little to report. I'm afraid, sir, we have something of a mystery man on our hands.'

'A dead mystery man,' Cathery muttered. 'That's what I don't like. Have you made contact with Europol?'

'I thought it inadvisable until we have further information to go on, sir.'

Sid Cathery scratched at his iron-grey, bristling hair in frustration. 'I want this bloody investigation concluded as quickly as possible. As for Europol — leave it to me. I'll use my own contacts. Get the de Vriess file — for what it's worth — to me and I'll see what I can churn up.'

O'Connor opened his mouth to protest. Assistant Chief Constable Sid Cathery glared at him. 'So? You want to say something?'

There was no point. Cathery was on a cavalry charge.

3

It was the night of the twenty-fifth day of the Chinese month and notifications had gone out to the relevant members on slips of red paper. No refusals had been received: it was well enough understood that a summons had to be obeyed, unless there were extenuating circumstances of which the Incense Master had been informed, and of which he approved. There were three new recruits to the Society of the Ghost Shadows: they had been strictly warned that to divulge information concerning the meeting would be visited with severe consequences. They had already arrived with their sponsors at the ceremonial room. They appeared as expected in the traditional manner, barefoot, with hair tousled and coats open, ready to swear their four ritual oaths and prepare to pass the Mountain of Knives.

Seated on his ceremonial chair in his long black robe the Dragon Head watched impassively as the young men were led through the rituals. The ceremony allowed him a period of reflection: he mused how things had been differently ordered in his day. When he had been inducted into the Red Flower Pavilion Society all those years ago in Hong Kong the Incense Master had taken him through a much more extensive ritual. But now, in more modern, less reflective times the ancient six-hour rituals had been debased, and to his regret had lost most of their meaning. He was forced to admit to himself that such changes had been necessary — rituals had to be shortened to avoid discovery in this Westernized society, where machines of incredible power could eavesdrop and view the most secret of activities. Perhaps more to the point, the old, complex ceremonies of his youth had become irrelevant to modern, Westernized, decadent Chinese recruits. They had grown up in a different society; they had less respect for the old ways, they lacked control, and failed to understand the relevance of the old disciplines.

The Dragon Head listened impassively as the Incense Master continued with the ceremonies. Lip service was still being paid in the rituals to the Circle of Heaven and Earth, the City of Willows, and the Hall of Universal Peace, but the ceremonies themselves had been considerably stripped down. The Ghost Shadows Society still insisted, under his direction, that the recruit should be dressed in a long white robe with a red sash tied around his head; the recruits were still required to proceed towards the altar with straw sandals on their feet. But the old, esoteric poems had now been dispensed with, the Buddhist and Taoist prayers and incantations of his own induction had been set aside, the long-revered earth gods and heroes of Triad traditional history ignored. It was the new way. The Dragon Head did not entirely approve, but he recognized that the Society could no longer afford the luxury of elaborate initiation ceremonies. Times had changed, the old ways forgotten, the ritual no longer possible in this new, urgent, Westernized society.

But at least the traditional thirty-six oaths were still used. Their importance had not been undermined, for on them lay the foundation of commitment to the Society and control of its brotherhood. He listened grimly as the white-robed Incense Master led the recruits through the ritual, heard the young men intone the oaths:

I shall not disclose the secrets of the Hung Society . . . I shall not be the cause of disharmony amongst my sworn brothers . . . I must not conspire with outsiders . . .

The words were of ancient origin, but their meaning was as relevant as it had ever been over the centuries. He took a grim satisfaction in acknowledging that the recruits knew as well as he did the reality of the threat lying behind the ancient penalties for oath-breaking:

I shall be killed by a myriad of swords . . . I shall be killed by five thunderbolts . . .

These were not empty threats. As the proceedings continued, the attention of the Dragon Head wandered. He narrowed his eyes in thought. He suspected that these new recruits were not of the calibre the Society had drawn in over the decades. Recent events had begun to concern him. The foot soldiers, the *sze kau*, they were committed to obeying orders from the hierarchy without question, within rigid rules. But some of them seemed to have become infected with the virus of violence. It was not the good way: the success of the Ghost Shadows, like the other societies such as the Red Turbans, the Small Sword Society, and the Black Eagles, lay in part upon strict controls that would keep a low profile, dissuade the *gwei-los* from interference in their activities, maintain a secret power in the endless search for profit. To that end the hierarchy of violence was controlled. Threats, humiliation, choppings — these were all part of the enforcement techniques encouraged by the Red Pole leaders of the *sze kau*, and permitted by senior officers of the Society. The Red Pole leaders of the fighting units, the *hung kwan*, acknowledged that they operated under instruction from above, but recently there had been occasions when members of the *hung kwan* had themselves disobeyed instructions, disregarded recognized systems and activities, taken upon themselves the decision to act, and go beyond what was advisable. Disobedience, acting independently in disregard of orders, this was a dangerous precedent. It undermined the strict foundation laid down by older, wiser men.

If a chopping was ordered, that was all that was needed. To kill was another matter.

To kill was not wise, not unless there were the strongest of reasons. It could only be a matter of last resort, after all other persuasions had failed. A killing could result in unwelcome repercussions, police involvement, disturbance of organizations, a redrawing of boundaries of mutual interest: such activity could even result in internecine warfare among the societies. A slight shudder of unwelcome memory ran along his spine: he recalled how he himself had been drawn into such an unwise practice two decades ago, when he had been younger, and less well versed in the advantages and intricacies of strategy and compromise. He had felt at the time it had been a necessary action, he had been losing face, the high prize was being torn from his grasp, but who knew when the storm caused by the fluttering of that butterfly's wings would bring retribution and destruction?

He dragged his thoughts back to the immediate present. The allegiance of the recruits was being sealed with blood and the cleansing tea was being drunk. The Dragon Head became aware of the hint of smoke in his nostrils, from the burning of the yellow paper. The shortened, fifteen-minute ceremony was coming to an end.

He stepped down from the raised dais at the end of the room, from which he had been silently observing the ceremony led by the Incense Master. Followed by the *fu shan chu*, the Deputy Master of the Mountain, the Dragon Head turned, twitching his long robe about him, and moved into the small room that lay beyond the red curtain. At the far end of the room was a simple wooden chair, with carved arms. He walked towards it, seated himself, adjusting his robe with care. The *fu shan chu* stood quietly by his side.

After a few moments the red curtain was drawn aside and the *heung chu*, the Incense Master, entered, followed by the young man who by all report had distinguished himself, and whom it had been decided to promote. He had come to the Society with glowing references, he had since demonstrated that he was possessed of significant skills, and now he had proved himself and his loyalty within the Ghost Shadows Society. The man abased himself, kneeling with his dark head bowed before the *lung tau*, the Dragon Head of the Ghost Shadows Society.

There was a short silence. A slow, cold bead of sweat trickled down the Dragon Head's back: he felt strangely cold under his robe. He stared at the man kneeling before him. He had come with a warm recommendation from the Black Eagles Society, but the Dragon Head remained nervous about men from outside the Ghost Shadows Society itself. The individual Triad societies had never shown themselves capable of working hand in glove, one with another: there were always elements of competition. Each had its own methods; each enjoyed its own territory, geographically and by way of profitable activity. But this man . . . he had special skills which were of considerable importance for the new ventures into which the Ghost Shadows were launching. And this man had already demonstrated, in a personal way, his loyalty and commitment to his brothers, and thus to the Ghost Shadows.

The recommendation had been promotion, a necessary promotion because of the status and power it involved, to the rank of *pak tze sin*, White Paper Fan. In that capacity he would join the ranks of those who held the real power within the Society: a leader of men, a business manager, a banker, adviser, strategist for the Society. He possessed the skills, and the experience, even though he was yet a young man. The Dragon Head felt cold, but he knew that this was the way of the modern world . . .

The Dragon Head raised his hand in a silent benediction. The Incense Master bowed, turned, and began to intone the oaths . . .

* * *

Two hours later, having discarded their robes and now dark-suited, the three senior officials of the Ghost Shadows Society sat in a private room at the back of the Regent Hotel. Tumblers of neat brandy were at their elbows and two of the men smoked fat, Cuban cigars. The meal had been a simple one, but a Cantonese repast which was different from the dishes served to Westernized taste in the specialist restaurant that offered Asian cuisine apart from the main restaurant. They had not discussed business during the meal: it was a social occasion, when they could talk about their families, recount old stories, boast about former glorious enterprises, indulge in nostalgia for the old days. Now, there was a companionable silence as they drank, and smoked and reflected.

'You have not expressed your concerns fully,' the Dragon Head said at last, quietly, to his second in command, his *fu shan chu*.

The Deputy Master of the Mountain drew on his cigar and stared at the glowing tip. He was clearly ill at ease, for obvious reasons. He was well aware of the close relationship between the Dragon Head and the Red Pole who had acted so recklessly. He spoke with obvious reluctance.

'The *hung kwan* of whom we have spoken earlier . . . it is agreed his behaviour was not necessary. The instructions were to deliver a chopping; the warning would have been sufficient, not only to the Dutchman, but also to his associates, the men who would work with him along the river once he established himself. We had interests to protect, that I recognize, but we all know, men of experience, we all know that while we remain unobtrusive, while we go about our business with circumspection, the police will not become too alarmed. But a killing changes all that. The *gweilos* will have been warned of our presence. Unwelcome attention will now be focused upon us. There could be difficult days ahead.'

'It was the action of youth,' the Incense Master murmured. 'An impetuous deed . . .'

His superior cast a contemptuous glance at him, aware of the man's weakness, an unwillingness to offend the Dragon Head. 'Such impetuosity could cost us dear. A chopping would have sufficed; a chopping was ordered. The *hung kwan* went too far, took upon himself a decision that was not his to make. He has shown himself to be stained with rebellion, with unnecessary violence. What was his purpose? To show us that he knows better than his elders? Or was it worse — a contempt for our ways?' He grunted, drew on his cigar. 'Nor do I need to remind you, if it had not been for the action of one not involved—'

'We have discussed this, and the person you mention has received his reward,' the Dragon Head intervened. He paused, his eyes glittering coldly. 'I hear what you both say; I am aware that we could be facing difficulties. But they are not insurmountable.' He turned his glance upon the Incense Master. 'This shall be your responsibility. There is no need for reprisal against the Red Pole in question. I think we should accept that it was youthful enthusiasm only that led him into error: but the Dutchman had become a threat to our enterprises. In this city we are entrenched, but still vulnerable, and the Dutchman could have severely damaged our enterprises, had his challenge to our monopoly been allowed to continue without check. So, for the errant *hung kwan* no reprisal, but a warning. You, *heung chu*, you will give it. You will make it clear. Such behaviour will not be tolerated again: it can spread unwisdom and disorder among his fellow *hung kwan*. Orders will in future be followed to the letter.' He paused. When he continued, his tone had hardened. 'It is your responsibility. The Red Poles are the leaders of our fighting units. They must be disciplined. You will make this clear: to *all* of them.'

The Incense Master took a deep breath, then nodded. He picked up his brandy glass. His eyes met those of the *fu shan chu*. In the glance of the Deputy Master of the Mountain he read a shadowed disagreement.

But the Dragon Head had spoken.

CHAPTER THREE

1

The request had come as a surprise to Arnold. He was called into Karen Stannard's office and found her with a quizzical look on her face. 'I've just had a call from Henry Wong,' she said as he entered the office. 'Has there been any problem with the items he suggested we claim under the Mannington bequest?'

Arnold shook his head. 'Not that I'm aware of. We've yet to collect them from the auction house, but that's because I'm still sorting out security for their housing. I thought maybe the best place, in the interim period, until we can get agreement on upgrading the museum at—'

'Never mind about that,' Karen cut in with a hint of irritation. 'I've already reported to the council, and they're more than happy about our acquisition. They'll want a valuation made in due course, and that'll be something you can get started on, but I'm pretty sure they won't argue about upgrading security costs.' She managed a cynical smile. 'It seems when money is really needed, and if involves an asset of the authority, then money can be found.' She sighed. 'If only the Deputy Chief Executive could be persuaded to shift himself. It makes one realize that Powell Frinton wasn't the pain in the backside we thought he was.'

What *some* of us thought he was, Arnold considered silently.

'Anyway, that's not the issue,' Karen continued. 'Mr Wong's been on the phone. He wants to be shown the site where we were thinking of building a centre to commemorate the sinking of the *Vendela*.'

Arnold raised his eyebrows. 'What's his interest in that?' he wondered.

Karen shrugged. 'Search me. It could be just that he's interested, in view of the fact that the Mannington collection was recovered from the wreck of the East Indiaman. But . . . What exactly do we know about Mr Wong?'

Arnold shrugged. 'Not a great deal. As you know, the connection came from Portia, by way of her former relationship with Wong's nephew, Jeremy Tan.'

'Who she's now dumped,' Karen reflected with a slight smile, 'in favour of Steven Sullivan. She gets around, that girl.'

Coolly, Arnold brought her back to the point. 'Apart from that, all I know about Mr Wong is that he's a collector of antiques—'

'And wealthy.'

'It seems so. From our brief conversations, it seems he's made his money in property development but that's about all I know. To be honest, it wasn't a major issue. I was just happy that he was prepared to lend a hand in choosing items from the Mannington collection. And from what we saw occur at the auction, he made some good choices for us.'

Mention of the auction caused a cloud to touch her eyes. He saw her shudder slightly. He could guess the reason for her reaction: she would be thinking about what happened after the auction, when they had made their disastrous visit to the Golden Palace. Her slim fingers strayed to her mouth, caressing her lips in thought. The recollections would be dark, he knew. 'He was a Dutchman, it seems,' she remarked after a short silence.

'The dead man?' Arnold nodded. 'It seems so. According to the newspapers he's finally been identified. Someone called

Charles de Vriess. But the details about him in the press are scanty: the police have issued no further information and they haven't put out anything at all about the hunt for his killer.'

'Who was so close to us in that restaurant . . . Let's hope they get their hands on that man soon. It was so cold, the way he murdered the Dutchman.' She took a deep, dismissive breath, pushing aside the memories, and glanced at Arnold. 'The police called you back for a second interview,' she continued. 'They haven't bothered me after I made my statement.'

'I think that'll be because they are convinced you didn't notice anything. DCI O'Connor is running the investigation, and wanted to talk to me. Not that I could help them much. I'd already told them what I saw, but it was all so fleeting. The best person to help them, I would have thought, was Steven Sullivan.'

She grimaced. 'What on earth *possessed* Sullivan to go charging after that man I can't imagine. It was reckless. He was taking his own life in his hands.'

'I think it was just pure instinct,' Arnold suggested. 'And he got clobbered for his pains.'

'Yes . . .' Karen was looking at him with an odd expression in her eyes. He felt uneasy: it was as though she was comparing Steven Sullivan's conduct with his own, and finding his wanting. Illogical, in view of her comment about Sullivan's recklessness. But, he reflected, women always wanted heroes. Slightly irritated, Arnold went on, 'Anyway, putting that aside, what about this Henry Wong request? What do you want me to do about it?'

She was silent for a few moments, tapping the desk in front of her, considering the matter. 'You'd better respond to him. But I think I'd better be there, to get a feeling at first-hand what his motivation is. I think maybe you should give him a ring, fix a suitable time and then escort him to the site. And . . . I think I'll come along at the same time.'

Another jaunt out of the office, Arnold thought. Not that the Deputy Chief Executive would even notice.

Arnold returned to his own office and checked in his desk for the card that Henry Wong had given him when they met at the martial arts centre. It was a private line, and Wong answered directly. 'Ah, Mr Landon, it is a pleasure to hear from you.'

'I understand you're interested in looking at our projected *Vendela* site,' Arnold explained. 'I'm ringing to see if we can fix a date when I could take you up there.'

'That is most kind of you,' the Chinese businessman purred. 'By all means let us fix a date and time. But there is no necessity for you to take me there. If you give me the appropriate directions I will get my driver to bring me to the site. It is better that way. It is not often I have the opportunity to visit your scenic Northumberland areas. And I am aware that you will be a busy man . . .'

* * *

Three days later Arnold led Karen down to the car park and drove them out of Morpeth, north along the A697.

Arnold had suggested they set off early to meet Henry Wong; it would give them the opportunity to make a detour into the Cheviots to visit a Romano-British site that was being worked on by a group from Sunderland, under the auspices of Newcastle University. They left Morpeth and headed for Wooler, before striking off left into the Simonside Hills. As they made their way towards the ridges of the Cheviots they passed the cotton-grass fringed gullies and peat-haggs that dominated the hills. Karen seemed relaxed, and more at ease in his presence than she had been for months, so that he was encouraged to draw her attention to the evocative sounds of the wild, treeless uplands, the bubbling call of the curlews that heralded the late arrival of the northern spring. There were glimpses of lapwings to be enjoyed and the high drifting spirals of buzzards, the almost motionless hovering of peregrine falcons. He was aware that she was somewhat amused by his enthusiasm, not least when he caught sight of some feral goats near the sandstone crags that formed a serrated line etched against the blue morning sky, and she laughed aloud. 'You're like a child!' she exclaimed, but there was no criticism in her tone.

'I've always thought it's a perquisite of the job that shouldn't be discounted,' he replied, grinning at her. 'You don't get out enough to enjoy it yourself.'

She humphed. 'As head of the department, there's too much admin stuff to do. You were well out of it, Arnold: it was a good decision not to go too hard for it yourself.'

It was the first time she had acknowledged that he had never really wanted the post she had won for herself: she had always seen him as a potential rival. It accounted for much of the animosity that seemed to bubble up intermittently between them. It was as though she felt he was always seeking to undermine her. It was never his intention. He slowed as the car crested the hill, and pointed out to her the crest of Raven Heugh. 'There's the site we're monitoring, just on that ridge over there.'

Karen stared at it. 'Not too far from here.'

'The road loops around — we've another couple of miles to go.'

'But if you pull in here, we could walk across to the ridge. Let's do that.'

Surprised, he guided the car on to a patch of rough moorland grass at the side of the road. Karen got out, took a deep breath, and hunched into her woollen jacket. 'Cool breeze up here. If we march, we won't notice it.'

She set off ahead of him, striding through clumps of heather and patches of bracken that grazing had failed to keep in check. She moved with an easy, lithe grace, and he was reminded once more of her elegance, and when she looked back at him her hair held reddish glints as it curled around the perfect lines of her face. He hurried to catch her up. A young grouse exploded from a clump of purple moor grass, with a chattering flight, and she laughed. 'I must be crazy to think of giving this up.'

'Are you serious?' he asked as he walked by her side. 'I know you said something the other day, but surely—'

She raised her head to feel the breeze on her cheek. She glanced at him: her eyes seemed hazel in colour, and a little sad. 'I don't know,' she said reluctantly. 'I feel as though I'm stuck in a rut sometimes. And, well, I don't know whether you've heard the news about the Chief Executive.'

'Powell Frinton? I knew he'd gone into hospital, but that's all.'

She wrinkled her nose. 'It seems he's suffering from bowel cancer. There's got to be doubt that he'll be able to return. And that puts the Deputy Chief Executive in a right panic, believe me. I doubt that he'd get the top job in any case, but the mere thought of having to be the interim Chief Executive is enough to make him yearn for early retirement.'

They stood on the rim of the sandstone outcrop, above rocky ledges sown with bell-heather and cowberry, looking across the intervening two hundred yards to the Romano-British dig. Arnold could see a group of students working on the exposed face. They had already unearthed bones and domestic rubbish at what would seem to have been a group of farm buildings. The hope was that they would find artefacts that would give rise to the suggestion of an extensive settlement, that would encourage further investment of time and money. He glanced at Karen. Her expression was solemn, and he gained the impression that she was hardly taking in the view.

'Would you really be thinking of applying for Powell Frinton's job?' he wondered. 'I mean, all that politicking, dealing with people you already despise.'

Perhaps he had gone too far. She frowned, glanced at him, and then waved a hand. 'Let's get across to the site.'

They spent an hour talking with the site manager, and being shown around the dig. Four trenches had been opened. The site manager explained that they had uncovered some worked flints, a few flagstone-type stones and a small quantity of charred wood, and burnt daub. The site manager explained they had already recovered some tack-like nails, shoe studs, and a rim sherd of a reeded mortarium. He suggested it dated from the first half of the fourth century, but Arnold was unable to raise any great enthusiasm. He hung back while Karen was shown the finds. He felt unsettled. When they left the site and climbed back up the hill he said little, kept his head down, paying no attention to the sedge-coloured, crumpled landscape about them.

They drove in silence away from the Cheviots and on towards the coast, to the cliffs beyond which the *Vendela* had met her doom. As Arnold negotiated the winding road down towards the flat, sheep-grazed plain that fronted the rocky beach beyond, he realized that Henry Wong had already arrived. A silver Jaguar was parked at the edge of the beach: two men were standing beside it, looking out towards the Black Needles that had broken the back of the East Indiaman. One of the men was Henry Wong, portly in a sheepskin jacket, collar raised against the offshore breezes, gesturing with his gold-headed stick. The other man was younger, slimmer.

'It's Jeremy Tan,' Arnold remarked. 'He must have driven Mr Wong up here.'

As Arnold drew his own vehicle alongside the Jaguar Henry Wong limped towards them, smiling. Arnold got out of the car, apologizing for having kept them waiting, but Henry Wong raised a placatory hand. 'Please do not disturb yourself. We have been here for minutes only. And I appreciate that you have work to do. But what a pleasant life you must have, being able to drive through this wonderful countryside, and enjoy such dramatic scenes as this.' He waved his hand seawards, to where the waves surged white and green over the Black Needles offshore.

'You know Miss Stannard, of course,' Arnold said.

'We met only briefly at the auction. I am delighted to meet you again, Miss Stannard,' Henry Wong beamed. He was wearing a broad-brimmed hat: he removed it and bowed slightly in an old-world manner. He glanced behind him: Jeremy Tan was standing a little way off. He had made no attempt to join them, but was staring out to sea. Henry Wong shrugged. 'He agreed to drive his old uncle up here, take time off from work, but Jeremy is a little out of sorts, today. Affairs of the heart, perhaps. What does an old man know?' He turned to Arnold. 'Now, I do not wish to waste your time, so perhaps you would like to explain to me your plans for this centre you mentioned to me.'

Arnold glanced at Karen, caught her nod of approval and commenced his explanation. 'The idea is to establish a base here, that would attract tourists, but also to be used as a research centre for this part of the coastline. The idea was to establish it as a memorial to the *Vendela*: it's the kind of thing that would be attractive to schools as well as tourists. We intended to have a photographic display relating to the days of the East Indiamen, the routes they took, the manner in which the *Vendela* came to grief and, naturally, displays of the kind of cargo the *Vendela* carried. The items you helped us choose from the Mannington collection would obviously figure prominently, though for reasons of security we would not be able to use them here as permanent exhibits. Occasional displays might be possible, but in the main they would have to be stored at a museum elsewhere. But this site would be used to spark interest in them . . .'

Henry Wong nodded gravely as Arnold showed him around the projected site, explained the need to construct a metalled track down from the main road, and showed him the sketches that had been prepared for the construction. Karen stood by, listening, but taking little part in the conversation. After a while, as Henry Wong continued to ask pertinent questions, his companion drifted back from where he was standing on the rocky beach and joined them, still standing a little apart, but listening to the conversation.

'This is all very interesting,' Wong commented with a furrowed brow, 'but I get the impression . . . you speak almost in the past tense. You say these *were* your plans . . .'

Arnold glanced at Karen. 'Perhaps Miss Stannard can explain the problems we're having with the funding.'

Henry Wong turned to her, and Karen began to tell him of the difficulties she was having with council funding. As she spoke, Arnold glanced towards Jeremy Tan. The young Chinese man was dressed in sharply cut black trousers and an anorak. There were bright spots of colour on his sallow cheeks and when he met Arnold's glance he nodded briefly, but his eyes were cold. He seemed irritated about something, as though he was disinclined to be here on the site. Arnold thought he had the appearance of a puppy that had been whipped.

'I see your problem, Miss Stannard,' Henry Wong was saying. 'And, of course, I appreciate the difficulties that are faced by local authorities in these days of financial restrictions. One sometimes feels that it is almost a duty that private enterprise should take upon itself . . .'

He was silent for a little while, turning his head, looking around the site, the black, louring cliffs, the offshore rocks, the crashing sea that centuries ago had torn the life out of the Dutch East Indiaman. In the silence, Jeremy Tan moved closer, his eyes fixed on the old man as though waiting for something to be said. Puzzled, Arnold glanced at Henry Wong as the old man turned, smiling at Karen Stannard.

'I should tell you, Miss Stannard, that I felt it an honour and a privilege that you should have turned to me when you needed advice about the Fowliang porcelain. I have long been a collector, but my worth and experience have never been so . . . *recognized*, before. I am also grateful that I had the opportunity to view the porcelain privately — to make the assessment of course — but also in order to make purchase decisions myself. But it is easy to talk of gratitude. I think it is also important that one should show one's thanks in a practical manner.'

His glance slipped past Karen to Arnold, and then to Jeremy Tan. 'When Jeremy agreed to drive me up here, I was still uncertain, but your explanations have now confirmed me in my intentions. You will be aware, Miss Stannard, that I have considerable interests in property development.'

Jeremy Tan spoke for the first time. 'Mr Wong is on the board of several development companies, and was responsible for the Stanway estate in County Durham.'

Henry Wong regarded the young Chinese man with a tolerant smile. 'My nephew will probably over-emphasize my importance in such business, but I admit not only to having been a successful entrepreneur in the field of property development, but also that I have had a yearning to . . . how do you say this? To put back something into the community, that is not linked by pure profit.'

Arnold felt a stirring in his veins. He was beginning to realize that Henry Wong's visit had not been dictated merely by curiosity.

'Such feelings are admirable,' Karen was saying. Her tone was careful, but Arnold knew that she too was feeling a surge of controlled excitement.

Henry Wong waved his hand expansively, taking in the site as a whole. 'The project you have described to me, the honouring of the *Vendela*, it seems to me it is a very worthy project. It is something I would wish to be involved in. Partly by way of thanking you for the opportunities you gave me, but perhaps even more because it satisfies my conscience towards the people of the north-east who have welcomed me to their land for so many decades.'

'I'm not sure what you're suggesting . . .' Karen began.

Henry Wong smiled blandly. 'I am suggesting that I be allowed to underwrite the *Vendela* project,' he said.

There was a short silence as Karen and Arnold stared at him. At last Karen found her tongue. 'That is very generous, Mr Wong, but—'

'Please.' He held up a pudgy hand. 'When I say underwrite, I should make it clear what I mean. Essentially, I will pay for the establishment of the *Vendela* centre.'

Karen gasped slightly. 'That's amazingly generous of you, Mr Wong.'

Wong bowed his head in embarrassed recognition. 'There will be certain conditions, of course.'

Hurriedly, Karen replied, 'Well, naturally, I would not expect that such generosity should come without certain restrictions.'

'Oh, they are not onerous,' Wong assured her. He glanced again at Jeremy Tan. 'I am prepared to invest a considerable amount of money, but to control costs I would wish my own company to undertake all the construction work. Naturally, I shall not interfere with the nature of the project, or attempt to change the plans you have already prepared, but work on site would have to be undertaken by my own people. And . . .' he smiled at his companion, 'since Jeremy here is experienced in the sourcing of materials, and organization of publicity, I would wish the firm he works for also to be involved with the project.'

Karen glanced at Arnold; there was a gleam of excited triumph in her eyes. 'I am certain we'll be able to come to the necessary arrangements, to the benefit of both parties. The name of the centre also, perhaps—'

Henry Wong forestalled her. 'I am too old to be interested in self-publicity,' he assured her. 'Such matters will remain in your hands. Perhaps I may suggest that my lawyers could meet you early next week.' He spread his hands wide. 'After all, why should we delay?'

'Mr Wong, I'm almost speechless,' Karen said.

The Chinese businessman smiled benignly. 'Please, do not overestimate the worth of my motives. I gain much from the transaction. A feeling of pleasure, and gratitude fulfilled. However . . .' He hesitated, smiling slightly. 'There is one other, personal consideration that I wish to add. A condition if you will.'

'Name it, Mr Wong,' Karen said firmly.

'I would like to make use of the services of your department.'

'How can we help?' Karen asked.

Henry Wong's glance turned to Arnold. He was smiling softly as he suggested, 'Perhaps you would be able to release Mr Landon from his duties, for the space of perhaps three weeks.'

Karen was puzzled. She shot a quick glance at Arnold. 'I don't understand.'

Henry Wong's tone was placatory. 'You might wish to regard it as a secondment. It would allow Mr Landon to work for me for this period, away from his current employment. If this could be arranged . . .'

Arnold became aware of a slight movement from Jeremy Tan. The man's eyes were firmly fixed on Henry Wong. The older man caught his glance, smiled slightly and nodded. 'And also, perhaps, since the work Mr Landon will undertake will be complicated, he would require an assistant. We would suggest, perhaps, Miss Portia Tyrrel?'

There was a short silence. Then Karen Stannard acquiesced. 'I feel certain that in the circumstances something can be arranged,' she replied firmly.

2

Portia Tyrrel was tight-lipped as she sat in Karen Stannard's office. Seated beside her, Arnold was very aware of the tension in her slim body. Her arms were folded, her eyes cold, as she listened while Karen, pacing around the room, brought them up to date.

'I've spoken to our *useless* Deputy Chief Executive and at least he's had the good sense to express no opinion and leave the matter up to my decision. I've trawled around the senior politicians and I've got the approval of the Leader of the Council.' She cocked an eye in Arnold's direction. 'Over drinks in the bar last night. You've no idea the kind of tricks I've got to employ to get things done sometimes.'

Arnold saw Portia stiffen. He realized that in the circumstances it was not the most sensible comment to make.

'Anyway,' Karen continued, 'I've taken soundings in the architects' department and the building department. Though both are a bit miffed — they think that the proposal derogates from their responsibility and authority though I don't see it myself since Wong won't change anything—'

'He's assured us of that,' Arnold added, glancing awkwardly at the silent Portia.

'—and the main thing is that we can move almost immediately on the project, since Henry Wong will be providing the machinery, the labour, the whole shebang. Work can start on the construction of the road immediately, it seems, since some of his work force is presently idle, and after that—'

'While this goes on what *exactly* are *we* supposed to be doing, Arnold and I?' Portia cut in peevishly.

Karen hesitated, frowning at the interruption. She glanced at Arnold and raised an interrogative eyebrow. She had clearly not realized things were going to be so difficult with Portia Tyrrel, and yet Arnold suspected Karen had a sneaking appreciation of the reason for Portia's annoyance: it was merely that she was unwilling to accept it. Carefully, aware he was treading on dangerous ground, Arnold said, 'Henry Wong has been a collector for the last twenty years. From what he's explained to me it's not just Chinese artefacts he's been collecting, like some of the *Vendela* porcelain he acquired at the sale. He's also put together a considerable amount of Celtic artefacts, some Romano-British items, a number of medieval weapons that he thinks might have been in co-existence with the Hung dynasty, and a series of parchments dating from the twelfth century. The deal he wants to strike with us—'

He caught Karen's angry glance, and corrected himself. 'The proposal Henry Wong has made to the department is that in return for his investment in the *Vendela* site, he wants assistance in cataloguing his collections, researching their interrelationship, identifying and checking the accuracy of the provenance of certain items . . . Karen feels you and I can be spared from the department for three weeks, and it seems a small enough price to pay for what Wong is prepared to do.'

'What Wong is asking us to do doesn't seem *Wight* to me,' Portia sneered.

'That's a cheap gibe,' Karen flashed. 'Just what's your problem, Portia?'

Portia Tyrrel glared at her. 'I'd have thought you would recognize exactly what the problem is! All right, I can understand why Arnold has been asked to undertake this task, but from what you've told me about the meeting up on the coast, and just how this deal was engineered, I've got suspicions about why I've been asked to go along with it!'

Karen Stannard had coloured slightly. She stopped pacing around the room and took a seat behind her desk, swivelled the chair uneasily and nodded. She shot a quick glance in Arnold's direction, then faced Portia. 'All right, I accept that there may be reasons behind the request that are . . . well, unusual.'

'Unusual? *Unethical* is more like it!'

Karen Stannard bridled. 'Oh, come on, Portia, lighten up a bit! Just because a man takes a fancy to you—'

Portia was seething. She unfolded her arms, put her hands on her slim knees and held Karen with a piercing look. 'Just because you're prepared to go creeping around politicians, taking drinks with them, chatting them up, indulging their little fantasies about getting into your knickers, that doesn't mean I have to do the same!'

'I resent that!' Karen snapped angrily. 'There's nothing wrong with indulging our bosses, as you put it. It's part of the game, playing them along to get what we need. And no one is saying that you—'

'No one is saying anything, but I'm not stupid!' Portia interrupted furiously. 'From what you let slip about your meeting up at the *Vendela* site, it's clear to me what's going on! Henry Wong wanted Arnold to do this work, but dragging me into it, that's nothing to do with the work involved, it's because he wants to indulge his bloody nephew Jeremy Tan! You know what I feel like about this, Karen? I feel I'm being treated like a slab of meat!'

There was a short silence. Arnold sat back in his seat. There was no way he was getting himself involved in this kind of argument. He felt way out of his depth. Portia took a deep breath, controlling herself. She swallowed hard. 'Look, a year ago I had a relationship with Jeremy Tan. I liked him, we had fun to begin with. We went out together; we had a good time. But, for me, as it went on, I felt it just wasn't going to work out. I can't explain exactly what was bothering me, but he began to get possessive, you know? Began to treat me as though I was just a chattel. There were times when we'd arranged to meet, and he didn't show. And he could get a bit . . . rough, if you know what I mean.' She glanced uncertainly at Arnold. 'I mean, I'm no shrinking violet as far as sex is concerned, but there are limits, you know what I mean?'

Arnold looked away. This was a conversation he didn't want to be party to.

'But more than that, it was attitude,' Portia continued. 'Maybe that's the way Chinese guys are — though I must say I never experienced that kind of behaviour when I was dating as a young kid in Singapore. The fact is I decided I couldn't take his way of handling me. So I gave him the word. I dumped him. He didn't take it too well at first, kept pestering me, but then it faded away as I stopped going to the nightclubs he frequented, the phone calls stopped, I got on with my life and I thought he got over his problem. So much so, I felt confident in getting in touch with him again, recently, to make the connection for the department with Henry Wong. As far as I was concerned we were still friends. But I never thought it would go further than that!'

'There's no reason why it should,' Karen murmured uncomfortably.

Portia shook her head in doubt. 'Mr Wong wanted Arnold's experience. My name came up, it seems to me, simply because it would give Jeremy an opportunity to get involved with me again.'

'I don't see how,' Arnold intervened cautiously. 'You and I will be working together. And Jeremy Tan doesn't work for Henry Wong — he's involved in some other business. As I recall, he's employed by Wong's business rival, Mr Cheung, that bullet-headed character who was bidding against Wong at the auction. There's no reason why the two of you should even bump into each other.'

Portia regarded him with a degree of contempt. 'I wish I could believe that, Arnold. Henry Wong doesn't employ Jeremy, but they're *family*! Look, I've moved on, I don't want to get tied in with Jeremy again. I've entered another relationship. It could get damaged — Steven and Jeremy know each other, and if Jeremy starts talking to Steven, locker room talk, particularly if he reckons he's seeing me again . . .' She paused, suddenly close to tears. 'I feel like I'm being *used*, Karen!'

There was a short, strained silence. Karen Stannard raised her head. It was clear she felt that Portia was overreacting. But there was little she could do to reassure her. She was used to using her own femininity to get what she wanted, but she always remained in control. Clearly, Portia didn't have the same kind of steel under the velvet. She shrugged, reluctantly. 'I'm sorry now that I even mentioned to you Jeremy Tan's involvement in the discussion at the site. To be honest, I thought it was a bit of a joke. It was just female intuition on my part that made me conclude Mr Wong was . . . indulging his nephew, as you put it. And clearly, if this is the way you feel, I can't force you to go along with Arnold to work on Wong's collection.' She hesitated. 'Of course . . . it's difficult to start raising questions about the conditions attached to Wong's offer, but I suppose if we point out the problem . . . I'm sure Henry Wong is a reasonable man, and will understand . . .'

Her voice faded away. The tension in the room was almost palpable. Arnold wriggled uncomfortably: he knew the unspoken question that was hanging there in front of them. If Portia refused to work with Arnold on this project, the whole deal with Henry Wong might collapse, if Wong felt affronted. The silence continued painfully.

At last Portia turned to Arnold. 'What do you think?' she asked dully. 'Am I reading too much into this situation?'

Arnold hesitated, aware that Karen was staring at him challengingly. 'Portia, as I see it, this is just a job,' he said quietly. 'We work on the collection for three weeks. I don't really see that there should be any difficulties . . .'

And he was certain that Steven Sullivan was sufficiently level-headed to ignore any gibes that his friend Jeremy Tan might make if they met at the martial arts centre. If there were even any to make.

Portia sighed, hesitated, then met Karen Stannard's eyes directly. She raised her chin. 'All right, Karen, I'll go along with it. But if I get the first hint of trouble from Jeremy Tan while I'm working with Arnold, if he starts coming around to Mr Wong's place to try to talk to me, or tries anything on, I'm out of there. Wong or no Wong.'

'I'm sure—' Karen began in relief.

'And let's be clear,' Portia interrupted her. 'After this, you *owe* me! You owe me big time!'

* * *

Some miles away, at Cambo, where Georgian landowners had laid out a new village to beautify their surroundings in 1740, the two police cars parked in the short, gravelled drive of the mock-Tudor house with its overgrown garden. The former ancient village had succumbed to famine, pestilence and the sixteenth-century change from plough to pasture. This house, built in 1790, had been the property of a minor landowner, seeking to ape his social betters; it had seen better days and now presented a sadly decayed appearance, but it was still a house of some quality, though somewhat isolated at the edge of the village.

Tracing its tenant to the house had been difficult. O'Connor had put three men from the crime room on to the task of discovering just where Charles de Vriess was based in the north-east. They'd discovered nothing from his credit card accounts other than that he had an address in Amsterdam which the Dutch police had informed them was only an accommodation address. They had traced two bank accounts in England, but the accounts had disclosed two different addresses which proved fruitless: de Vriess had made arrangements to manage his accounts online with the banks, and was sent no statements through the post. But there were considerable sums of money in those accounts, and the police had immediately obtained a magistrate's warrant to freeze them, pending further enquiries.

The breakthrough had come from an estate agent in Northumberland who had read of the murder of the Dutchman in the local press. He had recognized the name of the dead man. Farnsby had taken the call. It seemed that a house on the out-skirts of Cambo village in Northumberland had been leased by one of their clients, to the man known as Charles de Vriess. The estate agent was able to provide a key since they were acting as letting agents for the owner, who was working in South Africa.

O'Connor had detailed Farnsby and two other officers to join him in a visit to the premises rented by the deceased Dutchman.

O'Connor had noted the neglected air of the premises: he guessed de Vriess would have stayed here rarely. It was more like a safe house than a home. The estate agent had informed them that the lease had commenced some four months earlier, but if de Vriess had moved in then it seemed he had done little to make his stay comfortable. When they used the key supplied by the estate agent and entered the house O'Connor became aware of a musty odour that con-firmed his suspicion that the house had been little used. The curtains were drawn and the rooms were in darkness. Farnsby switched on the lights in the hallway. He picked up the small pile of post that lay just inside the front door, and riffled through it.

'Just junk mail, nothing personal,' he commented.

O'Connor nodded, gestured to the other officers. 'All right, you all know what to do. You two, take the upper floor. DI Farnsby and I will look over the situation here on the ground floor.'

'Are we looking for anything in particular, DCI?' one of the detective constables asked unwisely.

'What the hell do I know what we're looking for?' O'Connor snarled irritably. 'So far we've got absolutely nothing on this bastard except two bank accounts and a name that's probably not his own! All we know is he got removed, and guys don't get hit like that unless they have something funny in their background. So you go through everything, turn things inside out, and then we'll talk about what we've got!'

Chastened, the two officers made their way up the stairs. O'Connor glanced at Farnsby, impassive at his side. 'You take the rooms on this side. I'll take the others.'

O'Connor entered the sitting room. He switched on the light, walked across the room and drew back the heavy brocaded curtains. He stared around him: the furniture was unimpressive, standard equipment, he guessed, in a letting. A settee, two easy chairs, a couple of small tables, a roll-top bureau in the corner on top of which were placed three bottles. O'Connor inspected them: two whisky, one brandy. None had been touched, the seals still intact. If de Vriess had bought them for evening relaxation after a day's work, he clearly had spent little time in the house. It was puzzling. He had leased the house several months ago but there were no signs that he had actually used the place much.

He slid his hand down the sides of the chairs, and the settee. He encountered only fluff. He wandered around the room erratically, puzzled. He turned his attention to the bureau. The bureau was locked, but when he tugged at one of the drawers it opened; inside he found a small key. It fitted the lock of the roll-top. He turned the key, opened the desk. The pigeonholes were empty. On the flat desk itself there was a ring-bound notebook. He picked it up, opened it. It contained a list of names on the first page. There were none he recognized. On the subsequent pages there were other lists, some under headings which appeared to be of limited companies, or other businesses: Newtown Enterprises; The Blue Rose; Yeavering Construction. The names were unfamiliar. He checked back to the Blue Rose. There was a list of names, and a brief scribble below them. *Registered charity*.

He turned to the sixth page. It was the last on which any entries had been made. It was a brief list of five names. He stared at them, and a slow numbness crept through his veins. He was still staring at the page when he heard Farnsby call.

'DCI O'Connor! You'd better take a look at this.'

With the notebook in his hand, O'Connor turned and went back into the hallway. Farnsby had already searched the front room; he was standing in the kitchen doorway. O'Connor walked towards him. Farnsby held out a hand: it contained a box. O'Connor took it from him, inspected the label. 'It's a proprietary medicine. So? Maybe de Vriess had a stomach problem.'

'Pretty badly,' Farnsby commented in a dry tone. He beckoned to O'Connor to follow him. He had opened the doors of two of the kitchen cabinets. They were stacked with boxes of the same brand.

'So he was a pharmaceutical representative,' O'Connor remarked. 'We already knew that.'

Farnsby retrieved the box of pills from O'Connor and read the label. 'Klazo. You ever heard of them?'

'The makers? Can't say I have, But these days—'

'Bit like Glaxo, isn't it? Though not *exactly* the same.' Farnsby turned slowly, looked around the kitchen. 'But take a look in this cabinet.'

He opened it somewhat theatrically, like a conjuror proud of his handiwork. Stacked neatly on the shelves were small green and white boxes. Farnsby took one down. 'Tadalafil,' he said. 'Marketed under the name of Cialis. You'll probably be aware this drug's obtainable only on prescription in this country, to counter erectile dysfunction. But in the swinging club scene it's much prized as a sexual stimulant. If you want to keep going the whole weekend—'

'I get the picture,' O'Connor growled. 'So what are you suggesting?'

Farnsby shrugged. 'What was de Vriess doing with stuff like this, and in this amount, even if he was working for a pharmaceutical company? Why carry stock such as this?'

O'Connor grunted. 'Let's do the rest of the house.'

The two detectives came down from the upstairs rooms. 'Nothing up there except furniture, a few items of clothing, bed's been slept in, but no sign of the place being used very much.'

Thoughtfully, O'Connor tapped the notebook he was holding on his left wrist. Farnsby glanced at it curiously. O'Connor took the house keys from his pocket, nodded to Farnsby. 'Okay, just keep prowling around here. I'm going to take a look outside.' He pointed to one of the constables. 'You. Come with me.'

He led the way around to the side of the house. The garage had an up-and-over door. After a few moments he found the correct key, rolled back the door. The two men stood at the entrance, staring. The garage had never been used to hold a car. It was stacked with perhaps forty cardboard boxes, wrapped in plastic. O'Connor could guess what they held. 'Okay,' he nodded, 'let's lock up again.'

Farnsby was standing at the front door to the house. 'You find anything?'

'More of the same,' O'Connor replied. 'A hell of a lot more.'

'Are you thinking what I'm thinking?'

'That all this stuff is fake?' O'Connor took a deep breath. 'It would be my guess. It looks as though our deceased Dutchman was in the business of selling counterfeit medicines, probably shipping them in from Amsterdam. We'll have to get it checked out at the labs, of course, but it looks to me that we've now got a reason for the killing of Charles de Vriess.'

'He was horning in on someone else's territory?' Farnsby suggested.

'Or he was selling the stuff as the real McCoy, and somebody got upset about it when the truth came out. Right, let's get a few samples to take back with us, and then we'll send a team out to go over the house again, and cart the boxes I found in the garage back to the forensic labs.'

He tossed the keys to Farnsby so that he could lock up, turned and went back to the car. He climbed into the passenger seat and sat there, thinking. He was aware that the smuggling and sale of counterfeit medicines was a lucrative and highly dangerous sideline of the narcotics business. Proprietary medicines could be brought in as bulk, sold on, then split up to maximize profit, selling by doses. Sometimes the medicines were fake, sometimes they were past their sell-by date, old stock that was repackaged and remarketed under brand names, or names that sounded close to legitimate companies. The nightclubs were targeted, amphetamines, methamphetamines known as 'ice', and Ecstasy being the drugs of choice: O'Connor had little doubt that the boxes in the garage would contain a range of medicines and drugs to supply the underworld industry. The killing of de Vriess had the hallmarks of a gangland war. The driver's door opened and Farnsby got in beside him. 'Back to HQ?'

O'Connor nodded. As the car engine roared into life he realized he was still holding the notebook he had picked up from the roll-top desk.

'So what's that?' Farnsby asked, as he drove out from the gravelled drive into the main road into Cambo village.

'It was in the desk back there. Lists of names. We'll get them checked out back at headquarters,' O'Connor said dully. He slipped the notebook into his pocket, but the list of names on the last page was still burnt in his memory. At a guess, it comprised a list of patrons — the usual titled people who would lend their names to charities, but would have no real involvement with the charity in question other than attending the odd function to raise money.

Below that group there was another list of names: maybe the members of the board of management. It was one of those names that had leapt out at him, driven the breath from his chest, as though a fist had struck him in the solar plexus.

He froze in his seat, his mind whirling. What was the significance of this notebook in the roll-top desk in a house leased by Charles de Vriess in Cambo village? And what connection could the woman who engaged his thoughts and memories nightly have with the man gunned down in the Golden Palace?

Equally to the point: what the hell was he going to do about it?

3

Arnold and Portia were to begin work for Henry Wong at the beginning of the following week. They both had files to deal with before they vacated their offices; in Arnold's case he had to make a few quick visits to active sites in Northumberland in order to complete progress reports for Karen Stannard and for the departmental committee reporting to the council, but by the Friday he felt reasonably reassured that he was more or less up to date. There was a final meeting with Karen to discuss the development of the *Vendela* site, at which Portia seemed in a better, more relaxed mood. She had had a conversation with Arnold where she had begun by reiterating her anxieties, became angry once more at what she saw as a disregard of her personal feelings, but by the time she joined Arnold in Karen's room, it seemed she had come to terms with the situation, though Arnold from time to time detected a gleam of ice in her eyes as she glanced at her head of department.

During the weekend Arnold took the opportunity to clear his head. He felt curiously detached, to a certain degree unsettled, and he was unable to pinpoint the reason for his state of mind. He had been in the Department of Museums and Antiquities for a considerable number of years now, and on the whole he enjoyed the work there, apart from the occasional spats with Karen Stannard, who had never seemed to come to terms with their relative situations. She constantly seemed to feel under threat. But he had learned to handle all that. Yet he felt unsettled.

When he was a boy his father had taken him through the dales of Yorkshire, seeking out the traces of long-spent workings, lime-burning kilns with their dark, cave-like mouths and turret-like structures, silted bell-pits surrounded by their raised discs of waste, lead-washing mills, and half-demolished, gaunt engine houses that were the final vestiges of a long-gone pig-iron industry. From such beginnings he had developed his own interests, seeking out traces of much older societies, Roman trackways, cup and ring stones, Viking gravestones and hog-back monuments, until finally as a grown man he had found himself in an employment that allowed him to indulge his tastes, learn about wood and stone and architecture, take part in archaeological digs, and work alongside academic experts whom he had sometimes confounded with his own practical experience.

So this weekend he walked old, familiar trackways on the high fells of the Northumbrian uplands. He walked Clennell Street again, a drove road that some claimed had been a trading route in prehistoric and Roman times and was certainly used for transhumance to summer pastures in the twelfth century. He tramped what some had described as England's last wilderness where the wind was high and strong, where the mists had once hidden border reivers in their destructive fog-bound rides, where Viking settlements had been established, ancient rituals undertaken, and men suspected of crime had been thrown into marshy bogs, strangled, mutilated, left to die a slow, choking death.

Over the years he had seen many such sites, caught up in the toils of an ancient story, and he was nowhere near satiation: it was not that he felt jaded, or dissatisfied with his work, because there was always the clean, bracing, salt-tanged air of the fells to enjoy, with the distant glimpses of the sea and the panorama of sheep-grazed hills. So why was he ill at ease?

It had to be Karen Stannard. When she had first arrived at the department to work alongside him, he had been as stunned by her elegance and beauty as the other men in the office. After seeing disconsolate office Romeos and disenchanted politicians who believed office brought favours, he had not been surprised to hear rumours about her sexual preferences but he had discounted them and had tried to establish a sound working relationship with her. It had, of course, been affected by her in-built suspicions, her competitive instincts and finally, even by her promotion to head of the department. But he had once seen another side of her also, a warmer, more vulnerable side which had climaxed in a brief closeness, culminating in a merging of desires and bodies. And perhaps that was the problem. In spite of the sharpness, the contemptuous dismissals, the arguments, he still held at the back of his mind that one occasion in the hotel at Alnwick . . . And now she was thinking of leaving.

As he walked the fells he was forced to reach the obvious conclusion: he was unable to foresee life in the department without her, in spite of her arrogance, her claims to superiority, her backbiting in committee and council rooms. Had anyone asked him to describe his feelings for her, he'd have been unable. But the fact was, she was part of his life.

So, in a sense, the confusion of his mind was eased by the need to take on a new challenge, by leaving the office behind for a few weeks to work for Henry Wong.

Portia decided to travel with him on the Monday rather than take her own car. Arnold picked her up at the office in Morpeth and they headed for the coast. Arnold had checked on some of the business in which Wong was involved: his property development activity was extensive, but recently had been confined to an area in County Durham. His base, however, was at a converted seventeenth-century manor house just inland from Seaton Delaval, on a hilltop with views out over the sea. It would not be his only home, Arnold guessed;

possibly it was merely a weekend retreat in the country, providing an opportunity to escape the drudgery of meetings and conferences he would attend in Durham and Leeds, Manchester and Teesside, where his holdings would seem to extend.

When Arnold turned into the driveway, Portia murmured at his side. It was a sound of approval.

Arnold guessed that the building was older than the seventeenth century in its origins. Possibly it had begun life as a fortified pele house, a last defence against the border raiders, for he seemed to identify a remnant of a sturdy tower in the stonework on the west wing of the house. It was difficult to tell, in view of later additions and somewhat botched restoration, but at some stage a wealthy merchant or industrialist had cleaned the stone, added a Georgian-style portico and redeveloped the mullioned windows. The entrance beyond the long gravelled driveway was adorned with white-painted ironwork of intricate design; above the doorway was a balustraded terrace hung with clematis and Virginia creeper. It was an imposing introduction to the house itself. At the doorway they were met by a slight, middle-aged man of Chinese origin, who led them inside to the library.

'Mr Wong is in a meeting at the moment, but I will inform him of your arrival.'

Henry Wong did not keep them waiting long. Portia had stationed herself at the tall, high window and was gazing out over the lawn and the meadow where a small group of pheasants strutted, while Arnold was admiring the old oak shelves and the expensive bindings of the books lined up there like self-conscious proclamations of taste and style, when the door opened and Henry Wong entered the room. He wore a dark business suit, a white shirt, and sported a red rose in his buttonhole. His moon face beamed a welcome.

'I regret I was not immediately available to welcome you, but certain of my business acquaintances desired a meeting with me, and since I knew you were coming, I thought it best that they met here. But, forgive me, if I may make a brief introduction to you of my problems regarding my collection, I will then have to leave you again.'

Arnold raised a hand. 'Please, Mr Wong, we wouldn't want to interrupt you. We're aware you're a busy man.'

In spite of his protestations the Chinese businessman remained with them for the next half-hour. Clearly, he was not averse to escaping from his business commitments to spend some time explaining about his collections. They were obviously dear to his heart.

'There comes a time,' he explained seriously, 'when one looks around at one's life and decides the pleasure one obtains from work can be overridden by the need to surround oneself with beautiful things. Yet always there is a conflict: the organization of business, the need to earn one's bread, competing with the sensation, the pleasures, the excitation and stimulation of the intellect.'

He began by showing them some of the books he had collected, first editions, ancient texts and parchments. 'I have the mind of a grasshopper,' he regretted. Then he turned to the table where he picked up a folder. 'This comprises a list of my holdings. I think the first task I would wish you to undertake is to study this list to familiarize yourselves with its contents. Then, perhaps, you will join me and my other guests for lunch?'

After Henry Wong had returned to his guests elsewhere in the mansion house, Portia and Arnold began work. The first task, as Wong had suggested, was to familiarize themselves with the holdings. Arnold was surprised at the catholic range of items: they included bronzes from the Greek period, Romano-British artefacts, a few items of Celtic jewellery, some Italian nineteenth-century paintings — regarding which he immediately admitted to Portia he knew nothing — and various pieces of ancient pottery. Other papers in the file described the dates of purchase. Arnold noted some of them went back twenty years, and only a few of the dates were supported by details of the vendors or auction rooms which had handled the purchase by Henry Wong. Arnold was slightly puzzled however by the haphazard manner in which the files had been arranged. There seemed to be little or no order, no logical grouping of the items.

'If I had a collection like this,' Portia grumbled, 'I'd damned well make sure it was better ordered. And is he expecting us to sort out the provenance of these pieces?'

'That's about the size of it,' Arnold replied. 'So, after lunch, I suggest we try to match up these entries against the items themselves. If they are all actually held in this building, anyway. Which I doubt.'

Arnold raised the matter over lunch. He and Portia had been invited to join Mr Wong in the dining room, which turned out to be long, oak-panelled, and tastefully decorated. The stressed beechwood dining table was covered in white damask, places had been laid for a cold collation, and glittering glasses were available for the Pinot Grigio served by a white-gloved waiter.

Henry Wong had introduced three companions. Arnold was aware of a certain relief in Portia's smile when she realized that Jeremy Tan was not among them. Each was dressed in a dark business suit. Like Wong, they were Chinese, and from the cut of their suits, prosperous. Arnold had expected a degree of formality but Henry Wong beamed upon him and Portia as they sat at the table and announced, 'I have already told my colleagues that you will be working here for a few weeks, and I have never been one to stand on unnecessary formalities. My colleague Mr Tsui is known as Jimmy to his friends. I am sure he would not object to first name usage: it makes for a more convivial lunch.'

Mr Tsui, a slim, intense-looking man in his late forties, with hollow cheeks and a penetrating glance, ducked his head, and smiled assent.

'Jimmy is in the restaurant supplies business,' Wong explained. 'And my friend here, Mr Cheung, he is always known as Freddie.'

'I think I have seen Mr Cheung before,' Arnold said to the middle-aged man with the short-cropped, iron-grey hair.

'I believe you were at the auction with Mr Wong, when you were both bidding for Chinese porcelain from the Mannington collection.'

'I was indeed.' Freddie Cheung laughed, though it had an edge to it. He glanced at his host. 'I am not sure who triumphed that day, but I believe we both enjoyed the contest.'

'So you also are a collector?' Portia asked.

Freddie Cheung regarded her with approval. 'That is correct, young lady. Like my friend and business acquaintance Henry, I have come to appreciate things of beauty in my old age.' He raised his glass to Portia, his eyes fixed upon her. 'And I do my utmost to collect them.'

Arnold felt a little uneasy. He wondered whether the trouble for Portia might be coming not from the absent Jeremy Tan but from a Chinese man of a different generation. He observed the man carefully. Cheung's face was round, his eyes inexpressive and narrow, and his nose was broad and fleshy. His lips were full, with a hint of sensuality, and he had a short, thick neck. Arnold found him less than prepossessing, and he gained the impression that Portia had a similar view.

The younger man seated beside Arnold leaned forward. 'As the son of Freddie Cheung,' he smiled, 'I am always around to make sure that he observes the niceties of Western culture. He calls me Little Joe, but I must say I prefer to respond just to Joe.'

Their host chuckled. 'And of course, Arnold and Portia, you will stop calling me Mr Wong. It makes me feel old beyond my years. Henry it shall be.'

Arnold agreed it made for a more relaxed situation. Over lunch he learned that Freddie Cheung had made his money in the hotel business, both in England and overseas; he boasted of owning several Chinese hotels in Singapore, two of which were known to Portia, to her obvious delight. Joe Cheung acted as a manager in one of the Manchester hotels owed by the Cheung family.

It was not long before Henry Wong asked the obvious question. 'So what do you think about my collection?'

Arnold glanced at Portia. 'It's incredible in its range. It must have taken you years to complete. But I'm afraid you've given us quite a task. The cataloguing alone will take us a week: it's almost as though you've never been bothered to keep the books straight.' Hastily, to avoid offence, he added, 'And of course, we'll have a big task also linking up the entries with the actual artefacts, so there'll be plenty to do. I presume they aren't all kept here in this house.'

Henry Wong shook his head. Affably, he replied, 'No, you are right, I have been careless about my control systems. And I will identify the locations when you need them, so you will not be required to spend all your time in this house.'

Freddie Cheung shifted his bulk in the chair. Arnold became aware that one of his eyelids drooped lazily, giving him a slightly sinister air. 'Most important of all,' Cheung suggested mischievously, 'make a determined effort to confirm the provenance of the items. Henry may well have cut a few corners, legally speaking, in acquiring his brilliant collection.'

Henry Wong laughed, but there was something forced about it. Arnold glanced at Freddie Cheung: there was a smile on the man's sallow, coarse features, but Arnold thought he detected a hint of malice, a touch of brutality in the man's self-satisfied mouth. He began to think that Henry Wong and Freddie Cheung might be involved in business ventures together but the rivalry he had detected between them in their bidding at the auction room was perhaps more serious than was apparent on the surface.

'I didn't detect any tension of that kind,' Portia remarked later, when Arnold mentioned it to her. They had finished lunch and returned to the library to continue with the catalogues. 'As far as I was concerned, it was a pleasant occasion; Joe Cheung was rather sweet, and as for Henry and Freddie, they just seemed to me to be two jolly, successful businessmen. Freddie Cheung, no doubt, will be a bit of a bastard in his business dealings, or they wouldn't have achieved what they have. But I've met men like him before. And as for him and Henry Wong, I think they're just friends.'

Arnold was not so sure.

The rest of the week passed quickly. Portia and Arnold worked at the house for two days, checking the catalogue entries against the artefacts that were held there. For the following two days, they spent time in the Newcastle University Library, where they were able to undertake some research into the provenance of the Romano-British pieces. The Chinese porcelain was not a problem, of course: since these items came from the Mannington collection their provenance had already been confirmed. On the Friday they began their tour of the other locations identified by Henry Wong — the collection was scattered, between properties in Sunderland, Middlesbrough and Leeds. Each property was owned by Henry Wong, and Arnold began to realize that the Chinese businessman was a person of considerable wealth. He would be well able to afford the financial support he was giving to the *Vendela* project.

On the Friday evening, Arnold called back at the office in Morpeth after dropping Portia. He was surprised to see that Karen's car was still parked outside the office. He went to his own room, and dealt with a few memoranda and letters that had landed on his desk during his absence. When he left the room, he saw that there was a light at the end of the corridor where Karen worked. He hesitated, then walked down and tapped at her door.

She called to him to enter.

'Arnold!' she explained, leaning back in her chair and stretching her arms above her head and yawning. 'I'm surprised to see you. So how's it going?'

'Well enough. And there's certainly enough to keep us busy. The whole cataloguing situation is chaotic, and as for details of provenance . . . well, it's chaotic. It surprises me that a businessman such as Wong would leave his affairs in such a mess. In fact, if I didn't know better I'd think it's almost as though someone's deliberately messed up the whole system just to give us work to do.'

'I can hardly imagine that's what's happened.' She locked her hands behind her head; the movement tightened the white shirt she was wearing. It emphasized the swell of her breasts, and the slimness of her waist.

'Anyway, everything all right here?' Arnold asked.

'Fine,' she smiled gently. Her eyes seemed green this evening, provocative. 'We're managing to hold the fort.'

'You're working late.'

'I'm just about finished now.'

There was a tightness suddenly in his chest. He hesitated. 'Do you . . . do you fancy a drink?'

She regarded him soberly, her eyes holding his. Something moved in their depths, an uncertainty, perhaps a memory. There was a short silence. She unlocked her hands, placed her elbows on the desk in front of her, cupped her face in her hands. 'I'm not sure that would be a good idea, Arnold.'

'An opportunity to wind down,' he suggested in a tone he forced to be casual, his mouth suddenly dry.

Her glance fell away. 'You know what they say about business and pleasure, Arnold. So, I don't think so. Not tonight.' She paused, avoiding his eye. 'Another time, maybe.'

Or never.

CHAPTER FOUR

1

Jack O'Connor had visited Belton Hall on previous occasions. He recalled his thoughts on first seeing the entrance to the Hall with its giant portico and Ionic columns. The doorway was flanked with marble statues of Autumn and Spring and the building was imposing against the backdrop of the northern hills. It was on that first visit he had caught his first glimpse of Isabella Portland: clad in jodhpurs and riding boots and a white, open-necked shirt, she had taken his breath away. Her magnificent dark eyes, set in an oval face, had looked at him almost mockingly, perhaps aware of the impact she could make on men. And he remembered her later, her red-gold, luxuriant hair spilling upon the pillow in the darkness of an hotel room, her arms about him, her warm flesh and soft thighs against his. He shivered, aware of the movement of his body at the recollection, the memory that had constantly taunted him in his waking nights ever since.

And he remembered the horror of his last visit to Belton Hall, when her true personality was revealed to him. She had clung to him that day, almost protectively, but the gun in the hand of her leaden-faced husband had been turned to his own temple. O'Connor could still see in his mind's eye the blood, bone and flesh of Gordon Portland spattering across the room. He could still hear Isabella's scream of terror and dismay, and for a while thereafter the memories of their love-making had faded, as though it had been something enjoyed by two other people.

He had not seen Isabella since, but as the horror of that last day at Belton Hall faded, so did his recollections of Isabella herself come flooding back, insidiously, so that he would wake in the night, twisting with desire, unable to force her image from his mind and dreams.

He had deliberately stayed away from her since that day her husband had died, and she had made no attempt to get in touch with him. Even now the thought of renewing their acquaintance, of actually seeing her again, made him shiver, half dreading what he might see in her eyes, conscious that his own resolve where she was concerned could be weak, and indeterminate.

He had not disclosed to Farnsby the details on the page he had removed from the ring-bound notebook. His DI had known about O'Connor's relationship with Isabella Portland, and disapproved of it. Inevitably, if O'Connor had shown him the names on the torn-out page he would have warned O'Connor away, insisted that he himself should deal with the matter. And he would have been right, O'Connor knew that. It was crazy to follow the enquiry himself; mad-ness even to think of meeting Isabella again.

And yet, here he was, his heart thumping like a teenage schoolboy, his nerve ends tingling as he came down from the hill into the long drive that led to Belton Hall.

The elderly resident butler had not been replaced since Gordon Portland's death. When he opened the door he immediately recognized O'Connor and his mouth registered his shock. He recovered quickly, but his eyes were cold and disapproving.

'I'd like to see Mrs Portland,' O'Connor said quietly, stepping inside the door.

The butler hesitated. 'I'm not certain . . . I'll see if she's available to—'

'This isn't a private visit,' O'Connor remarked bluntly. 'It's a police matter.'

The butler stepped back a pace, his pouched eyes flickering as though seeking escape from a dilemma, then he gestured with his left hand. 'Perhaps you wouldn't mind waiting in the hall, Mr O'Connor, while I speak to Mrs Portland.'

O'Connor moved forward into the cool, tiled hallway, glancing up to the cupola-lit staircase. It was down those steps she had come, the first time he saw her. He thrust the thought away irritably. He reminded himself of the central reason why he was here, denying the subdued need to see her again. He waited, edgily, his pulse still racing. The butler had walked through to the breakfast room to the left. He glanced at his watch. He could imagine Isabella would be struggling in her own way, wondering what brought him here to Belton Hall. Perhaps it was now all over as far as she was concerned: after all, there had been lovers before him, as Gordon Portland had sneeringly informed him. There might have been a lover since. But perhaps that was not the way it was. There was still the possibility . . .

From the corner of his eye he caught a movement in the doorway of the breakfast room. He turned his head: Isabella stood there, saying something quietly to the butler, who glanced at O'Connor and then moved away into the depths of the house. Isabella stood there for a few moments, regarding him soberly, then she came forward towards O'Connor, with the same easy stride, the slow elegant swinging of the hips that he recalled so well, and when she spoke it was the slightly husky, melodious, faintly accented voice that had whispered to him on the pillow. Except that her tone was cool, and controlled, the voice of a stranger.

'Detective Chief Inspector O'Connor. Your visit is a surprise.' She raised an eyebrow, a hint of contempt in her eyes. 'And on official business, I understand.'

'I regret my intrusion,' he managed to say. His tongue was thick; his tone uncertain.

She regarded him speculatively for several moments, then turned aside. For a moment he thought she was going to lead him into the library, but then she checked, thought better of it because of the bloody memories it held for each of them, and moved away from the room where her husband had died. He followed her through to the back of the house, to the morning room. It was flooded with pale sunlight, and offered a view of the distant hills.

She turned to face him, still stiff and cold in her tone. 'Perhaps you would like to sit down, while you explain to me what you have come for.'

He was unable to help himself. 'Isabella, do we have to be so formal?' he blurted out.

She stood in front of him, very still. Her eyes were fixed on his; he read no warmth in her glance. 'It is months since my husband died,' she said quietly. 'I think you made your choice, made it very obvious.'

'Isabella, I—'

'You knew where I was. Once the enquiries were finished — and I went through hell, you know, but you were not there for me—'

'I was taken off the case,' he muttered. 'I was too closely involved.'

It was not strictly true. DI Farnsby had warned him: if he remained involved in the conclusion of the investigation it was inevitable that the truth about his relationship with Isabella would emerge. She was right. He *had* made a choice.

'You knew where I was,' she repeated coldly. 'You could have come to me, when things had quietened down, but you did not. Today, you are here for the first time, and it is on business.'

'You must understand,' he insisted defensively, 'I had to step back, and I wasn't sure . . . the things your husband said that day . . .' Gordon Portland's words came back to him, echoing in his skull. *You must know by now that my wife is nothing but a whore . . .* He swallowed hard. 'It seemed best to leave

125

things as they stood. But as the time went past, I couldn't get you out of my mind.'

'In spite of the lovers you had heard about?' she asked contemptuously. 'In spite of the view Gordon had of me? If you had come to help me in those black days after Gordon killed himself it could have been different, but things have changed, I have changed, and I've buried the past.'

Stung, he snapped, 'By taking a new lover perhaps?'

Her dark eyes seemed to glaze over momentarily. Her lips tightened and she seemed to be about to blaze at him in an angry denial, but she regained control, glanced behind her, took a seat in the easy chair facing him. She affected a look of indifference. 'I told you, I have changed. My marriage was a cage, but it no longer exists. The pressures have gone. You will be well aware that Gordon was a rich man: it was why my family in Italy persuaded me to marry him in the first place. Now that he is dead, I am a rich woman. I am a free woman. I do not *need* men.'

He detected the nuance — I do not need *you*. She sat stiff-backed, her long legs stretched out in front of her. 'I'm sorry. I wish it had been different. I wish I had come to see you,' he murmured.

She shrugged indifferently. 'You did not. But you are here now. And I am told your visit is connected with police business. I suggest you get on with what you have to do.'

He was silent for a few moments. There was a dull ache of resentment in his chest. He knew he was at fault, but she did not understand the way it had been for him. Any more than he had been able to appreciate the agonies she must have suffered, after that catastrophic day.

'Well?' she queried. 'Is it something to do with the death of my husband? I thought that was all over and done with.'

O'Connor shook his head. 'It is, all finished. The investigation I was involved with, in which your husband played a part, that's all completed. But now . . .' He raised his head, thrusting aside all thoughts of the past. 'You might have seen in the newspapers that a man was shot to death in a Chinese restaurant a few days ago.'

'I don't read the newspapers,' she replied with a studied indifference.

'We've discovered that the man's name was Charles de Vriess.'

He held her gaze. He waited. She gave the appearance of boredom.

'Is that supposed to mean something to me?' she asked, after a short silence, during which she appeared to be waiting for him to add further comment.

O'Connor's mouth was dry. He licked his lips. 'You didn't know him?'

She shook her head. 'I haven't even heard the name.'

O'Connor leaned back in his chair, suddenly feeling more in control now, watching her carefully. 'I remember your husband telling me he made his money in the construction business.'

'Among other things,' she replied carelessly.

'He also told me that he decided to retire from active work in his companies, to escape the cut-throat, dog-eat-dog aspects of it. He married you, and then began to relax—'

'Do we have to go over the history of my marriage?' she demanded with a flash of irritation.

O'Connor ploughed on doggedly. 'He also talked about how he began to collect paintings and sculptures—'

'I've sold them all now,' she interrupted.

For a moment he thought he detected a slight shudder: it would be because of the use Gordon Portland had made of one item in his collection. A broad-bladed Bowie knife. O'Connor dragged his thoughts back to the present. 'What else had he intended to do in his retirement? Collecting sculptures, yes . . .'

'Enjoying his possessions,' she added cynically. 'Me included.'

'But did he have any other interests? Did he get involved in any other kind of business or charitable activity?'

Isabella frowned. It detracted little from her beauty. 'I don't know what you're talking about. Is there a point to this conversation?'

'When did you get involved in the Starling Foundation?' he asked bluntly.

Surprised, she grimaced. 'I don't see that's any business of yours.'

'Was it after your husband's death? Had he been involved with the Foundation? Did you get dragged into it in his place?'

Paradoxically, the belligerence in his tone allowed her to relax. She leaned back in her chair slowly, crossing her long legs provocatively. She allowed a slight smile to touch her full lips. 'Is this an accepted interrogation technique?' she asked quietly. 'Ask questions to trap me into admissions, before telling me what this is all about?'

'Have you got something to hide?' he countered.

'Doesn't everyone?' she challenged. 'Don't you, for instance?'

Annoyed, he replied, 'When did you first meet Charles de Vriess?'

Her eyes widened. She was silent, staring at him with a slight amusement in her glance. 'I've already told you. I've never even heard of him.'

'Not even through the Starling Foundation?'

A contemptuous smile curved her lips, and she shook her head mockingly. Annoyed at the thought that she was playing with him, O'Connor thrust his hand into his jacket pocket and took out a folded sheet of paper. 'This is a photocopy of a page that I found in a notebook. The Starling Foundation is mentioned. And it's got your name on it.'

She seemed unfazed. When he handed her the sheet she took it carelessly, glanced at it and shrugged. 'Why, so it does. How nefarious of me, to keep from your knowledge a harmless, rather less than onerous, activity for my spare time.'

'You're named as a subscriber to the Starling Foundation.'

'It would seem so,' she sighed theatrically. 'But is helping a charity now to be regarded as a crime? Have you really been sent to question me because I have made a donation to a charitable foundation? Could you find no other excuse, no other reason to come here to visit me? What exactly is it you want?' She thrust the paper back at him. 'What exactly is this all about?'

Angry, he decided it was time to deflate her. 'I found the notebook, from which this page was . . . extracted. The notebook was in a desk, in the house rented by the dead man. And you still tell me you've never heard of Charles de Vriess?'

He had caught her attention. 'I've already told you twice! I've never heard of him,' she snapped. 'Besides, of what significance is it? I've subscribed to a charitable foundation. My name appears on a list. Why the hell that should be of interest to anyone I can't imagine. And why it should occasion a visit from such a senior officer as a detective chief inspector is beyond my comprehension!'

O'Connor sat stiffly in his chair, glaring at her. Slowly, he forced himself to relax. 'I think it would be helpful, Isabella,' he suggested, calming down, realizing that the tension between them was driving the conversation, 'if you could tell me how you got involved with the Starling Foundation.'

She recognized the gentleness in his tone, and frowned again, accepting that she too was more affected by this meeting than she was prepared to admit. She shrugged. 'Before he died, Gordon was involved in a number of charities, sat on their boards. People asked him, because he was wealthy, well known in the north-east.' She glanced around the room. 'Because he lived here, I suppose, as well. Belton Hall. Abode of the wealthy. Anyway, after his death, as a result of the scandal, several of them simply faded out of touch with the name Portland. One or two of the more thick-skinned did not. When they approached me to stand in his place, I turned the requests down.' Her dark eyes held his, coolly. 'I've never been a charitable person.'

He made no response.

'Then, a short while ago, one or two new charitable organizations, who perhaps were not aware of the scandals that had touched the name of Portland, approached me. I turned them down. But I did make a contribution to the Starling Foundation.'

'Why?' O'Connor demanded bluntly. 'What was different about them?'

She frowned in recollection. 'Perhaps they caught me at a weak moment. They wanted a donation of course, and I complied with their request. But the reason I responded to them . . . well, you've got to realize it was a time when I was down, emotionally, feeling very sorry for myself, withdrawn and lonely in this bloody mausoleum of a house, and when the news of the tsunami in Asia hit the headlines it brought me to my senses. Here were people who were far worse off than me. After all, they had lost everything. All I had lost was a husband — whom I disliked — and a lover.'

He was unable to hold her glance. 'The tsunami . . .' O'Connor said thoughtfully. 'Is that the reason why they approached you?'

Almost wearily, she replied, 'I got a letter stating they were commencing a fund to assist the people made homeless by the tsunami. It struck a chord with me. I agreed to make a contribution. They asked me if I would serve on their board. I refused that honour.'

'So you've not been involved with the charity very long?'

'I'm not *involved*. I simply made a contribution. But you're right — it's only been a few months.'

'But you were told of its activities. Tsunami relief . . . What material help does the charity offer to the tsunami victims?'

She frowned, and shrugged. 'I can't say I've paid a great deal of attention, other than to make the donation. The usual stuff. Clothing, blankets, food parcels—'

'Medical aid?' he asked sharply.

She caught the sudden change in tone. 'I don't know. I suppose so. I've told you, I've never really enquired closely.'

He watched her carefully as he stated, 'It's just odd that the Foundation, and your name, appears in a notebook owned by the dead man. We know now that Charles de Vriess seems to have been a pharmaceutical representative.'

Isabella waved a hand. 'I wouldn't know about that. But that's maybe why he had information about the Starling Foundation. Maybe his firm was involved in providing medical supplies, giving support to the charity.'

'You don't know that.'

Her eyes glittered. 'I agree. I don't know that. I've never heard of this man de Vriess. And I don't see that it's important that he had a copy of the list of large donations to the Foundation at his damned house.'

They were getting nowhere. She was probably right. He sat silently for a few moments. 'Have you had dealings with any of the officers or board members of the Starling Foundation?'

She shook her head. 'I only made a donation. I've received various communications from them, but I've just dumped them.'

O'Connor took a deep breath. He had made a bad mistake. When he had seen her name his reaction had been to remove the page from the notebook, discover what connection she had had with the dead man, but now it seemed there had been no real connection: it had all been innocent. There was no reason he could discern why de Vriess should have had the Starling Foundation in the notebook, but as far as he could see there was nothing suspicious to be gleaned from the fact of her involvement. And she had not known Charles de Vriess.

'So is that all?' she asked coldly.

He was reluctant to leave. He wanted to stay longer, perhaps hoping for a thawing, a relaxation of the tension that still lay between them. But there were no more questions to ask. He felt edgy, uncertain. He stood up. 'I'm sorry I had to bother you.'

She made no immediate reply. She rose from her chair, preceded him into the hallway. He was aware of the scent of her perfume as she brushed past him, opened the door at the main entrance. She hesitated for a moment, as he stood awkwardly on the front steps below the portico, and then she extended her hand. He took it; it was cool, slim. He recalled those slim fingers in his hair, on his body . . .

'Goodbye,' she said.

He found no glimmer of hope in her tone.

He returned to his car. He started the engine, reversed in the drive, and as he turned to drive away he looked back. Isabella Portland was still standing in the doorway, watching. She did not raise her hand to wave. But she was still there when he drove into the bend in the drive, still there until he was lost to view.

He was barely aware of the return to Ponteland. He was on automatic pilot mentally, engrossed still in his meeting with Isabella. He went over what had been said, cursing himself for his clumsiness, his inability to blurt out what he was really feeling, angry that he had been unable to tell her the way it had been, the way it still was. And yet in a sense it was of no significance: Isabella Portland's coolness suggested she wanted no return to the way it had been between them.

He was almost surprised when he found himself driving into the car park at headquarters. He got out, locked the car, and went up to his office. He sat down in his chair behind the desk, and put his head back, trying to clear his mind of the past. After a while he put his hand in his pocket, pulled out the crumpled piece of paper on which he had photocopied the page torn from the notebook. He stared at the names for a while, then shook his head. He crumpled the paper still further, then flicked it into the waste-paper basket. After a moment, he opened the desk drawer, fished inside for the original entry from the notebook. He should never have torn it out. But it was too late now. He would have to destroy it. Too late to go back. Explanations would be difficult.

There was a tap on the door. He looked up. It was Detective Inspector Farnsby. There was the light of triumph on his saturnine features. 'Looks as though we were right,' he announced.

Casually, O'Connor slipped the page he was holding into the drawer of his desk, covered it with a file. 'Right about what?'

'Those medical products we found at the house rented by Charles de Vriess. I've just had the lab report: they've tested a number of samples. The stuff is all counterfeit. And as for most of the really expensive stuff, well, they were just placebos in the main.'

'So it looks as though de Vriess was on a smuggling and counterfeiting run, from Amsterdam,' O'Connor suggested.

'That's about the size of it.'

'Well, it gives us a lead we can follow anyway. We've got motive. It's a matter now of cracking down on anyone whom we suspect of dealing in—'

The door burst open behind Farnsby, forcing him to step aside, as the bull-necked, heavily built Assistant Chief Constable barged into the room. Sid Cathery's broad features were empurpled, and he glared in barely controlled fury at the two officers facing him. 'You two working on the de Vriess case?' he demanded.

'We were just discussing the fact that it seems he was dealing in counterfeit medicines—'

'Bollocks to that! You can forget about it.' Cathery took a deep breath, controlling himself, and O'Connor suddenly realized that while they were experiencing his anger, it was not in fact directed at them. Cathery stabbed a thick finger at O'Connor and then was turning, heading back down the corridor. 'You'd better both come along to my office. There's someone you need to meet.'

Puzzled, O'Connor raised his eyebrows, shot a startled glance at Farnsby and rose to his feet. Farnsby was already heading for the door. The two men hurried after Cathery, barging his way along the corridor, then up the stairs to his office. Cathery slammed the heel of his hand into the half-open door, bursting it wide, and then held it open. He glowered at the man seated to one side of his desk. 'You can make your own introductions. I'm getting myself a cup of coffee.'

The heavily built, dark-haired man with the sleepy eyes rising from the chair in Cathery's office glanced at Farnsby, and then at O'Connor. 'I believe,' he said, smiling slightly, 'you and I have already met.'

133

2

O'Connor stared at the man in front of him in surprise. He recalled how he had thought of him as a coiled serpent; the impression was reinforced now, as he stood with an air of complacency before them, cool, casual, dangerous. He glanced at Farnsby. 'This is Mr Garland. He works for the Federal Bureau of Narcotics and Dangerous Drugs.'

'In the good old US of A,' Garland added, somewhat unnecessarily. He nodded to Farnsby, making no effort to shake hands, and sat down again. 'Mr Garland sounds a bit formal and British. Maybe you should just call me Bob.' He gestured towards the seats beside him. 'You might as well rest the feet. Looks like your Assistant Chief Constable won't be back for a while. Does he always get that riled so easy?'

The two men did as he suggested. O'Connor shrugged. 'Mr Cathery has a somewhat short fuse. Depends what's happened to upset him.'

Garland grinned, making no attempt to disguise his indifference to the tantrums of the Assistant Chief Constable. His heavy-lidded eyes glanced from one man to the other. 'Well, I don't know why he should get so upset. After all, I'm only here to take some weight off your shoulders.'

'In what way would that be?' Farnsby enquired in a crisp, somewhat dismissive tone.

'You guys are investigating the death of Charles de Vriess, aren't you?' Garland smiled easily. 'I'm here to help you cut some corners.'

There was a short, strained silence. O'Connor frowned. 'I don't quite understand.'

Garland raised an eyebrow, lazily, confident. 'That's your problem. You really *don't* understand, and you're running down wrong tracks. I got information you don't.'

O'Connor considered the matter for a moment, then said, 'As far as we can make out, Charles de Vriess was smuggling and dealing with fake drugs. Is that why you're involved with this? Because the FBNDD has information?' He stared levelly at Garland. 'What exactly is your status in this enquiry?'

Bob Garland snorted. 'Status. You guys are so uptight. I think that's why your ACC got so riled up when I walked into his office — with the blessing of your Chief Constable, I might add.' He leaned back, crossing one leg over the other. He nodded to O'Connor. 'You'll recall I was having a chat with you at the conference in Padua. I approached your Chief after I'd seen you leaving, and he told me about your little problem here. I got on to some of our people and obtained the full details; they filled me in and asked me to handle the FinCen side of things.'

'FinCen?' Farnsby enquired.

'Financial Crimes Enforcement Network,' O'Connor explained in a quiet voice. To Garland, he said, 'I don't see what your FinCen organization has to do with this. De Vriess was dealing in narcotics and—'

Garland interrupted him smoothly. 'After I spoke to the FinCen people in Washington, and they gave me the go-ahead, I got in touch with your Home Office in London, and then your Chief Constable. He told me I could step into the breach, plug a few holes, that sort of thing.'

O'Connor understood why Cathery would be annoyed. The Chief Constable would have told him after Garland's arrival, and Cathery would not be best pleased at the thought of an American agent working on his patch. Farnsby seemed irritated also, as much by Garland's studied casualness as by his presence in the investigation. 'I suppose you're going to tell us you know who killed de Vriess, and why he was killed.'

The heavy-lidded eyes held an arrogant gleam. 'Well, you might say that, son. Fact is, I got a pretty good idea who's behind the killing. Who ordered it. Why the hit was made.'

Farnsby was silent, but his mouth was grim with disbelief. He looked at O'Connor, who remarked, 'You seem pretty confident, Mr Garland. At Padua, you were talking about the influence of the Triads. Are we to assume you're laying the de Vriess killing at the doors of a Triad society?'

'Exactly that.' A trace of bitterness entered Garland's voice, and O'Connor was reminded of his first impression of the FBNND man. 'You've come across the Ghost Shadows Society?'

'Never heard of them,' Farnsby snapped. 'We've no record of Triad activity here in the north-east.'

'That doesn't mean they don't exist.' Garland's tone had hardened. 'You British police, you're too damn slow to see what's happening under your noses.' He glanced at O'Connor. 'You heard what was said in Padua. You heard how important this campaign is. It's one we've taken seriously in the States. We used our RICO statutes to bring down the Italian mobs and now we're targeting the Triads. But you guys in Europe are slow.'

'What exactly are the RICO statutes?' Farnsby enquired stiffly.

'Racketeer Influenced and Corrupt Organization legislation. The statutes allow for swingeing asset confiscation, financial investigations not just of the guys convicted but their associates and families also. Heavy prison sentences, crippling fines. But in Europe you're still sucking your thumbs,' Garland said contemptuously. 'All right, you made a start with money-laundering laws but you guys are still reluctant to admit Triad power: you think it's just a local problem of a few thugs ripping off restaurant owners—'

Farnsby bristled. He was about to make an angry retort. O'Connor forestalled him. 'All right. You asked us about the Ghost Shadows Society.'

Garland turned his glance to O'Connor, permitted himself a slight smile. 'Bit of a long story. It's one we've been following in the FBNND. The story of a guy called Freddie Cheung.'

The name was unfamiliar to O'Connor. He watched as Garland took a silver case from his pocket. He extracted from it a thin cigar, brought out a lighter, flicked it and lit up. He made no attempt to ask whether either Farnsby or O'Connor objected. More in control, O'Connor wondered what sort of explosion they might get from Sid Cathery when he returned and sniffed cigar smoke. 'Perhaps you'd better tell us about this man,' he suggested quietly.

'Cheung's of Hakka descent, born about 1947 in the New Territories outside Hong Kong. Like many young men at the time, he got involved in Triad activity. He was ruthless and ambitious and he rose quickly through the ranks. It looks as though he became head of a Triad sub-group in Kowloon, dealing in narcotics. But by 1975 things got too hot for him. He followed the same route as many Triad members: he became a climber on the Golden Mountain.' Garland smiled thinly, drew on his cigar with obvious satisfaction. 'It's how the Triads referred to San Francisco. In other words, Freddie Cheung came to the States. But when our crackdown started he came to Europe. More specifically, the UK.'

'How do you know all this?' Farnsby demanded frostily.

'We've had our problems in the States. And we dealt with them, not least through the RICO statutes. And we made a study of the Triads. Fact is, we know that Cheung came to UK in 1987.' He inspected the glowing end of the cigar reflectively. 'Of course, once he made his way into Europe we lost sight of him for a while. And we can't be absolutely certain of his progress when he came to Britain. But we *think* what happened is this. He found a number of disparate Triad groups already in existence outside of the main centres in London and Liverpool, and he began to reorganize them. He pulled in their Dragon Heads, took control of their foot soldiers, and our guess is that's when he took over the Ghost Shadows Society. No doubt there were initial power struggles, a few choppings, a killing or two — though well outside the UK — but our information suggests that by 1995 the Ghost Shadows were a tightly organized bunch. It's our guess that Freddie Cheung became *shan chu*, controlling the society, well-connected with lawyers and key political friends, mediating in Triad disputes and keeping the Triad peace.'

O'Connor observed how Farnsby's coldness seemed to have deserted him; a gleam of interest was now apparent in his eyes. For himself, a dull misery seemed to have seeped into his bones, though he was unable to identify the cause. He pulled himself together. 'Your interest — the FBNND — it will have been because of international narcotics smuggling, I suppose.'

'Correct. Cheung was well placed when the poppy crop in the Golden Triangle failed. In Europe the Triads lost out at first, they were quickly usurped by Turkish, Iranian and Pakistani producers operating out of the Golden Crescent — mainly Afghanistan. But Cheung had connections: the Ghost Shadows ended up getting their heroin — and also morphine base — by working with Cheung's sources in Laos. They set up a tight organization. Cheung followed the usual pattern, of course: set up legitimate enterprises in the UK as cover but maintained branches for his illegal activities. In 1990 he was challenged by a guy called Ricky Chan, who even tried to bring him into court. Cheung had him killed in Macau, putting out the story he had double-crossed the Ghost Shadows over a heroin shipment. In fact it was just a power struggle. Once Cheung was secure in the UK he made business contacts with the Vietnamese in France, the

Mafia in Naples, Rome, Milan and Turin, as well as emerging Triads in Spain, and Germany.'

'Cheung controls a European *empire*?' Farnsby asked in astonishment.

'Naw, not in that sense,' Garland snapped in irritation. 'They're linked, but each operation is independent of the other.' Blue smoke drifted in the air as he took another pull on his slim cigar. 'We now have agents established in each of these countries; my job is to work with police forces in the UK. And we had information that a centre is being established up here, with a lodge in Newcastle. The Ghost Shadows. They're already shaking down every Chinese business in the north.'

'Shaking down?' O'Connor queried.

'Extortion, loan-sharking, smuggling drugs.'

'So how did de Vriess fit in? He was a Dutchman.'

Something moved, deep in Garland's eyes, a hint of malice. His lids drooped as though he were reluctant to disclose his feelings. 'He got hit because Cheung thought he was setting up in opposition, bringing in fake medicines.' He was silent for a moment. 'It was a mistake. A bad decision. Ordinarily, the opposition gets warned, threatened, maybe chopped. A killing like that, it was unusual. Either Cheung's lost his sense of balance, or one of his foot soldiers got over-excited.'

'Why a bad decision?' Farnsby asked.

'Because it's put a spotlight on the organization,' Garland replied coldly. 'It's not the way they like to do things. They prefer staying in the shadows.'

'Are you *certain* of all this?' O'Connor asked doubtfully, almost dreading the reply.

Before Garland could reply, they were interrupted. The door burst open, and Assistant Chief Constable Sid Cathery barged into the room. He had taken a cup of coffee to calm down, O'Connor surmised, but it had done little to assuage him. He had lost some of his high colour, but his shoulders were still rigidly set and as he walked past the American narcotics agent his mouth was grimly set. He slumped down in the chair behind his desk and glared at Garland. 'You been bringing them up to speed?'

'Sort of,' Garland replied languidly.

'You told them about what the Chief wants us to concentrate on?'

Garland hesitated, then nodded. 'I was about to get around to that.' He regarded the two men seated beside him. 'Narcotics is one thing, but our information would suggest that the Ghost Shadows Society has begun to move into other areas. Not just counterfeit drugs, but financial fraud.'

'You mean credit card theft?' Farnsby asked.

'That's been going on for some time, using fraudulent assistants in shops or restaurants. Middle-ranking Society members carry out card-making, with templates and a pretty high degree of technological skill. It usually involves borrowing genuine cards for the templates in order to obtain the information encoded on the magnetic strip.'

'How is all this counterfeiting financed?' O'Connor asked.

Garland shrugged. 'Through dirty money obtained from narcotics or other illegal activity. And the counterfeiting profits are then invested in other organized crimes, or in legitimate business activity such as property development.'

Sid Cathery was glaring at the cigar still smouldering in Garland's fingers. 'Would you mind putting that bloody thing out!' he snarled.

Garland was unmoved. 'You should've told me you objected.' He looked around for an ashtray, saw none and finally pinched the ash with quick fingers. He seemed indifferent to the fact that the ash fell on the carpeted floor. Cathery's colour was rising again. O'Connor spoke quickly, to avert another outburst.

'What happens to the money from all this counterfeiting activity?'

Garland slipped the remains of the cigar into his top pocket. 'The Triads are wealthy from this kind of trade, but the money, well, they invest in companies run by legitimate organizations or individuals, where the returns are not spectacular but steady. Some investments are made in high-risk, speculative commercial activity such as stock, commodity or currency markets. That's why you need laws that allow you to trace the money. If profits are reinvested in legitimate activity it's difficult to follow; illegal investments are made from illegal income before laundering into legit business. Keeping the two apart confuses the police and thwarts the seizure of assets. You guys in Europe have made a start with money-laundering laws, but there's a ways to go.'

'And that's what our friend here from the States is suggesting we start to concentrate on,' Cathery intervened sneeringly. 'Forget things like narcotics—'

'No,' Garland said swiftly. 'Not forget it, just recognize that's not the way to kill the activity.'

'I stand corrected,' Cathery announced sarcastically. 'Mr Garland suggests we keep dragging in the dealers, but we should spend more time looking at the ways in which his Ghost Shadows Society launders the money they make.'

'The fact is,' Garland continued, 'you guys have to try to get ahead of the game. You got to target the laundering of money obtained illegally, but you got to take a look at what is known as cyber-crime as well. From the information we got, it seems the Ghost Shadows are about to set up a new criminal activity. They're about to start targeting commercial computers and they'll be using the cutting edge of computer technology. They've recently acquired equipment that can fire bursts of electronic power to disrupt computer circuitry from long distances. They can destroy hard disks. They can hide logic bombs — you know, encrypted algorithms — in computer systems. In other words they can hijack computer systems.'

'With what aims?' Farnsby asked.

'Mr Garland suggests that the idea,' Cathery muttered, 'is to hijack the system, then contact the owner and demand a ransom in exchange for the code which will reverse the encryption process.'

'It's known as a DoS attack,' Garland added. 'Denial of Service attacks. And from what we understand, the Ghost Shadows are already recruiting experts to help them to do just this in the north of England.'

'There haven't been any complaints from financial institutions,' Farnsby objected.

'They're always keeping tight-lipped about it,' Garland explained. 'They don't like the negative publicity that would arise if it was known their systems were insecure. But it's on record that more than three million was paid in blackmail recently by a merchant bank in London and finance companies have suffered more than sixty such blackmail attempts. Our information is it's about to happen up here in the north.' He grunted sourly. 'But like I said, the finance houses don't talk too much about it. Bad for business.'

Farnsby cleared his throat. 'All right, so we'll have new priorities up here soon. But right now, we're supposed to be dealing with the killing of the Dutchman de Vriess. You say you know who's responsible for the killing, but how do we pin it on this man Cheung? We don't even know who Charles de Vriess was. We don't know what organization he was working for. We've no clue to his real identity. Surely, that's the first thing we need to establish.'

Assistant Chief Constable Sid Cathery gave a cynical, explosive laugh. He turned his gaze upon the FBNND man across the desk. 'You haven't got around to giving them that little titbit yet, then?'

Garland eyed him coldly. 'I can see you're bursting to inform them. I've done all I need to do for the moment. I've other matters to attend to.'

'Like informing next of kin?' Cathery sneered.

Garland rose without replying. He nodded to O'Connor and Farnsby and walked towards the door. It closed quietly behind him. O'Connor watched him leave, then swung around to look at Cathery. 'What's going on?' he asked. 'I don't understand.'

'What's going on?' Cathery exclaimed. 'That's what I'd bloody well like to know! It's a fine kettle of fish when the bloody Yanks just walk into our back yard and do what the hell they please, without telling anyone who's responsible for law and order in this country! We're the bloody front-line troops and no one tells us bugger all. The Chief just walks in here and almost casually tells me about this bastard Garland and what he's been up to, so long after the event that it's useless for us to raise a squawk!'

Farnsby looked bewildered. 'Am I missing something here?'

Cathery's tone was scornful. 'We're treated as though we're just babes in the flaming wood! We've just been given priorities that we've had no opportunity to question or influence. We have a murder enquiry on our hands and we're told to put our efforts elsewhere, not worry too much about the killing, because it'll all get sorted out if we can put the finger on this character Freddie Cheung. Desk work, that's what it's called. That's what Garland actually called us — desk jockeys!'

Frowning, O'Connor suddenly recalled something that had been said in the heated argument that had blown up in Padua, between the FBNDD man, Garland, and Franklin, from the Home Office.

. . . Indeed, the US Embassy in London even maintained a resident officer who gathered intelligence on drug traffickers, infiltrated operations and identified couriers . . . While that officer worked hand in glove with the British authorities there was a . . . er . . . certain falling out over the matter of his methods . . .

'Bob Garland implied we needn't dig into the background of this man Charles de Vriess,' O'Connor said slowly. 'He said he knew all about him . . . could identify him.'

'Too bloody right,' Cathery snarled.

'Are you saying . . . ?'

'I'm telling you what Garland obviously didn't get around to putting on the table. We can lay off the identity of de Vriess because that man Garland already has a full dossier on him. He knows who he was, where he came from, what he was up to, and what his bloody *mission* was!'

'Mission?' Farnsby queried.

'Wake up, DI Farnsby! Hasn't it sunk in yet? Charles de Vriess has been smuggling fake medicines into the north-east right under our very noses, and we were told nothing about it. Why? Because that bloody man Garland thinks we're incompetent, unable to run our own show, and because he thought he knew the answers, knew how best to bring his pet target Freddie Cheung to book! Charles de Vriess was horning in on the fringes of Triad activity not just to rouse up the Ghost Shadows Society. He was hoping to rile them into maybe doing a deal with him, although it's a bloody wild hope he'd achieve that as far as I can see. The *theory* was that he could in some way get closer to the Ghost Shadows, even get taken over by them, infiltrate the Society, not as a member, of course, but as a link man. It was a set-up. But it blew up in Garland's face when someone put a bullet into Charles de Vriess's throat. As if, in spite of what Garland says, it would never have been anything other than inevitable!'

'Charles de Vriess was a plant,' O'Connor muttered, almost to himself.

Sid Cathery's mouth was grim. 'Too damned right. Charles de Vriess was well known to Garland because he recruited him, ran him, arranged for his supplies of fake designer drugs. Charles de Vriess was an undercover agent, employed by our American friend Garland. He was an agent for the Federal Bureau for Narcotics and Dangerous Drugs. Working here on our patch, for God's sake, without our bloody knowledge!'

3

The lounge in the Black Horse was thinly populated. Arnold had been somewhat surprised when Portia had suggested, after they had finished for the day at Henry Wong's house, that they have a drink together. He was even more surprised when she had proposed that they should get back to Morpeth and go to the Black Horse. On arrival at the pub she had left him to order the drinks, while she excused herself to make a phone call. When she returned to join him at the table near the window, she was a little flushed, but clearly pleased with herself in a nervous kind of way.

She slid into the seat beside him, and thanked him for the gin and tonic he had placed in front of her. 'So,' he said, 'tomorrow it'll be Sunderland for me. I'll need to take a close look at those bronzes Henry Wong has in the house there. I'm not at all sure the description in his list matches up well with the suggested provenance. Have you got anywhere with the identification of the paintings?'

She pulled a face. 'Like you, I'm no expert, but they seem to check out all right. I just hope we don't find out later that they appear in some police file as having been stolen from somebody else's private collection.'

'You think Mr Wong would stoop to such behaviour?' Arnold asked, smiling.

She eyed him slyly. 'Hey, you can never tell with the Chinese — and I can say that because I'm half Chinese myself. But seriously, there's always the possibility that Mr Wong could have been sold stolen goods without his realizing it.'

'I think it unlikely,' Arnold mused. 'He wouldn't have taken a chance in asking us to go over his collection.'

'I guess so,' she agreed. She glanced at her watch, then sipped her drink, a little on edge. 'But it still amazes me that he could raise such a great collection, and yet keep such careless records.'

'Privilege of the rich.' Arnold saw her glance again at her watch. 'It's only been about thirteen seconds,' he said.

'What do you mean?' she asked, startled.

'Since you last checked the time. You supposed to be somewhere else?'

She hesitated. He was curious. He had known Portia for several years now and he had seen her as a confident, professional woman, skilled in her subject, manipulative in her dealings with men, competitive in her reaction to Karen Stannard. But since she had agreed to take on the assignment for Henry Wong she had shown a different side to her personality. She had worked hard, as he would have expected, but there were moments when she would seem to be daydreaming, edgy, uncertain. Now, when she made no immediate reply to his question, he asked, 'Is there a reason for our meeting like this? I was surprised to be invited. We don't normally socialize after work.'

She bared her perfect teeth in an attempt at a smile. Somewhat sheepishly, she admitted, 'Actually, I've got a date.'

'Apart from me?' he mocked her. 'I thought tonight I was the man in your life.'

'Don't be stupid, Arnold,' she snapped, with a flash of irritation. Then, relenting, she added, 'That was the phone call I made.'

'Putting him off?' Arnold asked drily.

She tapped him lightly on the shoulder, aware of his teasing. 'No. I rang him to tell him I was here. At the Black Horse.' A little nervously she added, 'He should be here in a few minutes.'

'At which point I will be expected to graciously retire,' Arnold remarked. 'So what was the point of inviting me in the first place?'

She wriggled her slim body, anxiously. 'I sort of . . . well, I wanted some moral support.' When she could see he was puzzled, she went on, 'I thought, maybe when Steven arrived and joined us, maybe we could talk about the work we're doing.'

'Steven Sullivan?' So the rumours, and his guesses, were true. 'Why would he be interested in what we're doing for Henry Wong?'

'I don't suppose he is, really,' she said somewhat gloomily. 'But it'll help break the ice, you know, so I can find out what he's been hearing.'

Puzzled, Arnold half turned in his seat to look at her squarely. 'What's the problem, Portia? What's this all about?'

She hesitated, then she ducked her head, looked a little sheepish. 'Look, Arnold, I know you've got views about me. You and I once, well, we sort of got . . . carried away . . .'

It was not the way he would have described the briefest of physical relationships they had enjoyed. She had always been in control on that occasion, and ever since. He was surprised now to see that she was nervous.

'The fact is,' she muttered, 'I really *like* Steven. We've got a good thing going, and I don't want it disturbed. You'll remember that when it was first suggested, I didn't want to get tied into this work for Henry Wong. There was always the chance that Jeremy Tan would show up . . . and I'm sure it was his idea. I think he suggested to his uncle that I joined you.'

'We've seen neither hide nor hair of Jeremy,' Arnold reminded her.

'That's true, but I know him, there's always the chance he could have been talking to Steven when they meet at that damned martial arts centre, and I'm afraid Jeremy will say things, sour what I've got going with Steven. I wouldn't want that to happen.'

'So how am I supposed to help?' Arnold wondered.

A pleading note entered her voice. 'Well, if we sort of talk generally about the work we're doing, and then we get around to mentioning Jeremy, maybe you could tease out of Steven — sort of man's talk, you know — whether Jeremy's *said* anything.'

'About what?'

'About me and Jeremy of course! You know, the relationship we had before I met Steven.'

Arnold shook his head, and smiled. 'I really think this is a bit silly, Portia, and I don't see how—'

'Hush! Here he is.'

Portia was rising to her feet. Steven Sullivan was striding across to join them. He looked very handsome, Arnold thought; a dark business suit, white shirt, carefully knotted tie. His dark hair was carefully combed back, his blue eyes bright with pleasure as he advanced towards Portia. They kissed in greeting, and as he watched them embrace Arnold concluded they made a perfect couple. Then Sullivan was turning to Arnold, extended his hand. His grip was firm. 'Mr Landon. Good to see you again. Can I get you a drink?'

As Arnold hesitated, Portia ignored her previous seat and took one opposite Arnold. 'We'll both have the same again, Steve,' she suggested. As Sullivan nodded and walked across to the bar to place the orders, she half whispered, in a dramatic tone, 'Once we've got the ball rolling, Arnold, I'll find an excuse to slip away for a few minutes.'

Arnold was of the opinion the whole situation was developing into little short of a farce, but, half amused, he decided to play along with the strategy. As it happened, once Sullivan returned, he opened up the field for them immediately. 'So, how are things going with your work for Henry Wong?'

Arnold leaned back casually in his seat and began to describe what they were doing, but it wasn't long before Portia, bright-eyed, broke in and began to chatter about their work in detail. Steven Sullivan listened politely; Arnold was unable to determine whether he was really interested in what she was saying, but his eyes rarely strayed from her face, and it was clear to Arnold that the young corporate accountant reciprocated the feelings that Portia Tyrrel had for him. Arnold felt more than ever that this was going to be a waste of time, that Portia had been overreacting, seeing dragons where there were none to be slain. He was on the point of giving up and leaving when Portia turned to him, smiled, and said, 'Would you two mind if I leave you for a moment? Powder my nose, that sort of thing.'

That kind of arch comment went out when Singapore was still a colony, Arnold thought sourly.

Sullivan watched her go with a slight smile, admiration in his glance. He turned back, picked up his drink. 'So you've just got a week or so to go,' he commented.

'With Mr Wong? Yes, that's right.'

'What then?'

It was an odd question. Arnold shrugged. 'Return to the usual stuff, I suppose, back in the department.' Aware that time was somewhat limited, he asked, 'Do you see much of Jeremy Tan these days?'

'Jeremy?' Steven Sullivan scratched at his ear. 'Not really. In fact, I haven't met him since . . . since that night at the martial arts centre.'

Portia would breathe a sigh of relief at that, Arnold thought. 'Doesn't he work out there anymore?'

'Oh, he probably does,' Sullivan asserted. 'But I've sort of dropped out. It was a way of keeping fit, but I've been pretty busy of late, putting in new computer systems at work. It's a sort of roving commission I've got — I'm wandering around the country a bit, working for various corporate clients. And, of course, there's Portia. We've been seeing quite a lot of each other.' He sipped at his brandy and soda. 'So there's not much time left for boys' games.'

So Portia's fears were groundless. 'Jeremy's pretty keen at the martial arts, is he?'

Sullivan grinned. 'You might say that. It's another reason for dropping out. We met at the club, became friendly, and sort of worked out together. But he's rather too competitive. There were times when he kind of took things a bit too seriously for me. I've got bruises to show for it!' He shook his head, chuckling. 'As they say, when they begin to catch you, time to give it up.'

They lapsed into a slightly awkward silence; they had little in common, Arnold realized. The young corporate accountant had better things to do than socialize with a man who spent his days digging around ancient earthworks. He caught a glimpse of movement near the door; looking up, he saw Portia standing there. She raised her eyebrows questioningly. Arnold shrugged.

'Ah, here she is!' Sullivan announced, scrambling to his feet as Portia rejoined them.

'Sit down, sit down,' Portia beamed. 'Finish your drinks. No need to rush away.' She glanced at Arnold. He smiled, shook his head slightly. She took it as encouragement. 'So what have you two been talking about, putting the world to rights?'

Casually, Arnold murmured, 'Talking about bruising activities with Jeremy Tan, really. Steven's sort of given up the martial arts stuff.'

There was a glint of relief in Portia's dark eyes. 'I always told him it was stupid. There was always the danger of getting interesting bits broken off.'

Sullivan laughed. The two of them began to indulge in good-hearted, somewhat risqué badinage, and Arnold's attention wandered. He glanced around the room; it had begun to fill up, he noted. Then he stiffened. There was a man standing at the bar, someone he recognized. He was staring at them. Another surprise for the evening, Arnold thought. Detective Chief Inspector Jack O'Connor. Next moment he felt a tug of dismay in his chest. O'Connor had picked up his drink and was walking across the room towards them.

A few moments later he was standing at their table, regarding them owlishly, his glass half raised. 'DCI O'Connor,' Arnold said quietly.

'Well, well, well, the three major suspects, conspiring together. What are you all cooking up now?'

Sullivan turned his head, looking up at the police officer. He put out a hand, taking Portia's in his. 'What was that?'

'It was a joke, man, a little witticism,' O'Connor replied, grinning. 'What I should have said was two witnesses and the *hero*!' He was weaving slightly on his feet. 'You know, come to think about it, that's the kind of conduct we don't strictly approve of. Members of the public dashing about after guys with guns. I mean, too many people like you, chasing after criminals, and we coppers would be done out of a job. Either that, or the funeral parlours would be working overtime.'

Arnold realized O'Connor had been drinking hard; if he wasn't already inebriated, he was well on the way to it. 'How is the investigation going, Mr O'Connor?'

'*Mister* O'Connor!' O'Connor beamed, winked at Sullivan. 'There's respect for you, young Sullivan. Not often you get that, when you're a copper. Even from your own people.' He turned back to Arnold. 'The investigation? Hey, it's going fine. Almost over.'

Sullivan's head came up. 'You've found the person who killed that Dutchman?' he asked in surprise.

'Not exactly that,' O'Connor admitted. 'But we know who called for the hit. So, after that, it's just a matter of time before it'll be all over bar the shouting. 'Course, when it comes to trial you three had better be ready to make statements. I mean, you were the ones who saw the killing, weren't you? The witnesses, and the *hero*.' He pulled up a chair, sat down beside Portia. 'Don't see too many of them, these days. Heroes. That Dutchman, now. Some would say maybe *he* was a kind of hero. Got killed for it, too.' A shadow seemed to pass over his eyes suddenly, and he lapsed into silence, frowning. Arnold guessed maybe the man had realized he was talking too much.

Portia was rising to her feet. 'It's time we went, Steve,' she suggested.

Sullivan rose with her. Arnold gained the brief impression he was somewhat reluctant to leave, interested in what O'Connor was saying. He gave O'Connor an odd look, then nodded. 'Yes, we'd better go. Mr Landon, good to see you. DCI O'Connor . . . good luck with your investigation.'

O'Connor looked up at him, nodded vaguely. 'Yeah. See you.'

After they had gone he stared at Arnold. There was a hint of belligerence in his tone. 'Happens when you're a copper, you know. The unwelcome guest, hey, corpse at the feast? Still, that's seen two of the company off. Now it's just me and you. So, you want a drink?'

Arnold shook his head. 'No thanks.'

O'Connor inspected his empty glass. 'You could get me one.'

'I think, DCI O'Connor, maybe another drink wouldn't be a good idea.'

He was curious. His previous experiences with O'Connor had left him with the impression that he was a reserved, somewhat introspective man who was devoted to his job, committed, perhaps a little dour in his dealings with people. He was not a man who would make friends easily. And he was a person unlikely to get drunk so openly, unless he was under considerable stress of some kind.

'This investigation into the death of the Dutchman, it's not going well?' Arnold asked tentatively.

'Well?' O'Connor snorted. 'I told you. Almost bloody wound up. And yet it's a bloody farce.' He shook his head in annoyance. 'But what the hell am I doing even talking about it? What's your interest in the business, apart from the fact you were there when the man took the bloody bullet? You know, Landon, there are times when a man gets sick of the work he does. He gets pulled so many ways. You know my father's in a home? You know he's got Alzheimer's? What a bloody way to go! Recognizing no one. Living his childhood all over again. I don't get to see him, no point is there? And then there's your job. You get pulled this way . . . and that.' He glowered at Arnold. 'You get satisfaction in your work?'

'Essentially, yes,' Arnold admitted.

'So did I, so did I. But now . . .'

O'Connor frowned, then lapsed into a gloomy, introspective silence. Arnold stood up slowly. 'I'd better be on my way. Are you . . . ?' He hesitated. 'Are you going to be all right?'

'Me?' O'Connor growled. 'Right as rain.'

* * *

But after Arnold Landon had left him, DCI Jack O'Connor knew that he had been far from truthful. He certainly was not right as rain.

It was difficult to know at what precise point it had all started to go wrong. It could have been that first day a year ago at Belton Hall, when he caught sight of Isabella Portland. Or the day when she had picked him up at Newcastle station: he'd been faced with a choice at that moment, when he could have walked away. Instead, he had accepted her offer of a lift and they had started their affair.

There had been other opportunities for choice, but he had made the wrong decisions. The ring-bound notebook in the house rented by Charles de Vriess. He had held it in his hand, but he hadn't shown it to Farnsby. And he had torn out the last page. There had been another opportunity when Garland had left Cathery's room, and the Assistant Chief Constable had ranted at the both of them, giving way to his rage. The words still echoed in his head.

'There's no way we're going to lie down under this kind of insult! The bloody Home Office must have approved this undercover operation, but we weren't informed until it had all blown up in smithereens with de Vriess being shot. On our patch! It's all very well the Chief Constable coming along and saying what's what, it's happened, but Garland had approval from high up, and we've just got to go along, co-operate with the whole business that's going on. That's not the way I see it. I'm not having a Yankee operation getting under way right under our noses, making us look like fools, treating us with contempt. No! No bloody way!'

He had pointed an angry finger at O'Connor. 'You, and Farnsby here, you're going to grab this thing by the throat! Garland's told us de Vriess was feeding him information on the Ghost Shadows Society, how they were operating, the businesses and charities they were using as cover, and Garland's told us who he reckons is responsible for the murder of his undercover agent, but what the hell does *he* know? This is our patch! So he wants us to find the links, get the goods on this bloody man called Freddie Cheung, and that's what we're bloody well going to do! But more than that, you're going to set up your teams and you're going to roust out every dealer you know on the street, every loan shark along the river, and you're going to grind the bastards. If Garland's right, and there is a Triad up here, this bloody Ghost Shadows nonsense working in the north-east, then we've got to make it damned hot for them, too hot to feel comfortable. We'll nail Freddie Cheung — and that means finding out every business he operates in, every possible money-laundering company he's tied to — and we'll make these sorry Chinese bastards wish they'd never seen the Tyne! International danger, my arse! Not up here! Not in our manor!'

He had still been raging along the corridor when Farnsby followed O'Connor and joined him in the DCI's office. 'I've never seen Cathery so mad,' Farnsby sighed. 'Still, at least he's given us a licence to operate with.' Then he had fallen silent, watching O'Connor quietly. 'You think we'd better take another look at that place de Vriess rented?'

'What for?'

'Just in case we might have missed something.'

He had had the choice open to him then. He could have told Farnsby about the page he had removed from the notebook. He had not done so. Instead, O'Connor felt a finger of ice along his spine. He failed to meet Farnsby's eyes. 'Don't see how we could have overlooked anything. The forensic team went in after us. They'd have covered everything.'

'It was just a thought,' Farnsby said quietly, his eyes still fixed on O'Connor. After a short silence, he added, 'I'll start briefing a team. Garland's given Cathery a list of possible operations we need to look at. The names of firms provided by de Vriess.'

'Yeah. You do that.'

After Farnsby had gone, O'Connor still felt uncertain. He felt he had detected a challenge in Farnsby's tone, but he pushed the thought aside as fanciful. The sheet he had torn from the notebook was still in his desk. He took it out now, looked at it, then slowly began to tear it into pieces. He pushed the scraps of paper into his pocket, and then remained at his desk for a long time after that, cold, gloomy, uncertain.

Finally, he roused himself from his torpor and left the office. He drove into the town. He made the call from a public telephone in the street, not trusting his own mobile, or the headquarters system. He wanted no traceable record of the call. When she answered, he found it difficult to speak for a few moments. His mouth was dry.

'Isabella? We need to meet. We've got to talk.'

In the street he found a litter bin. He dropped the shredded sheet from the notebook into the bin. The action itself left a leaden feeling in his stomach. It was a kind of betrayal, a denial of all that he had prided himself in, his career, his commitment, his loyalty.

It was then that he had decided he wanted to get drunk.

CHAPTER FIVE

1

The work at the *Vendela* site was progressing well. Arnold met Karen Stannard on the cliffs; they had arrived separately in their own cars and they now stood on the grassy headland overlooking the cove that opened out to the menacing half-submerged Black Needles offshore. He had brought with him the detailed plans for the site, and they could check out what was happening in the cove below them. Arnold pointed out where the construction team had already completed the stone track running in from the main road almost half a mile away. And the footings of the exhibition centre had already been put in place: breeze-block walls were currently in the process of erection. It was a scene of almost frantic activity. Henry Wong had clearly recruited his own labour force, largely, as far as Arnold could make out, of Asian origin. They worked speedily, and with commitment.

'So Mr Wong's been as good as his word,' Karen commented, brushing away stray locks of her hair as the sea breeze blew them across her eyes. 'Just shows what can happen if the owner lends his weight to a project. These guys must have been working like crazy.'

'It's been a good bargain for the department,' Arnold suggested. 'But you have to wonder whether it's been really worth it, from Wong's point of view.'

Karen glanced at him curiously. 'I thought you said there was plenty of work with all this cataloguing and checking you've been doing.'

'Don't get me wrong, there is,' Arnold assured her quickly. 'And there's a good week's work left to do. But you have to ask the question. There are what, ten men working down there? Five still on the road completion, and another five building the walls of the exhibition centre itself. Then there are all the materials to take account of, quite apart from the heavy machinery. All in return for me and Portia spending three weeks checking on Wong's collection of antiques. It hardly balances out, does it?'

'You're not taking into account one more element,' Karen commented. 'Philanthropy. This has never been about striking a commercial bargain. It's clear to me that Henry Wong is taken by the idea of making a contribution, indulging his interests — not least in the *Vendela* as the carrier of his Chinese porcelain purchase — and building something worthwhile for the community. No, I agree it isn't a sensible commercial bargain he's made, the trade-off between his construction company and our department, but it was never really about that, was it?' She raised her head, sniffing at the salty breeze. 'We could do with a few more men like Henry Wong around.'

Arnold guessed she was right. They stood there for a little while on the cliff top, watching the work at the site, then she said, in a lower, more sombre tone, 'I don't know whether you've heard. Powell Frinton won't be coming back. That's certain now. The leader of the council spoke to me about it yesterday.'

Arnold eyed her warily. 'He's retiring?'

She nodded. 'The leader told me the Deputy Chief Executive will also be standing down. Which is no surprise to any of us. The leader told me the first trawl for replacements will be made internally. All heads of department will be asked to attend for interview. It's a formality, of course: the job will go to a lawyer, in my opinion, from outside. But, I suppose they'll want to go through the motions . . .' She shook her head suddenly, as anger gripped her. 'As for the department, I'm fed up with it, Arnold, sick of all the bloody shenanigans that go on, the politicking, the backbiting . . . I've had enough of it. I feel there's got to be something more worthwhile to do.'

He made no reply. He'd seen the signs for some time; he'd guessed this was coming. She glanced at him, warily. 'Cat got your tongue?'

He shrugged. 'It was a job I never wanted. You did, and you got it.'

'That sounds like a reproof,' she flashed at him.

'I didn't mean it that way. But this . . .' He gestured at the sea below them, the land rising behind them to the foothills of the distant Cheviots. '. . . this is what I've always enjoyed. A job that would take me out and about in countryside like this. But that's the way I'm made. Your ambitions have always been different.'

There was no way she was going to admit that she envied him his peace of mind, though he suspected that was the way she felt at this moment. But the feeling would no doubt pass. He knew her well. She was a beautiful, determined, ambitious woman and the Department of Museums and Antiquities would never hold her in the end. The thought made him uneasy, unsettled him in a strange way, but it was nevertheless what he believed to be the truth. He looked at her, was aware of the half-parted lips, the flawless skin, the classical profile, and he felt depression gnaw at him.

He glanced at his watch. 'I'd better get going. I need to be at Sunderland this afternoon.'

'And I'd better get back to the office,' she muttered.

* * *

The house in Sunderland was completely different from the imposing property that Arnold and Portia had been visiting in Northumberland. It was a Victorian villa, double-fronted, red-brick built, in a quiet street near the city centre. The other houses in the street all sported noticeboards announcing the activities of their owners: a few lawyers, some accountants, a dentist, a structural engineer and an estate agent. The house Arnold entered had its own discreet sign: *Cornelius Construction Company Ltd.*

The girl behind the desk in the reception area greeted him warmly. She had been expecting him. She was small, blonde, with a slight Sunderland accent. 'You'll find the articles you wish to see in the boardroom on the first floor, Mr Landon. There are some other items which you'll need to speak to Mr Edwards about, since they are kept locked away, but he will be able to let you have the key. I'll ring him now, so he can escort you upstairs. Would you mind waiting, please, while I ring him?'

Arnold nodded, and stepped into the small waiting room beside reception. It was sparsely furnished, a settee, two chairs, a desk strewn with construction magazines. He glanced at them idly as he waited. After a few moments he looked back to the receptionist: she was busy on the phone.

The office manager she had identified as Mr Edwards was clearly busy. Arnold sat down, picked up a magazine after a few minutes, and looked through its advertisements. He found one for Cornelius Construction. He was studying it when he became aware that someone had entered the reception area and was talking to the girl behind the desk.

The man's back was familiar: the set of the shoulders, the iron-grey cropped hair. The receptionist gestured towards the waiting room, and the man turned, glanced at Arnold, then came forward to join him.

'Mr Landon! I thought it was you.'

Freddie Cheung was beaming a welcome. It was strange, Arnold thought as he shook hands with the heavy-shouldered Chinese businessman, it made little difference in what mood

Cheung seemed to be — it was never reflected in his narrow, inexpressive eyes. They seemed to be blank, showing no real emotion, uneasy, constantly flickering glances about him as though seeking enemies. His full-lipped, lizard smile now held no real warmth: it was a weapon, to be brought out when it suited him. 'I was calling in to see my friend Mr Wong — I have one of my own offices just up the road — but I find you here in his place! We are well met, my friend.' He glanced at his watch. 'Have you lunched yet?'

Arnold shook his head. 'I've just driven down from the north, and there wasn't really time to stop. It's just a quick visit really, it shouldn't take me more than an hour or two, so I can wait till then.'

'You are speaking nonsense,' Cheung asserted, placing a hand on Arnold's arm. His grip was surprisingly strong. 'If Henry Wong knew that I was not offering you hospitality in such a situation, in his absence, he would think the less of me. Come, my club is not far from here. Join me for a light lunch. As you say, your work here will not be too arduous. You can do it after I have wined and dined you. After all, a friend of Mr Wong's cannot be left with an empty belly!'

Arnold tried to argue, having no desire to spend time in Cheung's company when he had work to do, but the chunky little man was insistent. He waved to the young blonde. 'Sally, explain things to Edwards. Tell him I will deliver Mr Landon, safe and sound, in about an hour or so. Please, Mr Landon, this way.'

To Arnold's embarrassment Freddie Cheung linked arms with him as they proceeded down the street. The man seemed impervious to Arnold's dismay, and chattered about business, the links he had made with various companies in the north, the admiration in which he held Henry Wong. 'A great man,' he emphasized. 'What some call a pillar in the community. This project he is supporting in Northumberland, for instance . . . admirable, admirable. When a man has wealth such as Henry's it is only right that he should use it for the public good. One day, perhaps, when

I have achieved the kind of business success that he has, perhaps I also shall undertake such activity. Not that I do not support charities now, of course . . . And there are families among recent Chinese immigrants to England whom I have been able to help, of course . . .'

He continued in a similar vein as they turned into a side street and Cheung drew him up the steps into the porticoed entrance to a private club. He led the way directly into the dining room. 'It is Western fare here,' he chuckled mirthlessly. 'None of that chicken and noodles that Henry likes so much. He is very pleased with you and your work,' he added as they were shown to their seats in a corner near the window. 'You must tell me all about it.'

He ignored Arnold for the next few minutes while he pored over the menu. Surreptitiously, Arnold observed him. The iron-grey hair had been recently cut, close to his skull. There were two white marks on his scalp, above the hairline, scars from some old injuries. His face was seamed and wrinkled, prematurely ageing, but there was a hardness about his mouth and jaw line that suggested determination. At some stage in his career his broad nose had been badly broken, and equally badly reset. 'So, my friend,' Freddie Cheung breathed, as he set his menu aside. 'You have chosen?'

The waiter stood by obsequiously. He was oriental, and he watched Cheung's every move, as though desperately eager to serve him. They ordered quickly: Arnold settled for some white fish, and insisted that was enough. Cheung ordered a bottle of white wine, but a tall glass of brandy appeared at his elbow almost immediately. The waiters here clearly knew what he required, without his asking for it. In this club, he was a man of consequence.

'I have known Henry Wong for many years, you know,' Cheung commented, after some minutes of meaningless conversation. 'From time to time we have found ourselves in competition, rivals you might say for various business deals. My tenders have usually won, but . . .' He grimaced, shrugging his powerful shoulders. 'Henry never needed the business anyway. He had already made his way here in this country before I arrived.'

'How long have you lived in England?' Arnold asked.

'Fifteen years, I suppose. Something like that.' He picked up his brandy glass and took a hefty mouthful. He looked at Arnold, his left eyelid drooping meaningfully. 'It is a Chinese vice, you know, brandy. But one learns to hold it. Learns not to let it affect one's judgement.' His suspicious eyes suddenly darted a glance at Arnold. 'I have made a judgement about you, Mr Landon.'

'And what might that be?' Arnold asked as the fish was placed in front of him.

'You are a man of perception and ability; of skill, experience and sensitivity, in your own line of work.'

Arnold smiled. 'That must be a snap judgement, not one strongly founded in reality.'

'I rarely make mistakes,' Cheung replied coolly, 'and certainly not about people to whom I wish to make an offer.'

Arnold stared at him in surprise. 'An offer? What do you mean?'

'An offer of employment,' Cheung said, leaning back in his chair, ignoring the pork dish placed in front of him, still toying with his brandy glass.

Arnold grunted in surprise, half smiling, then was silent for a few moments as Cheung picked up the bottle of Sauvignon Blanc and half filled the balloon glass in front of Arnold. Arnold shook his head. 'Why would you wish to employ me?'

'Because I have a high regard for your skills.'

'But employ me in what capacity?' Arnold asked, astonished.

Freddie Cheung put down his brandy glass, picked up his fork and began to attack his pork with relish. With his mouth half full, he gestured at Arnold with the fork. 'Let me put it like this. You will be aware that I, like my friend Henry, am a collector of beautiful things.'

Arnold smiled, nodded. 'I gathered that you had an enthusiasm for collection, when I saw the way you were bidding against each other for the Chinese porcelain at the auction sale.'

Freddie Cheung chomped greedily at his pork. 'Like Henry, I am getting older, and have enough money to surround myself with fine objects — for their beauty, of course, but also, I admit, as an investment. But I do not have Henry's advantages. He made his money before I came to England; he has a longer history of collection; he has a trained eye. For me, life has been different. I am of a poor Hakka background. I am uneducated. I do not have the kind of experience that Henry has enjoyed.'

'I still don't understand,' Arnold murmured.

'I have some kind of idea what you are paid — or should I say underpaid — in your present job in that museums department. I am confident that I could more than double that figure. And you must admit that you are wasted there. You must be frustrated at the way in which your skills are being thrown away on useless, mind-drugging banalities. I can offer you something different, more exciting. I can offer you the opportunity to apply your skills, and extend your experiences.'

Arnold's mind was in a whirl. He was confused. The hunched, powerful figure across the table from him seemed in earnest, and yet Arnold could hardly believe it was anything other than a joke, a misunderstanding. 'I'm very flattered by what you're saying, Mr Cheung, but at the same time I can't really understand what it is you'd want of me.'

'Travel,' Cheung said decisively. 'That's what I'm offering to you. The chance to travel as my agent. Here in the UK, in Europe, in Southeast Asia, wherever we get a hint of something of beauty that would be worth acquiring. Think of it, Mr Landon. If we hear of a piece appearing in an auction in Greece I would send you there. You would inspect it, caress it, evaluate it, bid for it. Another day it might be Turkey, or Bangkok. Should the right items arise in the market, I would send you there to acquire them.' There was a gleam in his narrow, beady eyes as he regarded Arnold. 'I want to establish a collection that would outshine any of my rivals here in England. You can help me do that. With my international connections, it can be achieved. And I would make it worth your while, Mr Landon.'

Arnold sipped his wine. He was shaken by the fierce driving tone in which Cheung had made his amazing offer. Arnold was thunderstruck. He could hardly believe what he was hearing. It was almost incomprehensible . . . and yet he suspected he could guess what lay behind it. He recalled the hint of enmity the two men had shown at the auction sale that day, the clear rivalry that lay between Freddie Cheung and Henry Wong, whatever business connections they might have. The suggestion being made seemed almost crazy to him, but at the same time he had been uneasy, unsettled of late, and maybe, like Karen Stannard, he was feeling he needed a change. 'This is a most interesting offer—' he began.

'One I would not wish to hold out for too long a period,' Cheung interrupted. He stroked his thick, bull neck thought-fully; his glance now was cold and direct. 'I would require an early answer.'

Arnold took a deep breath. 'You've taken me by surprise, Mr Cheung. I'd need time to think the matter over, consider it . . .'

There was a short silence. 'I can't wait too long,' Freddie Cheung announced stonily. 'I'd need an answer within two days.'

Arnold raised his eyebrows. 'I'm not sure I could keep to such a tight deadline—'

'There is a good reason for it. You will be working for Mr Wong, I believe, for just one more week.'

'That's so,' Arnold agreed, 'but I don't see that would cause a problem.'

'The fact is, I would want to reach an agreement while you are still working on your present assignment,' Freddie Cheung stated in a flat, yet meaningful tone.

Arnold was silent for a while, puzzled. He toyed with his fish. There was something odd about this conversation. He could not put his finger on the problem, but Cheung's offer was beginning to worry him.

'If you were to enter into an agreement with me,' Cheung said quietly, 'I would expect a high degree of loyalty, in return for significant rewards.'

Arnold met his gaze levelly. 'I'm not certain I understand you, Mr Cheung.'

The Chinese businessman laid down his fork, picked up his brandy again. As he held Arnold's glance over the rim of the glass his eyes held a strange hostility. 'If we can reach an agreement, within two days, while you are still working in Wong's house in Northumberland, there is something I would want you to do for me.'

'I don't understand,' Arnold replied warily. 'What has the house in Northumberland to do with this?'

Freddie Cheung let out a sound, halfway between a sigh and a hiss. 'You must understand, Mr Landon, I am a businessman. I am in a cut-throat business. It is one where the least advantage can be used to bring rich rewards. Now you . . . you have access to the house in Northumberland. At the moment I am engaged in certain delicate negotiations, the details of which need not concern you, but negotiations which, if they come to a successful conclusion, will bring me a great deal of money. Certain of my . . . ah . . . associates have been able to let me have information which I cannot make use of personally. But you . . .'

Arnold felt cold. His back stiffened. 'What exactly is it you want, Mr Cheung?'

Cheung lowered his voice. 'I am informed that on the first floor of Henry Wong's house in Northumberland there is a small office. I have visited the house myself but never seen that office. With your licence to move around the house, you will find it easily enough.'

Arnold remained silent, but his mouth was dry.

'Henry lacks imagination,' Cheung sneered. 'Or perhaps he has never watched Hollywood films. There is a painting on the wall, I am told. Behind it there is a wall safe.' He paused, eyeing Arnold carefully, gauging his reaction. 'My informants have obtained the combination to this safe. It will be a simple matter for you. I will give you the combination; you will open the safe. Inside you will find certain documents. I will tell you what details you will need to look for, and copy. That is all I would require. The rest of it, the travel, the salary, all that will be yours.' He took a swallow of brandy. Almost casually he added, 'This is not a difficult task, I think you will agree.'

There was a long silence. Arnold stared at his plate. He felt angry. He could not comprehend the crudity of the man's approach. At last he looked up. 'I think, Mr Cheung, you've approached the wrong person.'

'The offer I've made—'

'I would have to reject. You cannot really believe I would undertake this kind of dirty business!'

Freddie Cheung's laugh was short, a contemptuous, barking sound. 'Please, Mr Landon. Industrial espionage, commercial subterfuges, this kind of thing happens all the time, in the real world.'

'Not in my world,' Arnold replied angrily.

Freddie Cheung put down his brandy glass. He looked at his plate contemplatively. Then he raised his glance: malice lurked in the depths of his eyes. 'So you are not interested in my offer?'

'No,' Arnold replied sharply.

'Then I think you should enjoy the rest of your lunch, Mr Landon. I think we have nothing more to say to each other.'

Freddie Cheung took his table napkin from his knees and tossed it carelessly on the table. He reached across the table to a small silver tray on which lay a card: he scribbled his initials on it, then lumbered to his feet. 'Please feel free to finish the wine. I understand it is of a good vintage.'

Arnold sat stiffly in his seat, unable to move, a wide range of arguments coursing through his mind. He was still appalled by the proposition Cheung had put to him. He still hardly credited that the man could have broached such a crude proposal. Cheung had begin to move away, towards the door, but he suddenly paused, turned, came back. He dropped a hand on Arnold's shoulder, as though making a friendly farewell gesture, as he leaned to whisper in Arnold's ear.

'A word of warning, Mr Landon. You have chosen the path. You have turned down my offer, and my request. I wish to make it clear that, as far as I am concerned, this conversation never actually occurred. And do not consider reporting it to my friend Henry Wong. *Do not even think of it.* Such an action on your part could have unfortunate consequences.'

The hand on Arnold's shoulder was heavy, the fingers thick and powerful. They gripped, contracted, squeezed hard.

After Cheung had left the room Arnold was still aware of the throbbing menace of that grip. The bruise, and the threat, were still with him when he returned to Henry Wong's office and started the work he should never have allowed himself to be persuaded to leave.

2

The police crackdown on the Triad organizations had been launched throughout the northern regions with incredible speed.

The first briefing meeting was held in Manchester: O'Connor and Farnsby attended along with five Assistant Chief Constables and a grouping of senior detectives from each of the participating police forces. O'Connor was not surprised to see that the Home Office man Franklin, sour-faced, was present in the room, clearly holding a watching brief. Equally, he had more or less expected to see Bob Garland there. It was the American agent who led the meeting. Some of the sleepiness seemed to have gone from Garland's eyes: he was focused, determined, deliberate in his speech.

'I'm here today as a government officer seconded from the FBNDD to the Financial Crimes Enforcement Network, or FinCen as we're known,' Garland began. 'The British Government—' he glanced at Franklin, who was still clearly uneasy at having to work with the brash American agent whose tactics he deplored—' has given me authority to draw together the various forces represented here, and act as their adviser in a wide-ranging operation, designed to break the backs of the Triad organizations operating in the north.'

Franklin leaned forward to add a comment, in a super-cilious tone. 'To date some of the forces present have been concentrating, under a directive from the Home Office, on the range of street crime that we accept has become prev-alent through Triad operations: muscle and intimidation, protection rackets, loan-sharking . . .' He paused, his civil service sensitivities clearly offended at the requirement to use such American terms in his brief. '. . . debt collection, illegal gambling, vice and narcotics peddling. The involvement of FinCen, in the person of Mr Garland, changes the thrust and direction of our efforts . . .'

Bob Garland hunched his shoulders. 'FinCen concen-trates on the next, higher phase of operations. We're looking at what happens to the money earned from illegal activities. Your government is now persuaded that this is where we can hit the Triads hard, and hurt them, perhaps fatally. It's what we've done in the States, and we know it works. Here in the UK you need to damage their legitimate organizations, their legal companies which are funded by dirty money. It's time to concentrate on the white-collar crime syndicates, crack down on the investment companies and the firms that are used for money-laundering.' He paused, sweeping the room with a cold glance. 'Manchester is a Dragon City, like San Francisco in the States, Vancouver in Canada, and Perth in Australia. But powerful additional centres are now being established in Leeds, Newcastle and Teesside. Today, I will be providing you with a range of targets in each of these areas. For various reasons, I will be basing myself in Newcastle, in a co-ordinating role.'

'With the support of the Home Office,' Franklin rum-bled, unable to keep the disdain out of his tones.

Garland's own voice hardened. 'FinCen has had a num-ber of operatives working undercover in Britain for the last two years. We've acquired a mass of information, which is now available to you as police officers. But with the murder of one of those operatives, it's time information was now acted upon. Strongly.' His mouth was grim. 'The murder of the

FinCen operative, Charles de Vriess, was an unusual crime, because the Triads don't usually kill unless they're forced to, and we believe that as far as the Ghost Shadows, the Triad society behind the killing, were concerned our operative was merely an irritant, muscling in on their deals. We don't believe they knew he was an informant. Just competition. But his killing changes things. Before he died, de Vriess was able to provide us with details of a number of business operations which we should now crack down on. In Leeds, three restaurants and a taxi firm; on Teesside, a film production company and a printing firm as well as two video stores. In Newcastle, where the Ghost Shadows have been expanding their business, we'll be targeting a restaurant supplies firm, a civil engineering company, a film production firm and a group working on CD and CD-ROM production.'

He smiled thinly. 'Counterfeit, of course. And finally, we'll be raiding a large accountancy firm . . . because of the leading role it's going to be playing, targeting commercial computers, computer access codes to allow the illegal electronic transfer of funds into front companies that project themselves as legitimate operations. Now, gentlemen, you will be asked to join your own local groups for briefing. Our activities need to be co-ordinated; we need to strike these companies on a systematic basis. The project is named . . .' He glanced at Franklin.

Self-importantly, Franklin announced, 'Operation Dragon Head.'

* * *

Garland himself joined the north-east group of officers later for the more detailed briefing. He produced a list of companies that, according to the information supplied by de Vriess, were controlled by the Ghost Shadows Society.

'How did de Vriess get this information?' O'Connor queried doubtfully, as he studied the list.

Garland shrugged. 'By keeping his ear to the ground. By working as a dealer himself on the fringes. By trained observation. And . . .' He hesitated. 'And by keeping in touch with other operatives working under deeper cover.'

'You mean de Vriess wasn't working alone?' Farnsby asked in surprise.

Garland's eyes were blank. 'FinCen agents operate in various ways,' he replied evasively. 'Anyway, let me take you through the list of companies that we have in the north-east, as targets. Some of them you'll already recognize, from the list in the notebook discovered by DCI O'Connor at de Vriess's rented house. Clearly, it was the last list he compiled, to add to information already supplied. He just never had time to submit it to us. Anyway, these companies are used by the Ghost Shadows Society mainly to launder profits from street crime but as you'll see they present a legitimate face to the world. Our task will be to get behind the masks — and that means we hit hard, quickly, and decisively. We'll be raiding the companies, seizing their books, and arresting for interrogation everyone named as connected with them. The timetable I've laid down means we have to get all our teams ready within five days.'

Assistant Chief Constable Cathery rumbled his disapproval. 'An operation this size means pulling officers off other duties. This isn't going to be easy to organize—'

'Delay, and we lose the big fish,' Garland snapped. 'Now, as you'll be aware, the companies fall into three groups. I suggest you organize your men into discrete teams . . .' He listened as Cathery nominated men for the suggested groups. 'Now we already have some individual Ghost Shadows members to target. From what de Vriess was able to ascertain, it looks as though Freddie Cheung is closely involved as the leader. I've already told you about him, the Stockbroker.'

'The Stockbroker?' Cathery queried.

Garland smiled thinly, without humour. 'That was the joke in Hong Kong. Freddie Cheung broke the legs and fingers of anyone who crossed him. Hence the Stockbroker. Now, we can't move against him directly until the raids are under way: his arrest would spark a winding down

173

immediately of all their activities. The rats would run for cover immediately. Then there's Jimmy Tsui. We think that he's also a senior member of the society. Same thing applies to him. Co-ordination is the key: we hit the businesses, and within hours we haul in the big men in the Ghost Shadows.' He glanced at Cathery. 'You got the list. So it's over to you.'

From Cathery's displeased expression, it was clear he thought it was not before time that he was put entirely in charge. 'All right,' the Assistant Chief Constable said in an authoritative tone. 'We got the teams nominated. Now let's go through the schedules.' He paused. 'I suppose these are now complete?'

Garland hesitated. 'It's the full list of what we got from de Vriess. In fact, we were expecting another group of names and companies just before he died, but it hasn't surfaced, apart from the notebook list O'Connor found. We might still get it from another operative, but at the moment that's what we've got, and we can't afford to wait any longer.'

O'Connor shifted uncomfortably in his seat. The notebook he had found would have been the final list, but when he had handed it in he had already removed the last page.

His work done, Garland stood to leave the room. In the doorway, he turned. 'It may well be more stuff will come in within the next twenty-four hours. If so, I'll keep you informed.'

'That's no more than we would expect,' Sid Cathery growled.

As he inspected the schedule presented by Garland, O'Connor was aware of Farnsby at his side, looking over his own copy of the list of business firms. 'They all look pretty legit to me,' he muttered.

O'Connor said nothing. Avoiding any appearance of anxiety he checked again through the list Garland had given them. Some of the names he recognized as having appeared in the notebook he had found. A sense of relief flooded over him as he saw there was still no mention of the Starling Foundation — or of Isabella Portland. He glanced at Farnsby and shrugged. 'Like Garland said — maybe there'll be more to come later.'

O'Connor's mouth was dry. He was aware that Farnsby was staring at him, but he avoided looking at him, unwilling to allow any message to be read in his eyes. O'Connor grimaced. 'Anyway, we've got plenty to get on with.' His voice was shaky. He gritted his teeth. He had to keep control of himself. And there was no way that Farnsby could *know*.

* * *

O'Connor had met Isabella Portland in a small country pub near Ogle.

His head still thumping from the hangover, the result of the deliberate bender he had indulged in, he had been seated in the lounge when she walked in. She glanced around, caught sight of him, and walked slowly towards him. He rose, offering her a drink, but she shook her head. She sat down opposite him, raised a cool eyebrow. 'Just like old times,' she said ironically.

They had met here on several occasions previously, when their passion had been at its height. He recalled the evenings when they had lain in each other's arms, in the shuttered darkness, losing their other lives in the merging of minds and bodies and desires.

'So,' she said coldly, bringing him back to the present. 'You sounded mysterious on the phone.'

'I thought it important that we meet.'

'So you said. You didn't explain why.'

He hesitated. He could have said there was another agenda, one he could not resist, that he had stayed away from her for too long, that the hurt had not faded but the desire, the need to be with her was still strong. Instead, he murmured, 'I think you need to be warned about what might happen.'

She cocked her head to one side. 'About what?'

'The Starling Foundation.'

'Oh, that damned thing,' she said impatiently. 'Do you mean to tell me you've dragged me here just to talk about a donation I've made to a charitable foundation that I've really no interest in anyway?'

'You need to cut out any sort of involvement with it,' he replied.

She stared at him. Her eyes seemed large, steady in their gaze. He read curiosity there, but nothing of affection. She had still not forgiven him for what she saw as a spurning. 'What exactly is this all about?'

He grimaced, bit his lip thoughtfully. He was uneasy about what he was doing; it was dangerous, and it could affect his career. 'You've already explained you're not interested in this foundation. My advice — my *strong* advice — is that you should get shot of any connection with it immediately. It would be wise to have nothing to do with it.'

'I'm getting the message, but no reason for it,' Isabella muttered impatiently.

O'Connor took a deep breath. 'Look, I don't know how far I can go with this. The fact is, the man who died, de Vriess . . . well, he was an undercover agent. He was investigating criminal activities. And he was killed, shot in the throat. I searched his house. I found a notebook there, with a list of names . . . companies, people, charitable foundations. When I saw that your name was there, I came to see you because I had to find out what connection you might have had with de Vriess.'

'I told you, there was none. The charity people — they just wanted me for a subscription . . .'

O'Connor shook his head. 'No. You don't understand. They got money from you, as part of their legitimate activity. But there are other reasons for the foundation. The money you gave them, well, maybe it will end up helping tsunami victims. More likely, it won't. It will go into a large pot.'

'I don't understand,' Isabella said, bewildered.

'It's my guess that Charles de Vriess wrote the Starling Foundation into the notebook because he'd discovered it was a front for criminal activity.' He paused. 'It looks as though the foundation is probably used for money-laundering.'

Her eyes widened in shock and disbelief. 'The tsunami victims—'

'I've told you,' he snapped, irritated. 'That will be a scam. The foundation will be used to launder money into other, maybe legitimate businesses, but apart from your own contribution, and maybe that of a few other names on that sheet, who are there for prestige and cover purposes, the main income will be from illegal activity.'

She stared at him silently. There was a shadow of doubt in her eyes, which was gradually being replaced by something else. Slowly, she said, 'My name was on that sheet of paper you showed me. You told me you removed it from the note-book, belonging to the man who was killed . . . He will have passed the information to his contacts?'

O'Connor shook his head. 'I don't think so. I'll proba-bly find out soon. But I think that the last sheet — the one I removed — was probably something he was about to follow up. The notebook was there in his desk, but it looks as though he hadn't yet passed all the details on to his supervisor.'

Silence grew about them again. He felt uncomfortable under her gaze. He sipped his whisky, avoiding her eyes. At last, quietly, she said, 'You haven't passed this information — the list of names on that sheet — you haven't passed it to anyone else.'

He made no reply.

'If the other people involved in this . . . enquiry see it, they will want to talk to everyone named on that paper.'

He shrugged. 'I guess so. And that could mean . . . unpleasantness, at least. But there's no reason why you should have to go through that. Not now. I've already destroyed the sheet. The rest of the notebook names are being acted upon. But you're safe. You're out of it.'

She took a deep, reflective breath. Her tone was subdued. 'You did that to protect me?' She hesitated. 'Why would you *do* that?'

He made no reply. But when his glance met hers, she knew why he had acted the way he had. He had deliberately held back and destroyed a piece of evidence, merely to protect her from investigation. And she knew what that implied: danger for himself if his action were ever to be exposed.

'So, in spite of all that's happened,' she said in a soft, reflective voice, 'for you and me, nothing really has changed, has it?' As she spoke she put out her hand, touched his gently, forgivingly.

But for O'Connor things *had* changed. He had put his career at risk, and he was scarred with the suspicion that Farnsby had in some way guessed that he had suppressed evidence. But Farnsby could not know for certain.

Moreover, it was now clear from the list that Garland had provided of the organizations to be targeted in the Newcastle area, that de Vriess had not sent that last piece of information to the FinCen controller. The Starling Foundation did not appear on the list of operations controlled by the Ghost Shadows Society. Isabella Portland need not be involved in any scandal.

But it also meant that at least one Ghost Shadows organization would escape the net cast by Operation Dragon Head.

* * *

It was late afternoon when Arnold Landon returned to the manor house owned by Henry Wong in Northumberland. He had completed his work at Sunderland, followed it up with a look at some items in an apartment block in Durham, and it was time to enter his findings in the central catalogue being prepared by Portia. It was late afternoon when he left Durham, took the road through the Tyne Tunnel and made his way up the coast to the house near Seaton Delaval. When he entered the house, there was no sign of her. He checked the rooms downstairs, including the library, then stood at the bottom of the curving staircase and called her name. He heard her reply from upstairs. 'I'm in the office up here.'

Arnold climbed the stairs and sought her out. He found her seated at a large desk, a computer glowing greenly in front of her, the catalogue beside her left elbow. 'What are you doing up here?'

She grunted unpleasantly. 'Hiding, in part. I saw Jeremy's car turn in the drive earlier on, so I thought I'd better keep out of his way. He's still around somewhere, I think.'

'I didn't see his car.'

'Then hopefully he's buzzed off.'

Arnold glanced around him. With a sinking feeling he realized he was in the room that Freddie Cheung had described to him. His eyes strayed towards the far wall. He saw the painting, behind which a wall safe was concealed. A safe which held the business secrets of Henry Wong, a safe to which Freddie Cheung held the combination. Abruptly, he turned away. 'I'm going back downstairs. I'll take the catalogues with me. I've got details to add.'

'That's fine,' she murmured, distracted, her eyes on the screen in front of her. 'I'm just checking here . . . there's some holdings I hadn't realized we'd missed, and some sales too—'

'I'll see you downstairs,' Arnold interrupted, picking up the catalogue entries. He headed back down to the library.

He worked there for an hour or so, adding the checks he had carried out in Sunderland and Durham to the details held in the catalogues. His mind kept straying to his conversation with Freddie Cheung the previous day. It was clear that whatever friendship, or business agreements, might subsist between Wong and Cheung, the latter was more than a rival. He was prepared to subvert Arnold in order to undertake industrial espionage of some kind.

The question that bothered Arnold was: should he warn Henry Wong of Cheung's attempt at bribery?

Arnold continued his work in the library, entering details of the items he had inspected, and preparing a report on the holdings Wong had acquired and their sales provenance. He was still busy with the report an hour later when he heard a step in the hall. A few moments later Jeremy Tan opened the library door and looked in. 'Mr Wong back yet?' he enquired.

Arnold shook his head. 'Are you expecting him?' he asked.

Jeremy shrugged non-committally, glanced around the room and left, closing the door behind him. Arnold hesitated, wondering whether he should go upstairs to warn Portia, but then decided against it. She was overreacting, it seemed to him. She had had a relationship with Jeremy, it was over, and now she was going out with Tan's friend Steven Sullivan. It was not for Arnold to interfere. It was all a storm in a teacup, as far as he was concerned. Consequently he shrugged the matter aside, returned to his work and was soon immersed in the cataloguing.

Within ten minutes he was dragged rudely back to reality. The door burst open, and Portia Tyrrel stormed into the room. She was white-faced with anger, and she almost spat the words out as she faced Arnold. 'I *told* you what it would be like!'

'What's the matter? What's going on!'

Portia stabbed a finger in his direction. 'I knew it was going to be this way! I told you! I warned Karen! I told you both that this was all a set-up for Jeremy to get his hands on me.'

Arnold stood up away from the table. 'Portia, look, I don't know—'

'The bastard just came back. He came upstairs and he grabbed me!' She was almost incoherent with rage. 'He was laughing and he grabbed me and when I told him to lay off, get away from me, he just laughed, said he couldn't understand why I was running around, going out to Chinese restaurants with a milksop like Steven Sullivan! He said he could throw him across a room without twitching a finger, almost, and then he tried to handle me—' She took a deep breath. 'Look, Arnold, I've had it. I've done my fair share of this work with you but I'm not taking this sort of nonsense, not just to please the department. I've been waiting for this to happen, looking over my shoulder all the time, because I knew he'd take a flyer at me again, and I'm just not standing for it. I'm getting out. You can stuff this job. I'll see you back in Morpeth!'

She was gone, slamming the door loudly behind her. Arnold felt a cold sheen of perspiration on his brow. He shook his head. He still felt Portia was overreacting; she was mature enough to handle situations like this without causing a scene, so he was unable to understand why she couldn't have handled things differently. But she had gone up like a firecracker at Jeremy Tan's expected approach. It could only mean she thought a great deal of Steven Sullivan — but yet felt insecure in the relationship. He sighed. He had enough troubles of his own. But at least he had now made his decision about Henry Wong.

It was an hour before Henry Wong arrived at the house, just as Arnold was about to pack up for the day. Arnold heard his Jaguar in the drive and walked to the window. Jeremy Tan must have heard it too: he had come out of the house and was standing with Henry Wong in the driveway, speaking animatedly. Wong listened placidly, leaning on his stick, head lowered slightly, shoulders hunched. At last he raised his head, spoke a few placatory words to the younger man and waved him away. Wong stood watching his nephew drive away: the Porsche sent up a hail of gravel as it roared off down the drive. Shaking his head slightly, Henry Wong turned, caught sight of Arnold in the window, and raised a hand in greeting.

Arnold returned to stand beside the desk he had been working at and gathered up the papers into a file. He heard the tap of Wong's stick in the hallway; a few moments later the Chinese businessman entered the room. He was frowning, shaking his head in doubt. 'Young people . . .' he murmured. 'They are so impetuous, so . . . undisciplined.'

'There's been an argument,' Arnold advised.

Henry Wong raised a hand in agreement. 'Jeremy was just explaining to me, out there. He is a hot-headed young man; he lacks a sense of . . . balance. I knew he had been in a

181

relationship with Portia, but I did not expect that he would cause her distress in this manner. What did she say about it?'

Arnold shrugged. 'She was pretty angry. You may or may not be aware she's going out with an acquaintance of Jeremy's — Steven Sullivan. According to Portia, Jeremy sneered about him. Said she shouldn't go out to Chinese restaurants with a milksop like Sullivan. Tried to . . . well, renew their relationship, as far as I can gather. It didn't please her. And that's an understatement. So she's stormed off the job.' He hesitated. 'I don't think she'll be coming back.'

Henry Wong frowned. 'That is a pity. But I suppose . . .' He seemed vaguely preoccupied, as though concerned about her disappearance.

'There's something else,' Arnold said slowly. It was as good a time as any to bring it up. 'I need to tell you about my having lunch in Sunderland yesterday. With Freddie Cheung.'

Henry Wong managed a smile; it had a wintry edge to it. 'Ah, my friend and business rival. It is good you had lunch with him. He can be a good host.'

'And an untrustworthy friend,' Arnold ventured.

There was a short silence. Henry Wong's bland features seemed unmoved, but there was a darkness about his eyes, a tension in his shoulders. He turned, sought out a chair near the window and sat down, facing Arnold. He placed both chubby hands on the walking stick, supporting his chin on his knuckles. 'We have known each other a long time, Mr Cheung and I,' Wong said softly.

'He invited me to lunch. I thought at first it was a coincidence, his seeing me in the street, entering your premises. But I think it was planned. I think he got your receptionist to tell him when I arrived.'

Wong remained very still. 'Now why would Freddie do that?' he asked in a quiet voice.

'He wanted to offer me a bribe,' Arnold replied simply.

A slight smile touched Wong's full mouth. He raised his head, fixed his gaze on his hands on the top of his cane and regarded them thoughtfully for a few moments. Softly, he asked, 'What sort of bribe would that be?'

'Employment. Travel. The chance to seek out antiques for him, things of value. Things that would help him match your own collections, which he clearly envies.'

Henry Wong grunted softly. 'Ah, well, he was always my rival in such matters.' He glanced up at Arnold quizzically. 'You accepted his . . . offer?'

Arnold shook his head. 'No. It had conditions attached to it. It would mean breaking faith. To you.'

Henry Wong frowned slightly, as though puzzled. 'To me? You are seconded into my service, but I am not your employer. I don't understand what you mean.'

Arnold grimaced uncomfortably. 'I'm working here in your house, without supervision. That involves a degree of trust. I don't sneak around, looking into your personal or business affairs.'

'I would have expected no less,' Wong asserted. There was a brief silence between the two men. Wong's eyes were reflective. 'But that is what Freddie Cheung asked you to do?'

Arnold nodded. 'He told me about a safe upstairs in your office. He told me he could give me the combination. He wanted me to copy a document there.'

'What document?' Wong asked mildly.

'We didn't get that far. My guess is it would be a business document, something relating to a tender in which you're both involved. He clearly wants to get an inside track in some business bid . . .'

'Ha!' Wong nodded slowly, considering the matter. 'I think I know what this is about . . .' He sat silently for a little while. 'Why do you tell me this, Arnold?'

'I turned him down,' Arnold replied abruptly. 'For me, that's the end of the matter. But I felt you needed to be told. I needed to warn you. Not only that Freddie Cheung is trying to seek out some of your business secrets, and is prepared to suborn me to get at them, but also because someone on your staff is disloyal. Cheung said he had the combination to your safe. You need to be warned: someone close to you is untrustworthy.'

Henry Wong nodded slowly. He rose, turned, stared out of the window for a little while. Then he sighed, turned back to gaze at Arnold. 'You are an honourable man, Arnold, and I am grateful for this information. Freddie Cheung, my old friend . . .' He shook his head sadly. 'And this business with Miss Tyrrel. She will think I asked for her to work here, so that I would put her in the way of Jeremy?'

He was a perceptive old man. Arnold hesitated, then nodded. 'That's what she's been afraid of.'

Henry Wong sighed again, shook his head regretfully. 'I am sorry things have turned out this way. I seem to have lost my touch with people. It is the problem of age. One forgets . . .' He raised a podgy hand, massaged his temple. He seemed worried, uncertain. 'I am beginning to think I should never have ventured into these waters. It was a pleasure to have assisted you with the matter of the Chinese porcelain, but now . . . I am left with the feeling that perhaps I should never have asked you to work here.'

Arnold was about to say something in protest, but then remained silent.

Henry Wong removed his dark-rimmed glasses, inspected them, took a handkerchief from the top pocket of his suit, and slowly began to polish the lens. 'And I have not yet even been to the *Vendela* site, to inspect the progress . . .' He raised his spectacles to the light, then satisfied, replaced them on the bridge of his nose. His tone was regretful. 'I think perhaps we should consider your work here finished, Arnold. You have done enough. Your involvement has been greater than I could have expected.'

Surprised, Arnold said, 'I wasn't objecting to the work here. It was just that Portia . . .'

Henry Wong shook his head. He seemed concerned, anxious about what had happened. 'No, I think it best for all concerned that we now end the arrangement. And it is time I visited the *Vendela* site. I will need to determine what must be done to complete the project.' He regarded Arnold almost owlishly. 'I still intend to complete the *Vendela* project, of course. But you need not return to finish the work here. I think it best we end it now. So many complications . . .'

Arnold was puzzled, but felt there was nothing he could say to make the Chinese businessman change his mind. And in a sense he felt a certain relief. Things had become complicated: he had no desire to get involved with business matters between Henry Wong and the devious Freddie Cheung.

Henry Wong saw him to the door. As he stood in the doorway, Wong said, 'I would be grateful if you could perhaps be available to show me the *Vendela* site, so I may inspect progress. Tomorrow afternoon, perhaps?'

Arnold nodded. 'Of course.'

Wong frowned, pursed his lips. 'I fear it might be rather late in the day. I have certain commitments.'

'That's no problem,' Arnold assured him. 'Would you wish Miss Stannard to be present also?'

'Miss Stannard?' Henry Wong considered the matter gravely. 'She will have much to do. She is a busy lady. No, there is no need for her to be present. Nor, for that matter, Miss Tyrrel. Present to her my personal apologies for the distress occasioned her, and my thanks for her sterling work.' He smiled broadly. 'I know I can rely upon your expertise, Arnold. So, shall we say tomorrow, at perhaps five thirty?' He inclined his head in gratitude. 'And may I thank you also for the work you have done here for me. And for the information about my old *friend*, Freddie Cheung. It will be acted upon.'

The man's manner was still easy, his features bland, but for just a moment there was a hint of menace in Henry Wong's tone.

3

Karen Stannard swivelled in her chair and frowned at Arnold. She shook her head impatiently. 'Portia's already been in here, shouting the odds. Threatening me with all sort of things — sexual harassment, for one thing! Hell's flames, you'd have thought she was grown up enough to deal with some horny idiot's attempt to grope her! It's not as though she's Little Miss Innocent, after all!'

Uneasily, Arnold contended, 'I think she's a bit on edge. She's stuck on Steven Sullivan and doesn't want anything to damage the relationship. And even though it seems Sullivan and Jeremy Tan don't see much of each other these days, she's afraid they might get talking, things could get said . . .'

'Oh, for God's sake!' Karen groaned. 'It's about time she took a grip on her love life.' She threw down the pencil she was holding in her hand, and then watched it roll across the desk to the floor. She stared at it, making no attempt to retrieve it, glaring at it as though it was symptomatic of the way things were unravelling in her professional life. 'And now Henry Wong is pulling out.'

Arnold shook his head. 'He didn't exactly say that,' he demurred. 'The impression I got, it was that Portia's walking out was a kind of last straw on top of other worries he has. And telling me I could finish there too, well—'

'But he wants to take a look at the *Vendela* site,' Karen snapped. 'My bet is he wants to pull the plug on that commitment, and I reckon he'll have grounds, with Portia walking away. It was a condition of his support, after all.'

'I wouldn't go that far. Mr Wong hasn't visited the site since the work started. I think he just wants to see how it's progressed. Certainly, he didn't say he was pulling out.'

Karen's lip curled in contempt. 'Arnold, your optimism can sometimes be mistaken for an inability to face facts. You may not be aware of it, but not a single workman turned up at the site this morning. I got a phone call from the site manager. The construction gang simply didn't show. He's left the site as well. Everything's ground to a halt.'

Arnold stared at her in silence. It was bad news: maybe she was right, and Wong had decided to break his word regarding the *Vendela* project. But he could hardly credit that the reason for such a decision would be Portia's walking out on the research work in Wong's collection.

Karen squeezed the heels of her hands into her eyes, rubbing them in frustration. 'It's all happening at once,' she complained. 'The freeze on finance; Powell Frinton retiring; interviews for all of us heads of department about the future; Portia threatening action; and Henry Wong walking away from a project he'd offered to finance. It makes me wonder why I even *bother*!' She dropped her hands, leaned over to pick up the pencil, then threw it petulantly across the room, swearing under her breath. She glanced at her watch. 'What time did you say Wong asked to meet you?'

'Five thirty.'

'Well, you better get your skates on,' she muttered. 'It's four o'clock now. Better get up to the *Vendela* site and see what you can do to save something from all this chaos. Be as nice to the old man as you have to: if he's set on pulling out of the *Vendela* project that'll be a disaster I don't want to happen.' She fixed him with a glance; her eyes seemed like green fire. 'Arnold, it's up to you.'

* * *

At the Ponteland headquarters the clock from the church in the village chimed four times. O'Connor grunted, shoved aside the reports he had been working on and got up from behind his desk. He needed a cup of coffee, and his legs were stiff. For that matter, so was his back. He rubbed a hand along the muscles: it had been the unaccustomed sexual activity that had caused it. That, and the pent-up, bruising passion that characterized the occasion. It had been too long, and both he and Isabella had hungered to repeat the urgency of the lovemaking they had previously enjoyed.

He thrust the thoughts aside, guiltily. In spite of the renewal, there was an underlying rawness that still tore at him, and he was constantly reminded of it as the day had progressed and the reports had come in.

He walked down the stairs to the canteen, obtained a cup of coffee from the girl behind the counter and found himself a table near the door. There were few other officers in, which was hardly surprising: Operation Dragon Head had called out most of them in the early hours, and they would be either catching up on some sleep, or writing reports within their particular teams and units.

He leaned forward on his elbows, closed his eyes briefly, and tried to prevent memories of Isabella Portland intrude into his thoughts. He was vaguely aware of the sound of the canteen door opening but he did not turn his head. He heard someone at the counter. A short while later, a chair beside his table was scraped back. He looked up. It was Farnsby, his eyes red-rimmed. 'You look as though you've had a night of it,' O'Connor commented.

Farnsby grunted, twisting his saturnine features into a scowl. 'I can think of better things to do than run around with Sid Cathery. Why the hell he felt he had to barge into each raid at some point last night, I can't imagine.'

'Glory,' O'Connor muttered. 'Being seen. Wanting to feel he's useful.'

'He was bloody seen, all right.' Farnsby sipped at his tea noisily. 'I've had enough for the moment. It's me for home in an hour, provided Cathery doesn't start yelling for me to drive him again. Anyway, how are things looking?'

O'Connor ran a hand over his eyes. 'I've been co-ordinating the reports as they've come in. Everything seems to be going fairly smoothly. Down in Leeds, they've managed to pull in about twenty people: mainly small-time guys, looks like, but they've got a stack of documentation to go through. On Teesside they hit gold. In the printing firm they found a stash of counterfeit ten-quid notes, and some of the same kind of fake medicines that Garland's man de Vriess had in his garage. Here in Newcastle—'

'I know,' Farnsby cut in almost wearily. 'Cathery's crowing about it as though he did it all personally. They've got Jimmy Tsui in the cells — they found him in one of the restaurants they were raiding. And they have a lead on Freddie Cheung: they think he boarded the Bergen ferry this morning, so there'll be a welcome committee waiting for him when they berth.'

'Why the ferry, instead of flying out of Newcastle?' O'Connor wondered.

Farnsby shrugged. 'Low-key stuff, I guess. There's some evidence that birds are starting to scatter, as news of the raids got out. But it looks as though the Ghost Shadows are being hit hard.'

'Which will please our American FinCen friend,' O'Connor remarked. He cocked a quizzical eye at Farnsby. 'You agree with Garland? You think this Ghost Shadows business is the real thing?'

'No matter what I think. He's convinced. And he's got Cathery believing in the Yellow Peril of the Triad societies.'

'Cathery will jump on any bandwagon that will carry him along the promotion trail,' O'Connor suggested sourly.

'As long as the bandwagon carries him in a direction well away from me for the next few hours—'

'DI Farnsby!'

Both men looked around. A police constable was standing in the doorway of the canteen. 'DI Farnsby, the Assistant Chief Constable wants you in his office.'

'Aw, bloody hell,' Farnsby moaned. 'Tell him—'

'Like *now*, sir,' the constable interrupted nervously.

Farnsby swore, drained his tea and struggled to his feet. O'Connor was about to utter words of mock sympathy when the constable called out again from the doorway. 'And you too, DCI.'

There was a glint of malicious pleasure in Farnsby's eyes as he glanced, almost triumphantly, at O'Connor. 'So it's going to be two to the slaughter, hey?'

Gloomily the two men walked behind the police constable, up the stairs and along the corridor towards Sid Cathery's office. 'We actually know the way, sonny,' O'Connor said sarcastically. The young constable glanced over his shoulder, hesitated, then walked on, tapped at Cathery's office door, and when the Assistant Chief Constable bellowed to them to enter, he stepped aside.

O'Connor opened the door and entered the room, Farnsby close on his heels. Cathery was not alone.

Bob Garland, the man from FinCen, was standing near the window with his arms folded, and a determined jut to his jaw. Cathery himself was seated, but his colour was high, and O'Connor guessed that the two men, never at ease with each other, had had another heated discussion. 'O'Connor. Farnsby. Mr Garland has some news for us.' He spat out the words distastefully, as though they were sawdust in his mouth. 'It seems he knows more about our manor than we locals do ourselves.'

Garland's thin mouth twisted. 'That's not the issue, here, Assistant Chief Constable. I've already explained, I have sources of information—'

'Mr Garland,' Sid Cathery sneered, 'has sources of information, informants whose identity he keeps very close to his chest. He planted that man de Vriess on our patch without informing us—'

'I had clearance from the Home Office!' Garland snapped.

'—with the connivance of London-based civil servants who don't know their arses from their elbows,' Cathery ploughed on bitterly, 'and by keeping things quiet that way he got his man de Vriess killed. Now, it seems, de Vriess wasn't the only inside man he's had passing him little snippets from inside his precious Ghost Shadows Society, and only when there's a problem does he bring himself to inform us—'

'All this is beside the point,' Garland snarled angrily. He turned his cold eyes upon Farnsby and O'Connor. 'I understand you know a woman called Karen Stannard.'

O'Connor raised his eyebrows. 'Well, yes, we've come across her. She works in Morpeth, at the Department of Museums and Antiquities.'

'Which apparently,' Cathery submitted contemptuously, 'is a somewhat hazardous occupation.'

Farnsby frowned. 'What's that supposed to mean, sir?'

Garland stepped forward. 'The woman is in danger,' he announced.

Sid Cathery snorted. 'What our American friend means is she's going to get hit!'

'Sir?' O'Connor was puzzled. 'I don't understand.'

'According to Mr Garland, she's fallen foul of his favourite villains. He is informed that her life is in danger. Now, if that's the case,' Cathery continued, grimacing and spreading his beefy hands wide, 'there's an obvious solution, a clear action we should be taking. But that's not Mr Garland's way. Apparently, they do things differently in the States.'

He swung in his chair and glared at the American agent. 'It's what we've been discussing before you two came to join us. We've been talking about how best to deal with this situation. And so far, we've reached no bloody conclusion!'

4

The sky had darkened in the west, storm clouds building up on the horizon, and Arnold caught the flash of distant lightning, presaging a storm that was already building up way out to sea. He stood on the headland looking down on the site that was planned to become the *Vendela* centre. It presented a desolate appearance. The approach road had been completed, the tarmac glistening after the recent shower of rain, but the buildings that were intended to be the exhibition centre were unfinished. One of them had been roofed, but the other two linked constructions showed bare skeletal timbers open to the elements. The workmen employed by Henry Wong had worked quickly and efficiently, there was no doubt about that, completing what they had achieved in a matter of two weeks, but Karen's information had been correct: there was not a single workman on site now, and the work had come to a halt. Arnold was left with the sinking feeling that there was now the possibility that it would never be completed. For if Henry Wong pulled out from the project, it was clear that the funds would not be forthcoming from any other sources that he and Karen had been able to identify.

He had left his car down near the roofed building, and walked up to the headland to observe the site from above.

Now, hunched in his anorak, he caught the flash of distant headlights in the darkening air, so Arnold trudged gloomily back down the rocky slope towards the site. He glanced at his watch. It was almost six o'clock. Henry Wong was late, but at least he was on his way. The headlights would be his. Arnold wondered whether he was being driven by Jeremy Tan. There was a sour taste in his throat. The collapse of this project may well have been down to the young martial arts fanatic. If he hadn't upset Portia, this might not have occurred. And yet, it was such a trivial matter, to give rise to such serious consequences.

As he crossed the sandy stretch that led up to the *Vendela* site Arnold caught sight of the long silver car breasting the hill, turning to follow the track down towards the cove. The car headlights seemed to flicker and flash as the vehicle bounced across the beginning of the new road. Arnold stood at the entrance to the building and watched as the car slowly came to a halt beside his own vehicle. The Chinese businessman's car was bigger, sleeker and much more expensive than his. A silver Jaguar. Maybe the sort of car Arnold could have afforded if he had accepted the offer made by Freddie Cheung. There was a short pause, and then the driver's door opened, and Arnold realized that Henry Wong had used no chauffeur on this occasion. He had driven himself up to the cove where the East Indiaman had broken its back three centuries ago.

Henry Wong limped across the intervening space towards him. 'Arnold. I am sorry to be late. I hope I have not kept you waiting too long.'

Arnold was relieved to detect a certain easy affability in Henry Wong's tones. The two men shook hands. Wong was wearing a dark overcoat and a scarf around his throat: his eyes gleamed behind his dark-rimmed glasses, and he seemed to have lost some of the tension Arnold had noted the previous day. 'It's not a problem, Henry,' Arnold said. 'I didn't leave the office until it was fairly late. I've only been here for fifteen minutes or so.'

Henry Wong heaved a sigh, turned, took a long, slow look around the site. He pointed out to sea. 'So, the rocks out there, you told me before but . . . what did you call them again?'

'The Black Needles,' Arnold confirmed. 'That's where the *Vendela* went down, though not before some of the porcelain you bought at the sale was salvaged.'

'Ah, yes, a romantic provenance,' Wong commented, nodding gravely. 'It makes the porcelain so much more valuable — and attractive to own, don't you agree?'

'I suppose so.' Arnold was still on edge, uncertain what Henry Wong's intentions might be regarding the site. 'Anyway, as you can see, the road's been put in, the buildings part constructed . . .'

'Yes. My people have done well,' the Chinese businessman said reflectively, looking about him. A short silence fell as he seemed lost in thought.

'I was surprised to see you alone. I thought you'd have been driven up by Jeremy,' Arnold commented.

Henry Wong gave a short, barking laugh. 'Ah, my young nephew has other things to do, apart from making a nuisance of himself with young women who do not appreciate his attentions. Besides, from time to time I like to sit behind the wheel of a powerful car. It reminds me of my more adventurous — if penniless — youth.' He chuckled, shaking his head at private memories. 'Now then, perhaps you would explain to me the layout of the site, and show me the inside of the buildings that have been developed thus far.'

Arnold agreed readily. He felt a quickening of his pulse, a flash of hope that perhaps he and Karen had misread the situation, had worried unduly. Wong was clearly interested in the site, and maybe he was still prepared to continue his investment in the work. Arnold wondered whether he should ask Wong why the men had been pulled off the site, but after a moment's reflection thought better of it. He began to explain in some detail the way the site was envisaged, waving his arm to describe the sweep of the cove and the views

194

out to the Black Needles that would be commanded from the windows of the exhibition centre. They inspected the unroofed buildings, designed to comprise a reception area, a small sixty-seat video room where it was intended to show filmed reconstructions of the break-up of the East Indiaman and the salvage of her precious cargo.

'What materials would you be using?' Henry Wong wondered.

'We have various contemporary accounts,' Arnold explained. 'A number of sketches of the scene, by local artists. Inevitably, it will be a somewhat circumscribed account but it should give the flavour of what happened on that stormy night.'

'Perhaps like tonight,' Henry Wong murmured as they heard the distant rumble of the approaching storm.

Arnold walked around the site with the department's benefactor, endeavouring to inject as much enthusiasm as he could into his account, in the hope that if there were problems Henry Wong might still be persuaded to continue with his investment. Wong seemed interested, nodding vigorously as Arnold explained, and at last they turned into the roofed building that was to be the major centre for the *Vendela* project. 'This is to be the exhibition centre.'

The light was dim inside the vast unlit room, but there was sufficient illumination to allow Arnold to explain how it was to be laid out: showcases, a library, a computer room where students would be encouraged to undertake programmes built around the seventeenth-century trading operations, and a high wall with a back-projection unit which would be in constant display, showing shifting scenes of the Northumberland coastline in all its splendour, beauty and danger.

Arnold was still explaining the project enthusiastically when there was a flash of reflected light in the room, sending dancing shadows against the bare walls. Surprised, Arnold walked across to the open windows and looked out at the hill. Another car was making its way down the newly built road. There was the tapping of a cane as Henry Wong came to stand beside him.

'It seems we have company,' the older man said in a quiet tone.

Together they turned back to the empty doorway and watched as the car drew up beside Wong's Jaguar. When the car doors opened, Arnold saw to his surprise that it was Portia who emerged. He also recognized the tall young Eurasian who got out from behind the wheel. It was her boyfriend, Steven Sullivan.

They came forward towards them, hand in hand.

'Portia!' Arnold exclaimed. 'What are you doing up here?'

She glanced uncertainly at Henry Wong, then smiled. 'I've taken a few days off work. Steven's managed to take some time off also, and suggested we might go up to Berwick, find a nice restaurant, spend a few days together. Then, as we were passing nearby, and he expressed an interest in seeing the *Vendela* site, I suggested we make a detour.' She cast a glance at the sky. 'Not that we can stay long. Looks like a storm brewing up.'

A brief flurry of fine rain added emphasis to her words. Henry Wong stepped forward politely. 'Miss Portia, I haven't had the opportunity to express my personal unhappiness that you found it necessary to leave the cataloguing of my collection. But now you are here with Mr Sullivan, please, come inside and see what we have here.' He led the way. 'Mr Landon has been explaining how the exhibition centre will look finally.'

Will look, thought Arnold exultantly. Not *would* look. Wong was not going to pull out of the project.

They stood in the echoing, empty exhibition hall and Portia exclaimed: 'It will be magnificent, Mr Wong. Look, Steve, that far wall down there? That's to be a huge projected backdrop and . . .' She turned her heads to look at Sullivan. He had relinquished her hand. Now, with his eyes fixed on Henry Wong he took a step backward, away from her, so that he was standing just to Wong's right. He had an air of expectancy about him, his muscular shoulders tense under the leather jacket he wore. Arnold was reminded again of the martial arts background the man possessed. Sullivan stood there now, leaning slightly forward, staring almost hungrily at the moon-faced elderly Chinese man beside him.

Henry Wong glanced at him, sighed, then in a characteristic gesture removed his spectacles and began to wipe the lens with a handkerchief he had drawn from his overcoat pocket. He polished them busily, removing the light flurry of raindrops that had touched them. He replaced the glasses and smiled almost sadly at Arnold, and then at Portia. 'I must apologize. I have not been open with you. The truth is, I have arranged for you both to be here, under false pretences.'

'*Arranged*?' Portia stared at him, uncomprehendingly. She turned to Sullivan. 'Steven?'

Henry Wong raised a chubby-knuckled hand. 'Please, I should make it clear that Steven has no real interest in the *Vendela* site. And I fear he will not be taking you to Berwick. He is here, with you, at my request.' He paused, waved a hand. 'For me, my interest in this project has always been real. I was most interested in the concept: it seemed to me to be a worthy investment for the community which over the years has made me a wealthy man.' He sighed theatrically. 'But I fear that recent events mean that I shall be forced to withdraw my support. In fact I shall soon be leaving the country. China beckons me, and a life of peace and contentment. But before I go, it is important that certain . . . loose ends, I think you call them . . . loose ends should be tied up. Problems cleared away.'

Portia turned a stricken look upon Arnold. 'What's this about? I don't understand.' She faced Sullivan, a pleading note entering her tone. 'Steve, what's going on? He *arranged* for us to come here? Steven . . .'

Sullivan did not even look at her. His eyes were still fixed upon Henry Wong, a dog obeying his master. The light was dim but Arnold could see that the dog was almost quivering, waiting to be slipped from the leash.

Grimly, Arnold asked, 'What is this all about? Like Portia, I don't know what the hell is going on. Is this something to do with what I told you about Freddie Cheung?'

Henry Wong lifted a finger, toyed with his full lower lip thoughtfully. 'Only indirectly. I suppose it is only fair that I should explain. I regret that I was forced to test you in that manner, with Freddie Cheung's offer. You were working so well. But I needed to discover whether you could be loyal to me.'

Arnold frowned. 'I rejected Cheung's offer. I told you about the bribery.'

'Bribery?' Portia's voice had risen. 'What bribery?'

There was a short silence, as Henry Wong held Arnold's glance. There was a hint of reluctant admiration in his narrow eyes. Then he shrugged. 'Yes, it is true you turned down Freddie Cheung's offer. But it was never real anyway. I asked him to meet you at the office, make the suggestion, test you with his proposal.'

'But why?' Arnold demanded.

He hesitated, and began to speak further, but Wong forestalled him, holding up a commanding hand. 'Please. I've explained. It is a matter of regret that these things have occurred.' The Chinese businessman's glance slipped towards Portia. 'It is sad. This should never have happened. You should never have become involved in my business affairs. It is simply that you and Portia and Miss Stannard happened to be in the wrong place at the wrong time.' He slipped a quick glance at Steven Sullivan standing silently beside him. 'Steven now, his presence was a different matter. It was also a matter of chance, but it was fortunate. He was able to avoid an escalation of the problem.'

'The wrong place?' Arnold's mind was churning. He could make no sense of what Wong was saying. And then, slowly, a thought took root, began to grow. 'The Golden Palace,' he said slowly.

Henry Wong nodded. 'A bad business. The Dutchman, Charles de Vriess, was causing problems. He was dealing in

198

fake designer drugs. He needed to be shown a lesson. He was to have been chopped but . . . I made a mistake. I entrusted the task to a hot-headed young man, a relative of mine. And he went too far. He took matters into his own hands. He shot the Dutchman. For this, he was severely reprimanded.'

'Reprimanded?' Portia croaked. '*Reprimanded* for shooting someone?'

Henry Wong ignored her horrified outburst. He was staring sadly at Arnold. 'Of course,' he added, 'it was fortunate that Steven was there. He was quick-witted.' He slid a serpent glance at the young man hanging on his every word. 'He recognized Jeremy of course and—'

'Jeremy Tan?' Portia gasped.

Slightly irritated, Wong made a gesture to Sullivan, who half turned, stepped forward, gripped Portia's arm fiercely and shook her. Her eyes were wide, scared, and she stared at him as though he were a stranger. 'He recognized Jeremy,' Wong continued, 'heard the commotion in the kitchen and immediately ran after him. I understand there was a struggle there — a young cook had tried to prevent Jeremy leaving after the killing. He has since been dealt with, quietly. And the others in the kitchen, they know better than to talk. But at the time, there was a situation developing. Steven knocked the cook aside, followed Jeremy into the alleyway, and assisted his escape.'

Arnold's mouth was dry. 'But he was injured, stunned. I found him in the alley.'

Wong smiled, nodding at Sullivan approvingly. 'A simple subterfuge. Jeremy was told to hit Steven, not too hard of course, so Steven could delay any pursuit with his probably effective groaning. It was quick-witted, yes, and demonstrated the loyalty which we admired. He has had his reward, of course.' He cast an almost fond glance at Sullivan. 'He had come to us with recommendations. Now, he has been promoted. He holds a position of great responsibility in our Society. Which I hope he will be able to continue, after Freddie Cheung and I have left the country.'

'I can't believe this,' Portia wailed. 'Steven, tell me this isn't true!'

Sullivan was very still. He ignored her, waited for Henry Wong's orders. Arnold's heart was pounding in his chest. 'So what is it you want with us here? Why bring us to the cove this evening?'

Wong shrugged. 'I leave in the morning.' He raised his head and listened as a gust of wind beat at the roof, and rain began to lash at the outside walls. 'In better weather than this, I hope. But why are you both here? I told you. Loose ends. You see, I could not be sure, finally, whether, if prompted by other evidence, there would not be things you might remember about that night. I could not be sure you would not have recognized Jeremy. I was uncertain whether you were really fooled by Steven feigning injury. It is unlikely, but it was a possible eventuality . . . and Jeremy is not only a Society member. He is family, and family connections are important.'

Steven Sullivan shifted slightly, stirring as though he was becoming impatient.

'I thought,' Wong continued, 'that it would be useful to bring you both under observation, perhaps get to know you better. So I asked you and Portia to work for me for a while. Miss Stannard, Steven informed me, although present at the unfortunate business in the Golden Palace, probably saw nothing. Even so, she will also be taken care of. As a precaution. As for you, Arnold, yes, I got to know you, and I had hopes that none of this would become necessary. I even tested your loyalty by asking Freddie to tempt you. But in the end, I could not wait. Other things have been happening these last few days. Pressures have increased. As a result of the incident in the Golden Palace questions have been raised, the police have started an extensive investigation . . . and I am becoming an old man. It is time for me to seek rest and peace. My time as *lung tau* is coming to an end. It is better I move on. I had expected that my *fu shan chu* would take my place, but Jimmy Tsui has already been arrested, I understand. It all means I must leave, and tie up loose ends.'

The Chinese terms he had used were meaningless to Arnold. But the man had spoken of Karen Stannard. 'You arranged to meet me here. And . . . and Sullivan enticed Portia here. But Miss Stannard—'

'Other arrangements are being made for her,' Wong interrupted dismissively.

The wind was rising, buffeting at the roof, and a roaring sound was growing, the sea rising perhaps, but there was an odd rhythmic sound to it also. 'It is enough,' Wong said simply. 'I have regrets of course. I wish it could have been otherwise.' He glanced around him. 'I even regret the abandonment of this centre, in honour of the East Indiaman, the *Vendela*. It would have been a monument to me. But . . .' He half turned, looked at Steven Sullivan. There was a message in his eyes. As Arnold stood there, rooted to the spot, he saw Steven Sullivan reach inside his leather jacket. His right hand emerged holding a handgun. Its barrel gleamed dully in the fading light as the rhythmic beating of the storm-racked air outside the building grew to a crescendo.

Henry Wong nodded. 'It is time. The girl first, Steven.'

Steven Sullivan moved slightly, stepping back. He looked at Portia as she stood there wide-eyed. The gun muzzle rose. For a moment Arnold thought he detected a hint of regret in the young man's eyes. He heard Sullivan murmur something. 'I'm sorry, Portia . . .'

Portia screamed. Then the thunder of the explosion reverberated against the bare walls of the half-finished exhibition centre, echoing, fading into death.

5

It had seemed like a long day, but she put that down to the anxieties that had been plaguing her. She was worried about Arnold's meeting with Henry Wong: she knew that the collapse of the project would have implications for her. She had boasted to the politicians that she had been able to recover the position they had failed to support financially. Now, if Henry Wong pulled out of the investment it would hardly redound to her credit. Then there was the matter of Powell Frinton's retirement. She had felt unsettled for some time, thinking about leaving the department, maybe seeking an academic appointment, but they were few and far between, and now there was the post of Chief Executive falling vacant.

Did she want it? She was unable to make up her mind. It would mean an increase in salary, but that mattered for little. She could beat off the dust of the department, and that would be a good thing the way her mind was working these days. But perhaps more important, there would be more power in her hands to influence events. On the downside, she knew that it would mean a greater involvement with the elected members, and that was something she would not enjoy. Over the years they had come to accept that she was not going to sleep her way to power and influence, but that didn't mean efforts would not increase if she were to be appointed to Powell Frinton's job. There were some members who would want to argue that she'd been done favours; they would want to call for something in return.

She was in an unpleasant frame of mind when she left the office at five thirty. It had begun to rain, and the sky was darkening rapidly. She drove home to her apartment at the edge of the town, still mulling over the issues that bothered her, barely aware of her surroundings. She parked in the street outside the apartment block, and climbed the stairs to the first floor. She kicked the door closed behind her, and headed for the bedroom, taking off her coat and slinging it irritably on the bed. She felt out of sorts. She returned to the sitting room and poured herself a glass of gin, added the appropriate amount of tonic water and slumped in an easy chair. Most times, she enjoyed her own company. Not this evening.

There had been affairs of course. There had been plenty of offers she had turned down. There had been the brief time with Arnold . . . She grunted in irritation. Whichever way she twisted, it always seemed to come back in some way or another to Arnold Landon. He was always there in the department, and now he was intruding into her private space. She enjoyed living alone, but maybe she had lived alone too long.

She put her head back on the chair, sipped her drink, but there was something wrong. She was unsettled, irritable, tired after the day's work, but there was something else, an indefinable sense of an item out of place in her life, in her apartment, in her surroundings. She looked about her, searching for things that might have caused the feeling, but everything seemed normal, nothing unusual. Yet there was something . . .

She put down her glass, rose to her feet, prowled around the room, overtaken by a strange sense of unease. Her skin prickled, there was an odd tension in her shoulders, a coldness along her spine. Yet there was nothing she could identify to explain her uneasiness. Until her senses sharpened, and she caught the slight taint of an unfamiliar odour in her nostrils. Faint, but different.

She shook herself. She was being fanciful. She was being ridiculous. It could have been a woman's perfume, someone she had talked to today, a hint of perfume that had clung to her own clothing. But it was not a woman's perfume. She closed her eyes: it was a hint of a *male* smell; it was unfamiliar to her. And it was out of place in her apartment.

She turned, walked towards the bedroom again. Her coat was still lying there on the bed. She picked it up, touched it to her nostrils, but the odour had gone, she was no longer aware of it, and she clucked her tongue, telling herself she had been fanciful. Yet her pulse had quickened, she was uneasy, and her nerves were on edge.

Suddenly, her edginess grew too strong. She felt she didn't want to stay in the flat in her present mood. She slipped one arm into her coat, and headed back into the hall-way. She paused for a moment, thinking about the waiting gin and tonic, cursing herself for being foolish, female, but her edginess was too strong. There was a pub two streets away; she would go there for a drink, take a meal in the restaurant next door. Get over this silly wariness. She slipped her other arm into her coat, reached out to begin unlocking the door when she heard the slight sound behind her.

She froze for only a second, then she began to turn her head, her fingers still on the door lock. In that second she caught sight of something dark, a blurred vision of movement, and then an arm locked around her neck, and she was being dragged away from the door. Panic surged through her veins and she tried to scream but the muscled arm across her throat cut off the sound. Instinctively, she kicked backwards, and her heel cut into her assailant's shin, but the grip on her throat tightened, she was being dragged away from the door, unable to call for help, her senses swimming, panic rising in her throat as she tore at the man's arm, dragged at it, reached back with her long nails to score the face of the man attacking her, but it was all in vain, all useless as she felt herself slipping into unconsciousness. Her darkening sight gave her a glimpse of a man's hand; something glittering in his fist. The restraining arm across her throat was slackening, and as the knife came forward she knew she was going to die.

Then there was a violent flashing of lights, and she was falling. She heard voices shouting, she hit the carpeted floor and she rolled as feet trampled above her, men rushed into the apartment, there was an excited yelling, an explosion of sound, and then she could hold on no longer, as her anxieties faded away, her concerns disappeared, and a soothing darkness enveloped her, soft, soundless . . .

'Miss Stannard.'

The voice was small, distant, only half-heard. She was aware of someone holding her, arms about her shoulders, cradling her. Slowly, Karen opened her eyes. There was aching thickness in her throat, a swelling, and stabs of pain shot through her breast as she breathed shudderingly. The face of the man holding her was vaguely familiar. She glanced around; other men were there, dressed in padded jackets, caps. Someone was being bundled out of the hallway, half dragged, his feet trailing as though he was unconscious.

'Are you all right?'

O'Connor. His name was O'Connor. Karen nodded, raised a hand to stroke her throat. She struggled to speak. Her voice came out as a croak. 'Who . . . who was . . . ?'

'Don't worry about it now,' Jack O'Connor soothed her as he helped her to her feet, groggy, limbs shaking. 'Can you walk? Let's get you to the hospital, get you checked out.'

As she left the apartment with O'Connor half supporting her she heard two men arguing, someone saying angrily, 'We should have got here sooner. We should never have tried a stake-out!'

'How the hell could we know the bastard was already inside?'

* * *

Twenty miles north, as the wind came whirling, rain-laden, from the west, the helicopter came lurching in above the Black Needles, to hover above the rainswept new road, its rotors beating, the men inside the machine tense, ready to leap out as soon as the touchdown occurred.

They bundled out of the helicopter, each armed with an assault rifle, anonymous, dark-clothed figures, bent double as they ran towards the designated exhibition centre, fanning out in a wide group, ready for any emergency. Behind them came the American agent who had called out the group. He hurried forward, his hair quickly plastered to his skull by the swirling rain. At the gaping doorway he paused; two men waited, flashlights in hand, then at a given signal they dashed in through the open door.

The vast room was dim; the flashlights swung and danced their beams across the floor, the walls the ceiling. But Garland had already seen the tight little group standing in the centre of the room.

'Put the gun down! Put the gun down!'

There was a clattering sound. Garland pushed his way forward. The torch beams outlined the group, standing as though frozen. Arnold Landon, his arms around a woman, the Tyrrel girl. The tall Eurasian, Steven Sullivan, a few feet apart, his hands hanging loosely by his sides.

Lying on the concrete floor an elderly man dressed in a dark overcoat and scarf. Garland walked forward, stood over him, stared down at the man as the wind hammered and beat at the roof of the exhibition building. The mouth of the dead man was open, grimacing with a deathly rictus; the eyes were staring vacantly, almost as though surprise had been the last emotion experienced.

The back of his head would be a mess, from the exit wound, but there was barely a mark on his plump face. The single bullet had entered his forehead, and taken his life almost immediately. Garland had been wrong; de Vriess's information had been inaccurate. He had thought that the man who led the Ghost Shadows Society had been Freddie

Cheung. He had not been informed otherwise. He should have been told earlier that the *lung tau* was in reality Henry Wong. The man who lay dead at his feet: the Dragon Head.

Garland glared at the man called Steven Sullivan. 'What the hell happened here?' he snarled.

Steven Sullivan made no reply. He stood there silently, arms limp, seemingly drained of feeling or emotion, an automaton who had run down, listless and still. Garland stared at him, took a deep breath, then turned sharply to the men who had fanned out around him. 'Get him out of here, *fast*!'

He glanced at Arnold Landon, still standing stiffly with his arms around the sobbing, terrified girl. 'Get them all out of here! *Now*!'

There was going to be some explaining to do.

* * *

Twenty-four hours later, in the office vacated by the Chief Constable to allow the discussion to take place, the atmosphere was crackling with tension. DCI O'Connor and DI Farnsby stood stiffly in front of the desk, behind which Assistant Chief Constable Sid Cathery prowled like an angry bull. His heavy shoulders were hunched, his head lowered as though he was about to charge into the legalized mayhem of a rugby scrum in his prime. 'So,' he barked, 'the woman is okay?'

'Miss Stannard was kept in for observation overnight,' O'Connor replied, 'but she suffered no real injury. We got there just before Jeremy Tan used the knife.'

'Bloody cavalry charge!' Cathery sneered. 'Arriving at the last moment.'

O'Connor's head came up angrily. 'We were following your instructions, sir. After the discussion with Garland you agreed that we should stake out the premises, attempt to get Tan when he entered the building. Then Miss Stannard arrived, went inside, and we were in a quandary. In the end, I felt we had to take the initiative, even if it meant scaring off the killer. Karen Stannard was being used as bait, but it wasn't right: we couldn't take the chance. And we were right. We entered the building on my order, and when we heard the sounds of struggle inside we kicked down the door, and collared the bastard. But you agreed the stake-out in the first instance, rather than proceeding directly to inform Karen Stannard of the danger she was in, and bring her in.'

Cathery glowered at him. He was right, of course, but Cathery was reluctant to admit it. Bloody Garland . . . He should never have listened to him in the first instance. He grunted, shaking his head. 'And the other two?'

Farnsby cleared his throat. 'Traumatized, of course, but otherwise unharmed. Landon was protecting the girl when we arrived. Sullivan gave no trouble. But . . .' He hesitated. 'He was taken aboard the helicopter, under arrest, but after that . . . I mean, he wasn't brought to headquarters, so I don't know . . .' His voice died away uncertainly. Cathery gave him a glance edged with malice, and picked up the phone on his desk. 'Is Garland in the building yet?'

He slammed down the phone, muttering to himself. 'He's on the way. He'll be here in a moment. With more than a few bloody explanations, I hope. This is something the Chief should be handling. Why I've been hung out to dry—'

There was a light tap on the door, and as though in answer to Cathery's prayers the Chief Constable entered the room. Behind him was Bob Garland. Cathery and the two detectives stiffened to attention. The Chief Constable waved a casual hand, and said, 'No ceremony, please, gentlemen. This will be a brief meeting. Mr Garland will be leaving us this afternoon. His role in this affair is over. The Ghost Shadows Society has, it seems, been taken apart. It's unlikely it will recover. The head of the organization is dead; his two senior officers Jimmy Tsui and Freddie Cheung have been arrested and are now in custody. The murderer of Charles de Vriess is also in custody—'

'Jeremy Tan,' Sid Cathery grated, in spite of himself.

The Chief Constable paused, eyed him coolly and nodded. 'That is correct.'

'And Steven Sullivan?' Cathery demanded.

There was a short silence. The Chief Constable walked forward, perched one haunch on the edge of Cathery's desk, and murmured, 'Mr Garland will fill us in with as much as we need to know. As you'll be aware, this operation has had the backing of the Home Office. The collaboration between FinCen and ourselves was cleared at the highest level. Of course, there have been a few . . . misunderstandings, but I am sure Mr Garland, before he leaves, will be able to clear them up.'

Bob Garland stepped forward, shooting a sharp glance at Farnsby and O'Connor. Then he faced Sid Cathery. 'You already know the way we work. We've set up arrangements in several countries in Europe. We've got the experience and the expertise in dealing with Triad societies. And we've learned there's only one way to root them out, break up the organization, cut off the Dragon Head, and send the members scuttling off or into long prison terms. The key is infiltration.'

Sid Cathery opened his mouth to say something angrily, but the Chief Constable's cold eye stopped him in his tracks.

'You were already aware that Charles de Vriess was a FinCen agent,' Garland continued.

'Only after he got killed!' Cathery snapped in spite of himself.

'Information of that kind is on a need-to-know basis,' Garland replied coldly. 'The undercover operation de Vriess ran meant he was able to give us a deal of information on the activities of the Ghost Shadows Society on the street, and he was able to name for us the likely leaders of the Society. But we needed someone else who could get deeper into the organization, deal with the top men, be in a position to blow the whole shebang sky-high. We had already found such a man in the States. A trained money man, with skills at finance that would make him invaluable to the Triad. He was already a member of a Triad society, the Black Eagles, in the States but he defected to us. But it meant he could come to the UK with a recommendation: Triad membership. He was not immediately acceptable to the Ghost Shadows, of course, he was still on trial in the Society, when he got lucky. He was present the night Charles de Vriess got hit.'

'*He* was lucky,' Cathery glowered. 'De Vriess wasn't.' Then, as the Chief Constable frowned at him, Cathery's eyes lit up in sudden understanding. 'Are you telling us that Steven Sullivan—'

'Was a FinCen agent. Of course. It was he who fed us the important information regarding the central operators. He got promoted to handle central funding business and money-laundering after he assisted Jeremy Tan's escape. He was now held in high regard. It meant that when we had enough information, and started the raids, he was able to tell us that the Dragon Head had ordered the elimination of the three other people who were at the Golden Palace that night. He told us Karen Stannard was going to be hit. He informed us Arnold Landon would be killed up at the *Vendela* site. And he made sure he'd be there, by offering to bring Portia Tyrrel along, so she could be taken out at the same time. So, he was given the task. Jeremy Tan would get to remove Karen Stannard; Sullivan was to be hit man for Landon and Portia Tyrrel.'

There was a short silence. O'Connor shifted on his feet. 'We almost missed Tan at Karen Stannard's apartment.'

Garland shrugged, almost indifferently. 'I didn't want him scared off. I thought if we staked out the place, we'd get him before he entered.'

'You got that one wrong,' Cathery sneered.

Bob Garland's mouth was grim. 'It worked out in the end.'

'Like it worked out at the cove?' Cathery demanded.

The Chief Constable twitched uncomfortably. He glanced at his watch. 'We haven't got much time before Mr Garland leaves us to make his reports . . . elsewhere. If we could just rein in our tempers somewhat, and listen to what he has to say.'

'Like how things got ballsed up at the *Vendela* site?' Cathery asked coldly, his eyes glittering as he glared at

Garland, ignoring the Chief Constable's emollient comments. 'Tell us! Sullivan must have been there to prevent Wong killing anyone. He was there to nail Wong, hold him until the task force arrived. Wong was unarmed. So how the hell did the Dragon Head end up with a bullet in his head?'

The silence grew around them, heavy with subdued anger. Reluctantly, Garland said, 'We didn't actually know it would be Wong. We believed the Dragon Head was Freddie Cheung. Sullivan didn't disabuse us of that. It seems . . . it seems Sullivan had his own private agenda.'

'He was a FinCen officer, under your control, wasn't he?'

'That's so,' Garland admitted unwillingly. 'But when we recruited him from the Black Eagles Society in the States, we didn't know his complete history.'

'What's that supposed to mean?'

Garland grimaced his reluctance to explain. 'Steven Sullivan was born to an Irish girl, Eileen Sullivan. His father was Chinese, a man called Ricky Chan, who was heavily involved with Triad activity.' He hesitated. 'Ricky Chan had a wife in Hong Kong, and it wasn't uncommon for Chinese men to have concubines. Whether Eileen knew at first that he was tied in with criminal activity we don't know, but it might have been why she took the boy to the States when he was in his early teens. But by then . . .' He glanced around the silent group of men. 'Ricky Chan had aspirations in the Triad. He was picked out to become *lung tau*, the Dragon Head. But he wasn't the only one with ambition. A young man called Henry Wong settled the matter: he had his henchman murder Ricky Chan when he had gone back to Hong Kong for his usual annual visit, to see his wife and other family, and conduct business. The hit took place in Macau, when Chan was visiting the casino. We didn't know about all this when we recruited Steven Sullivan from the Black Eagles Society in the States.'

'So what did you recruit Sullivan for?' Farnsby asked curiously.

'There's a new wave of criminal activity within Triad societies. It's big money. Denial of service operations. Sullivan is not just computer literate: he's extremely skilled in software systems and he knows how to use logic bombs, encryption techniques, the works. We took him in because we knew he could infiltrate easily, and would be useful in Europe. So we brought him over, and he joined the Ghost Shadows Society. Our motive was to insert him into the top echelons by reasons of his skills, determine who was pulling the puppet strings, feed us — and your Home Office — the information and give us the opportunity to kill off the Triads. That suited Sullivan fine — but what we didn't know was that Sullivan had another motive. It was his way of getting close to the Dragon Head of the Ghost Shadows Society — and get revenge for the murder of his father.'

The Chief Constable humphed uncomfortably. He stood up from the edge of the desk, glanced again at his watch. 'Your car will be downstairs, Mr Garland. Your plane will be leaving in an hour. Now that matters have been resolved, I think we can leave things there for the moment and—'

'One moment, sir,' O'Connor objected. 'There's the matter of what's to happen to Steven Sullivan.'

The Chief Constable's eyes seemed to glaze over. 'I think we can leave that for now.'

O'Connor frowned, about to argue, but Sid Cathery butted in, still angry, and suddenly smelling a rat. 'We don't have him in custody, sir. The man may have been working as an undercover agent, but the killing of Henry Wong, it was done in cold blood. Sullivan was the only man in that building who was armed. He will have to stand trial and—'

'No.' Garland's tone suggested he would brook no discussion of the matter.

Sid Cathery bristled predictably. 'What the hell do you mean? This isn't the bloody Wild West! This is our jurisdiction, and your bloody operative gunned down someone for his own personal motives! You don't think we can let you walk away from that, do you?'

The Chief Constable's features were pale. 'I think we must leave it, Sid. The Home Office—'

'Bugger the Home Office,' Cathery flashed, now out of control. 'This is a murder whichever way you look at it and we don't even have the killer in custody! What's going on here? Where is Sullivan?'

There was a short silence. The Chief Constable, irritated by Cathery's outburst but unable to challenge it, turned to the silent FinCen man.

'He's no longer in the country,' Garland said harshly.

Cathery's eyebrows shot up in surprise. He was stunned for a moment, then opened his fleshy mouth to protest, but was forestalled by the American agent.

'You got to understand, Mr Cathery,' Garland said quietly. 'Steven Sullivan is a FinCen man. And we look after our own. That's all there is to it.'

As he walked out of the room, O'Connor was reminded yet again of the comment made in Padua, by the Home Office man, Franklin: *We could not countenance some of the methods used . . .*

* * *

The Chief Constable left the room hurriedly, accompanying the American agent. It was left to O'Connor and Farnsby to experience the raging, swearing, stamping performance of the enraged Assistant Chief Constable. Cathery had got close to the line with the Chief Constable, O'Connor thought: his arguing could have brought him up on a disciplinary charge. But both he and Farnsby had sympathy for Cathery's position. It was just a pity that they had to bear the brunt of the Assistant Chief Constable's fury.

Gradually, Sid Cathery regained control. 'Anyway, I suppose there's nothing we can bloody well do, but leave it to those chicken-hearted Home Office civil servants to lie down with their legs in the air and let the Yanks trample all over them.' He took a deep breath. 'At least, it's up to us to finish the cleaning up of the stables. Wong is dead; Freddie Cheung was arrested this morning in Amsterdam; Jimmy Tsui will face a long prison term here, and the rest of these murderous thugs, once we get hold of them, will be chucked inside as well, or deported, or both. Garland's left us a file on the financial side of things. Prepared by Steven Sullivan, it seems,' he sneered, 'from information supplied by Charles de Vriess. These are all front organizations for money-laundering. We can crack down on them. Farnsby, you'll be heading it up. So that's it. Now get the hell out of here so I can heal my bruises in peace.'

It was the end of the day. O'Connor walked back to his office. He glanced at his watch. An hour's drive north, and he would be with Isabella. Somehow, the thought did not excite him the way it should. Things were different. Perhaps too much had happened for it ever to be possible to get back to where they had been. He looked up as the door opened, and DI Farnsby peered into the room.

'Ah. Thought I might just catch you before you left.'

He did not enter the room, but remained standing in the open doorway. 'I've got the list of companies from Cathery. Before I get on with organizing the investigations I thought I might ask you if you've got any thoughts about it.'

'Thoughts?' O'Connor wrinkled his brow. 'Such as?'

Farnsby's tone was cold. 'I just wondered whether there was anything you might add. Something like that.'

'I don't know what you mean,' O'Connor said quietly, but something moved in his gut. 'Why should I want to add anything to the list?'

There was a short silence. 'I've looked closely at the notebook you found in de Vriess's house,' Farnsby said in a frosty tone. 'I talked it over with forensic as well, after they'd finished with it.'

'And?' O'Connor challenged, meeting Farnsby's glance.

'They confirmed my suspicion. They reckon a sheet was torn out of the notebook. Maybe the last sheet.'

'It was ring-bound,' O'Connor commented casually. 'Maybe de Vriess tore it out, threw it away.'

'Or maybe someone else did.' Farnsby's glance was hostile. He hesitated, then said, 'It was you found the book. You didn't show it to me until we were on the way back in the car.'

O'Connor lifted his chin defiantly. 'Just what are you trying to say, Farnsby?'

The detective inspector stared at him, struggling to bring out his suspicions, but O'Connor knew he had nothing to go on, nothing *except* suspicions. At last, Farnsby muttered in a tone marked with contempt, 'I think you tampered with that notebook. I don't know why. Maybe if I probed a bit more, maybe I'd find out. But that's not the way we work together, is it? Coppers like us, we got to trust each other, or the system breaks down. But I'll tell you this, DCI. This is the last time.'

'The last time for what?' O'Connor queried, dry-mouthed.

Farnsby's tone was bitter. 'I covered for you once before, over that Isabella Portland business. I don't know what it is you removed from that notebook, but I'm pretty sure you did take out something. But I want to make it clear, DCI O'Connor. This is the last time. The last time I cover for you.'

After he had gone O'Connor stared out of the window, seeing nothing. Removing the name of the Starling Foundation had meant that at least one of the Triad money-laundering scams would go undetected. But it also meant that he had been able to get together with Isabella once more.

The question was . . . Was it something he really wanted anymore?

* * *

The lounge bar in the Coach and Horses in Morpeth was quiet. It was early in the evening: the regulars would not arrive for another half-hour or so, the restaurant would not commence serving until six thirty. Karen had booked a table for the three of them, and suggested they leave the office early, to walk across to the pub and have a drink before dinner.

Portia Tyrrel seemed diminished in some way. Her usual sparkle, the confidence that Arnold had always connected with her, seemed to have been dissipated. Perhaps that was why to Arnold's surprise Karen had invited them to dinner: it was certainly an unusual gesture. As they sat in the lounge it was hardly a cheerful occasion: each of them was subdued, concerned only with their own thoughts. Uncharacteristically, Karen stretched out a hand, laid it on Portia's and in a sympathetic tone asked, 'Have you heard anything from Steven?'

Portia hesitated, then shook her dark head. 'No. Nor do I expect to. When those men arrived, and took him away, I didn't even have a chance to speak to him. The last thing he said to me was that he was sorry. Sorry for what?' Something of the old spark flashed briefly in her almond eyes. 'Sorry for leading me up the garden path, making me think we had something good between us? Sorry for using me? Or sorry for letting me see the brutal thing he was about to do?'

'I don't think he used you,' Arnold intervened. 'And remember, Henry Wong had instructed him to kill you, and then me. Instead, he turned the gun on Wong. My guess is your relationship developed . . . he had an agenda of his own but I don't think he was able to prevent what was happening between you.'

'But there was something more important to him than our relationship,' Portia argued in a sudden passion. 'Murdering his employer!'

'He saved your life, Portia,' Arnold reminded her gently.

The silence that followed was broken by Karen. She sighed. 'I don't think we should talk any more about what happened up at the *Vendela* site. Or about what happened to me at my apartment.' She shuddered slightly. 'I can't go back there now. I've put it up for sale. I'm moving on. And that's why I wanted us to get together this evening.' She shook her head. 'I feel that with what's happened recently, the department's been sort of torn apart.'

Arnold knew what she meant. He had been unsettled for weeks, he had been disturbed by the offer from Freddie

Cheung, and his feelings about Karen were still in a confused state. 'So where will you move to?' he asked.

Karen shook her head. 'It depends. I've decided I might as well have a crack at Powell Frinton's job. There are certain councillors who feel I'm in with a good chance. Or maybe I'll get out altogether. There's a job in the archaeology department at York University. I'm thinking about it. But in any case I want out.' She flicked a glance at Arnold: her eyes seemed uncertain, indeterminate in colour. He had never quite decided what colour her eyes were . . . 'If you wanted my job, Arnold, you'd have my support.'

He had never wanted her job. He accepted now, in spite of all the problems that had entered their relationship, he didn't want to see her leave. As for himself . . . his mind drifted back over the years, to the excitement of discovering the *sudarium*, the experience of unearthing the *Kvernbiter*, feeling history under his fingers, tasting salt on his tongue as he sailed near the rocks where the East Indiaman had gone down, three hundred years ago . . . There were other things out there to discover. He did not really want his life to change.

When they finally made their way into the restaurant, to be the first patrons of the evening, Karen glanced back over her shoulder.

'Let's hope, this time, we don't get disturbed by some nutter with a gun,' she said.

It was, Arnold considered, a comment in very bad taste.

THE END

ALSO BY ROY LEWIS

Thank you for reading this book.

If you enjoyed it please leave feedback on Amazon or Goodreads, and if there is anything we missed or you have a question about, then please get in touch. We appreciate you choosing our book.

Founded in 2014 in Shoreditch, London, we at Joffe Books pride ourselves on our history of innovative publishing. We were thrilled to be shortlisted for Independent Publisher of the Year at the British Book Awards.

www.joffebooks.com

We're very grateful to eagle-eyed readers who take the time to contact us. Please send any errors you find to corrections@joffebooks.com. We'll get them fixed ASAP.